Marrying Daisy was supposed to alleviate his loneliness, not confuse him.

He gained a sense of accomplishment when he helped her or the twins do something. Just being on the property to protect them brought him peace. More than once last night he'd looked out the barn door and checked to be certain everything was as it should be at the cabin. It was his duty as her friend.

But watching Daisy cry tugged at the edges of his hardened heart. Tucker was trying to be patient and not make her uncomfortable, but he wasn't accustomed to a woman's tears. It was a hard thing to watch without offering comfort. Yet she rejected his attempt to comfort her when he touched her shoulders. He'd need to remember not to do that again.

His heart broke for her over all her suffering. At the same time he wa̶n̶t̶ ̶ her senseless whe̶ everything.

Where had that th̶ want him to touch to kiss her. And he w̶a̶s̶n̶'̶t̶ about to open himself up to more rejection. Better to keep a safe distance.

ANGEL MOORE

fell in love with romance in elementary school when she read the story of Robin Hood and Maid Marian. A Harlequin novel, usually Betty Neels, accompanied her to school every day as a teen, where she'd finish all her schoolwork and escape to a happily-ever-after world.

As a pastor's wife she is dedicated to the work of her local church ministries, serving with the children and worship teams.

The joy of her life is her family. Married to her best friend, she has two wonderful sons, a lovely daughter-in-law, and three grands. She loves sharing her faith and the hope she knows is real because of God's goodness to her.

Conveniently Wed

ANGEL MOORE

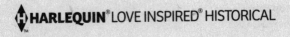

HARLEQUIN® LOVE INSPIRED® HISTORICAL

LOVE INSPIRED BOOKS

ISBN-13: 978-0-373-28293-7

Conveniently Wed

Copyright © 2014 by Angelissa J. Moore

www.Harlequin.com

Printed in U.S.A.

But they that wait upon the Lord shall renew their strength;
they shall mount up with wings as eagles;
they shall run, and not be weary;
and they shall walk, and not faint.
—*Isaiah* 40:31

To Tina James for the time and encouragement
she invested in my first sale.

To the friends and family who read the drafts
along the way.

To Austin for being my champion on
the adventure of entering the writing world.

To Bob for believing in me and motivating me
to write my first manuscript.

And to God for His mercy and constant help.

Chapter One

Daisy Mosley pulled back both hammers on the shotgun, lowered the barrel onto the windowsill and aimed at the center of the rider's chest. No stranger had been down the lane since her husband, Murdock, had been killed by horse thieves three weeks earlier. Daisy was determined that no harm would come to James and John. She could hear the eight-year-old twins shushing each other as they scurried under her bed in the far corner of the cabin.

Watching carefully, she followed the rider's slow approach with her gun. Very tall and broad with a straight back, a worn Stetson and red hair, he was definitely not a local. His mount was the prettiest pinto she'd ever seen. He was almost close enough for her to shoot when he stopped. He leaned forward in the saddle, his face still shielded by the Stetson.

"Daisy Marie, put that gun down before you hurt somebody."

"Who are you?" Daisy didn't flinch. "And how do you know my name?"

The stranger chuckled. "You know who I am. Have for years. And you know I don't trust you with a gun. Not after what happened when your papa was trying to teach you to shoot."

"Oh, my goodness!" In one swift movement, Daisy lowered the gun, released the hammers and put it in the rack over the mantel. "Boys, come meet Tucker Barlow!" she called to her sons as she unbolted the door and raced across the porch, barely skimming the steps.

Tucker dismounted just in time to brace against the impact of Daisy throwing herself into his arms. She remembered fondly that, even though she carried quite a lot of momentum for such a petite lady, she was no match for his strength. Not many could stand against the power of her exuberance. He lifted her and swung her around in a circle before setting her on the dusty ground. He held her hands, and she leaned back to look up at him.

"Daisy, you are a sight. And what kind of welcome was that for you to think about shooting me before I even met these fine-looking men you've got here?"

James and John stood behind their mother, timid of the big stranger.

Daisy withdrew her hands from Tucker's and turned to the twins. "James, John, meet Mr. Barlow. Mr. Barlow, these are my sons."

"Strong Bible names. Glad to meet you both." He held out a hand for James to shake and then turned to John. "I'm glad you've got that freckle over your lip, John. Otherwise, I might never know who I was talking to."

John ducked his head shyly. "It's a birthmark. Momma

said God put it there so she wouldn't mix us up when we were babies."

James spoke up. "If he didn't have it, we could trick people and trade places and stuff."

Daisy chuckled. "They look alike, but it doesn't take long to find out how different they are." She smiled at Tucker. "Boys, Mr. Barlow works for Papa Warren. He was a good friend to me when I was a girl. I haven't seen him since I moved here when me and your papa got married over ten years ago."

Looking directly at the young boys, Tucker said, "You don't need to call me Mr. Barlow. We're gonna be working side by side as men. You can call me Tucker."

"What are you talking about, Tucker?" Daisy rested her hands on the boys' shoulders as they flanked her and watched the giant stranger.

Tucker removed his hat and lowered his gaze to the ground reverently. "Your father felt it was for the best—given the circumstances and all."

The excitement of having a visitor gave way to sadness as her little family remembered their fresh grief. Daisy appreciated Tucker's respect of Murdock's memory.

"Boys, why don't you go fetch a cool drink of water from the well while me and your momma talk in private?"

Daisy nudged the twins toward the side yard and looked into Tucker's face, shading her eyes against the sun with one hand. She didn't remember him being so tall. "What are you talking about, 'Papa says it's for the best'?"

"Now, Daisy, just hear me out." The tapping of her

toe rustled the hem of her skirt. She wasn't in the mood to be patient—not that she ever was.

"I'm waiting…" Her words provoked Tucker to explain.

"Your father came to me the day he got your telegraph about Murdock's murder. He was so concerned about you and the boys. He wanted to know how you were holding up under such a tragic loss. Would the men who killed Murdock come back and harm you or the boys? Would you lose your land? He was beside himself." Tucker paused as if choosing his next words carefully. "We talked for a long time that night." Tucker stopped and drew in a deep breath.

"And…" Daisy's toes still tapped, and now she folded her arms across her chest, anticipating she wouldn't like the next part of the conversation.

Tucker looked at the hat in his hands and smoothed the brim. "And…" His mouth set in a firm line, and his eyes raised to meet her stare. "We think it would be best for you and the boys if you and I get married." His words spilled out in a rush.

Daisy shook her head and turned one ear toward him with her brows wrinkled in confusion. "Who thinks what for who?"

Tucker could hear the disbelief in her voice. Thinking she might take it better when she realized it was her father's idea, he emphasized Mr. Warren's perspective.

"Your father—and I've come to agree with him— thinks it would be best if you and I get married. Today."

"Wait just one minute. I'm not following your train of thought. Why would you think this?" Daisy said, sounding befuddled.

"Not just me," Tucker reiterated. "Me and your father. We both know a lot about what you're facing now. Your father lost your mother and had to raise you girls alone. He knows the pain you're in. And my father passed away when I was young. I know how the boys are feeling." Tucker maintained a calm demeanor. He knew how quickly Daisy could go from confused to angry or indignant. Many times he'd seen her jump from one emotion to another.

"Just because you think you know what I'm feeling doesn't mean I need to marry you." Daisy's voice rose a bit.

"It's not just about that, Daisy. You've got two sons to raise. You'll need help with that."

Tucker proceeded with caution, trying not to set her off before she understood his motive. "You've got the farm, too. It's too much to do alone. I remember what my mother went through after my father died. She worked herself to death. Those boys need you." He couldn't imagine Daisy suffering as his mother had. He'd been too young to save his mother. But he wouldn't risk this woman—who he'd once hoped would love him—falling to the same fate.

Daisy lowered her arms and clenched her fists at her sides. "I am managing this farm just fine. And my boys are okay, too. They've just been through a lot, that's all." Her words couldn't hide the concern in her voice, which revealed how badly she must want to believe what she was saying. Tucker knew she wasn't convinced. "I don't know who put this fool notion in your head, but marriage is not what I need right now." She stopped and thought for a moment. "And why would you want to marry me in the first place?"

"It's not a fool notion. Your father and I talked and prayed about this before I decided to come. I'd have been here a couple of weeks ago, but it took time to tie up some business in East River." With a grin and imploring gaze he added, "We've always been friends. We get along and understand one another. That's what you need now." He'd given up on love a long time ago. At thirty-one he knew his chance at being anyone's true love was behind him. His youthful efforts to love and be loved had taught him well. This chance at marriage to a good friend would give him comfort from the loneliness he'd known for so long.

Daisy unclenched her fists and reached her hands to his. She went up on her tiptoes and placed a small kiss on his cheek. "Oh, Tucker. Thank you." She spoke sweetly near his ear. "You're such a dear friend." She released his hands and backed away. "But I disagree with you and Papa."

Tucker saw the resigned strength in her eyes. She'd always plowed full steam ahead into whatever she set her mind to do. No doubt she was determined to survive and take care of James and John by herself.

"Daisy, we're concerned about you and the boys. It's too much—"

She cut him off, her tone indignant. "Did you and Papa think you could just come here and tell me what to do like I'm still a child? I'm a grown woman with responsibilities."

"I want to help with those responsibilities." Tucker kept his voice calm with great effort. "Think about it. Who'd ever marry me? I'm too old and set in my ways. You and I are friends. We'll be good for each other. I'll help you with the boys and the farm. You'll keep me from being a lonely old man." He smiled, hoping to break through her resistance. "And you're too fine a Christian woman to have a man here on the farm who isn't your husband."

Daisy was quiet for a moment. He saw the hesitation in her eyes as she pondered all they'd talked about.

"Tell you what. You just read this. Then we'll talk." He pulled an envelope from the inside pocket of his leather vest and handed it to her. "I'll go keep the boys occupied. You come find us when you're ready." He settled his hat back on his head, took the pinto by the reins and headed to the well, stirring up a path of dust as he went.

Daisy turned the envelope over in her hand. The wax seal was her father's unique design. The curling vines woven together in a heart pattern represented the things her dad loved best—his three daughters, all named after flowers and whom he collectively called "Papa's Garden." She walked to the porch and sat on the wooden rocker Murdock had made when he'd found out they were going to have a baby.

Daisy carefully broke the seal and removed the fragile paper. Unfolding it she braced herself for the first communication she'd received from him since his telegraph of sympathy after Murdock was killed.

Tears spilled over her lashes as she read her father's concern by relating it to her mother's death. They now shared the common thread of the loss of the love of their life. His words about how prayer had helped to heal his grief gave her comfort.

She pondered his main concern about the boys needing a man in their lives. Her eyes lit on the paragraph warning her she could lose her land in spite of the new laws assuring women in Texas could own land outright. Her heart clenched at the thought of losing everything Murdock had worked so hard to build for the future of their sons.

The letter ended by confirming his wishes that she marry Tucker. He wanted her to do it today, so Tucker's presence on the farm wouldn't reflect poorly on her reputation in town. He'd given Tucker his gift to them of money for a wedding supper to share in town that afternoon. He assured her it was all for her own good.

The sound of boots on the porch caused Daisy to look up as she finished the last line.

Tucker leaned against the porch railing and folded his arms. Pushing his hat back so she could see his face, he asked, "Well, Daisy? What do you say?"

"What do I say?" The chair rocked violently as she practically leaped from it. "What do I say?" Daisy stomped down the steps and across the yard in the direction of the barn. She caught a glimpse of the boys playing behind the corral.

Emotions raced through her mind and heart. She was reacting like the schoolgirl she'd once been. She used to tromp off into the woods to be alone when her feelings were hurt or her father hadn't let her get her way. Oh, to be that girl again and kick against the grass and head to the edge of the stream by her childhood home after being scolded for some prank she'd pulled on her sisters. Her mind took her to the times when she needed to get some emotion or event out of her system. Tucker was a shadow in the background then. Today he followed her in silence.

Without warning Daisy turned on him. "What do I say?" She shook the letter in her hand near his face. "I haven't even had time to process this silly idea of Papa's, and you want to know what I say?" Just as quickly she turned and marched away.

After going only a few feet, she stopped and stared into the sky. Her vision blurred as tears filled her eyes. Sobbing and clutching the letter to her heart, Daisy wailed, "Why, Papa? Why did Murdock have to die? I miss him so badly! And I need you here now."

Daisy felt Tucker's hands settle on her shoulders. "I'm so sorry, Daisy. Your father's health kept him from being here for you. His heart was breaking for you when I left. And no one knows why bad things happen like Murdock dying. Life isn't fair sometimes. You've been through an awful lot. Taking care of the land and raising those boys…you shouldn't have to do it alone."

He gently turned her around to face him. He knelt down on one knee as he held her hands in his. "Daisy, I'm asking you to do me the honor of marrying me. I promise to take care of you and James and John. I'll do my best to be a good husband to you. Your papa asked me to come here, but I'd be obliged if you'd let me stay." Was there an unsettledness in his expression? What would make him want to marry a grieving widow with two young sons?

"Oh, Tucker, I can't let you do that. You've got your own life to live. The boys and I will be fine." She pulled against his grip, but he didn't let go.

She was reeling inside. This morning she awoke with a world of responsibilities on her and God alone. Now someone was offering a lifeline of friendship and help, but she couldn't accept. She still loved Murdock—with every piece of her broken heart.

"Daisy, I'm not doing this because your father asked

me. I'm doing it because it's the right thing to do. Think about the future...your boys...this land. Those boys need a man to look up to. I'm not their father, but I promise to be a good example to them. Your father is right about the land and the new laws. You don't want everything you and Murdock worked for to be taken away." He tugged gently on her hands and smiled up at her. "Please say yes. For the boys. For the land. For you. For me? I know we can make it work. We were good friends before. We can be again. But only if you want me here. I won't stay if you don't."

Daisy looked into Tucker's green eyes and saw the sincerity of his offer. Many times in her youth she had found comfort in his friendship. More than once he'd rescued her from some scheme she'd thought up, either by helping her out of the dilemma she caused or by preventing her from doing something in the first place. She knew she could trust him. Four years older than her twenty-seven, she wondered if he was still as resolute as ever. Her papa said he was a great foreman because he was quick to make decisions and to handle situations. Would he try to handle her? Or her sons?

Daisy's mind swam with all the things she faced— twin boys to raise, running a farm, the possibility she couldn't keep the land without a husband. She considered herself to be a strong woman, but the workload was overwhelming. She'd hoped it would ease as she adjusted to doing everything without Murdock. It hadn't.

She also realized the value of the sacrifice Tucker was making to give up his freedom to help her raise another man's sons. How many times as a girl had she longed for a mother? Her father had been good to her and her sisters, but she'd ached for a woman's nurturing touch. She didn't want her sons to grow up without a father. Tucker was a good man. But she wanted her sons to know the value of a loving marriage. Could she grow to love Tucker as she had loved Murdock? Not now. The very idea was unfathomable. Could anyone have two chances at perfection?

"Okay." Daisy heard herself speak without realizing she was going to agree.

"Okay?" Tucker tilted his head to one side, and his brow puckered. "You're sure?"

"Okay." A new resolve at saying it aloud settled in her soul. "Let's do it. Why not? I haven't had control of anything in my life for the last month. Why should today be any different? Let's get married." Daisy pulled her hands free and smoothed her father's crumpled letter. "I'm sure Reverend Dismuke will be happy to accommodate us today. He can perform the ceremony, and his wife can be our witness."

She headed to the house almost at a trot, beckoning to the boys as she went. Then she stopped and looked at him over her shoulder. "Are you just going to kneel there in the dirt, or are you going to go get cleaned up for your wedding? You should find everything you need in the tack room in the barn." In an instant she was off again, picking up her skirt in both hands to keep from tripping.

"Impetuous as ever," Tucker called out behind her. The echo of his whistle caught the breeze and followed her up the porch steps and into the house.

Daisy sat at the foot of the table in the center of the small cabin. At the side of the table, James and John climbed onto the bench they had helped their father build.

"Boys, we need to talk." She wasn't sure exactly what to tell them first. "We've all been through a lot in the last few weeks. You have been such good boys. And you know I'd do anything in the world for you."

"Yes, ma'am," they answered in unison.

She took her father's letter from the pocket of her skirt. "You know how happy your papa was when you did something he asked you to do?" They both nodded, then looked at each other curiously before turning back to her and crossing their arms on the table in front of them. Matching brows drew together to join mirrored frowns.

"This is a letter from Papa Warren." She laid the letter on the table and smoothed it with her palm. A breeze lifted the lace curtain at the window by the door, causing the pages to flutter. The air's freshness helped her draw the breath for her next bit of news.

"He wants me to do something that will help us keep our home and make a way for you boys to still have this land when you're grown up—just like your papa wanted." The lack of understanding in their eyes caused Daisy to move straight to the point.

"I'm going to marry Mr. Barlow."

"Why, Momma?" There was a chorus of disbelief. "You can't! You're already married to Papa. You can't marry somebody else!"

Tears formed in her eyes, to be quickly blinked away. Daisy swallowed and reached out to the twins, inviting them into her embrace. They scrambled to her, and she wrapped them in her arms. "I know you don't understand. I did marry your papa. He and I loved each other very much." She pulled back and cupped one chin in each hand so James and John would see directly into her eyes. "I will always love your papa—just like you will. It hurts me as much as it hurts the two of you that he isn't here anymore. We know he's with Jesus."

Small tear-stained faces waited for her to continue. "Papa worked hard for this land. He wouldn't want us to lose everything because he isn't here anymore. That could happen if I don't marry again. It doesn't mean I don't love your papa. It means I love him so much that I want to make sure his dreams come true for you boys."

James spoke. As the firstborn he usually took the lead, and John rarely objected. "How could we lose our house, Momma?" Clearly the eight-year-old didn't understand.

"The government controls who gets to keep a house. Ladies have problems owning land that men don't have. It's complicated, so you're going to have to trust that Papa Warren knows best."

"Are you sure, Momma?" John's concern reflected in his small face. "Can't we keep it? It's ours now."

Daisy drew the boys back into a hug and kissed both blond heads. "I wish we could, but because of the laws of the state of Texas, this is the best way. I promise." Again she felt the press of helplessness that had threatened to overwhelm her since Murdock had been killed. It went against her stubborn nature to need someone else to rescue her.

"Mr. Barlow is a good man," she assured. "I've known him for many years. He's a godly man, like your papa. He'll take good care of us. He'll teach you things I can't. Like how to plow a field or take care of a broken wagon wheel. There's so much you'll need to know that only a man can teach you."

James and John leaned back and looked at her. "Are you sure, Momma?" James asked.

"I'm sure, son." Daisy smiled at them. "And you'll grow to love him, too. He's a respectable man."

The twins looked at each other in resignation and dropped their heads. Her amazement at their matching mannerisms never dimmed. "Okay, Momma. But it's gonna take a bit for us to get used to having another man around here." John paused. "We just got used to being the only men. Now we've got to train another one. He can show us how to fix wagon wheels and plow, but we'll teach him how to take care of the farm like Papa did."

Laughing, she released them and tussled each head with one hand. "Now I'm going to get ready for our trip to town. I need you boys to get washed up and put on your Sunday best." She rose from the chair and smoothed her skirt. "I certainly can't get married looking like this." She shooed them both outside to the well.

The twins brought water in and then dressed in their room. Satisfied with their appearance, she sent them to wait on the porch.

Daisy freshened up using the washbasin and mirror behind the screen in the corner of the cabin. Murdock had given her the screen as a gift, wanting her to have some privacy in the cabin full of males. She stood back to stare at her reflection. The lost weight from the pain and stress of the past three weeks did nothing to improve her appearance. Dark brown eyes looked hollow and bruised in her slightly freckled face. The gentle wave of her blond hair pulled tendrils loose from the pins she'd pushed in this morning before attempting to do the chores of two people. The weeks without him had worn her down more than she'd realized.

Daisy knew marrying Tucker would be the easiest solution to her problems, but she wondered if she could muster the strength to go through with the wedding. She still ached for Murdock.

Tucker was a good man and a good friend. Could she be patient while he adjusted to marriage? He'd never answered to anyone except a boss. Would he be willing to work alongside her? Or would his natural tendency to take charge make her more defensive of her boys and the farm?

Lord, I'm trusting You and Papa now. I am starting to think this is Your plan for my life. Help me get it right.

Taking a deep breath, Daisy went to the chest at the foot of the bed she and Murdock had shared and lifted the lid. She pulled out her best dress and, lifting it by the shoulders, let the breeze catch it as it floated onto the bed. Smoothing the soft, sea-green cotton, she thought about the last time she'd worn it. She and Murdock had gone to the spring social at church. They had strolled by the river, arm in arm, laughing and talking, while the boys played ball with their friends in the churchyard. Murdock had bought the dress for her birthday and told her to be happy on the days she wore it.

A tear slid down her cheek as she knew in her heart he'd want her to have a happy future. She would have wanted him to move on with his life if the situation had been reversed. However, knowing she should move forward was easier than actually taking the steps to do it.

Daisy wiped her face with the back of her hand. "I will not cry in the dress bought to make me happy." And then she put it on. Could she take the joy of her past into a future that offered contentment, but not true love?

The heaviness of Tucker's boots sounded on the porch

steps as she took a final look in the mirror. Her hand trembled as she reached up to touch the delicate white lace collar at her neck—and then she saw it. Her wedding band.

Daisy's knees buckled, and she collapsed to sit on the side of the bed. She held her hand out to look at the ring. The plain gold band had been there so long it was like a part of her. Murdock had given it to her on their first anniversary. The scratches and worn places testified to the hard work and commitment of their relationship. Spinning it on her finger and rubbing the cool smoothness of it, she blew out a determined breath and pulled the ring from her hand. She went to the chest and found the small velvet bag the ring had come in. She kissed the ring and slid it inside. With the pull of the drawstring she tied her past into a bow and lovingly placed it in the chest before lowering the lid.

Digging deep inside for energy she wasn't sure she had, Daisy pushed against the closed chest to stand. With her shoulders back and head held high, she straightened the ribbons of the bow that held her Sunday hat in place. Numbness froze her countenance in resignation. Her father's letter was tucked inside her small reticule for comfort as she journeyed forward into the day's events.

Sunlight sliced into the cabin when she opened the front door.

James and John sat on the front steps, looking into the fields. Tucker leaned against the porch railing staring at the door. He stood to his full height as Daisy joined them on the porch. Hat in hand he smiled at her.

"Miss Daisy, you look lovely." He took a step closer to her and hesitated, turning the Stetson in his hands.

"I took the liberty of hitching my horse to your wagon for the trip into town."

With a curt nod in his direction, Daisy said, "Thank you, Tucker," before turning to her sons. "Well, boys, let's go. Hop up into the back of the wagon." Daisy set the boys into motion with her no-nonsense tone. Hands in his pockets, James kicked at the dirt as he walked. John scampered ahead of his brother and vaulted into the wagon.

Daisy cautioned her eldest. "James, mind your manners and do as you're told."

His "Yes, ma'am" was muttered so quietly Tucker almost couldn't hear it. Tucker walked down the steps ahead of her and turned to offer his hand as she followed. He didn't meet her gaze. He took her small gloved hand in his calloused one and assisted her down the steps. She immediately withdrew it when her feet touched the ground. He watched her twist the drawstrings on her reticule around her fingers as they slowly walked to the wagon.

Again Tucker offered a hand to steady her as she climbed into the wagon. Again she permitted only the briefest of contact and settled into the seat while he walked in front of his horse to climb up beside her. He was a bit surprised by how quickly she'd agreed to marry him. When it was all said and done, he was a friend from so far in her past she had not recognized him when he rode onto her land a mere hour ago.

Grabbing the reins and sending the horse forward, he said, "I'll see about getting a couple of horses next week. We'll need them for working the farm. Mack here is more for riding than pulling a wagon. He's a ranch horse."

Daisy kept her eyes straight ahead and her voice low so James and John wouldn't hear her above the sounds of the wagon on the narrow lane leading to the main road. "If you don't mind, I'd like to keep to the topic of the day. We can talk about such business later. I don't want to remind the boys of the loss of their papa and our horses."

"Good idea." Tucker matched her volume. "I'm sorry I brought it up."

"It's not a problem," she said between taut lips. "It's just that so much is happening today. I don't want to add to the weight of all that's already on their minds. They've had a rough go of it."

"I understand." He turned the wagon onto the main road and signaled his horse to pick up speed as they headed toward town. They traveled in silence for a few minutes.

"If you don't mind, I'd like to be married in the church, not the parsonage." Daisy began to rattle off details for the afternoon's agenda. "We can have a nice supper at the local hotel. It's a very impressive establishment for a town as small as Pine Haven. The food is very good. I'd also like to stop in at the general store. The boys haven't had a treat in a long time. I think this is just the occasion for it."

"Whoa, Daisy. Seems like you've got this all planned out in your head already. Mind if I interject some thoughts?"

"Interject away." She lifted her arm in a sweeping gesture. "It's not like any of this was my idea in the first place. I was just trying to make the most of it."

"Oh, good. That'll help." Tucker kept his eyes on the road ahead. "Sarcasm will be just the right spice to add to today. Keep it up and James will be back to kicking dirt by the time we get to town." He grinned to let her know he was teasing her the way he had when she was a teenager. He turned and winked at her. He saw the corners of her mouth tug into a smile before he looked back to the road.

"You always had a knack for getting me out of a mood." She settled her hands in her lap again and looked up into the bright sky, appearing to relax for the first time since he'd ridden onto the farm just after lunch. She took in a deep breath and let it out in a whoosh. The boys had curled up on the hay in the back of the wagon and fallen asleep in the sunshine. Their clothes would be wrinkled, but he was glad to see they'd settled down.

"How are you, Daisy? Really?"

"I'm better now. Not over it by any means, but better. Working the farm will take the stress out of you if you let it." The underlying sadness in her voice revealed the true depth of her pain.

"If you ever need to talk about it, I'll listen."

Daisy put one gloved hand on his arm and he felt her gaze on him as he drove. "I remember many times when you did just that. Thank you, Tucker." She cleared her throat. "Not just for being a friend who's willing to listen, but for everything. I know what a sacrifice it is for you to give up your life to help me and the boys."

"Don't you worry about that for one minute. I'm sorry those little fellows lost their papa. I know what it's like to grow up without a father. You might remember mine was gone before I was old enough to know much about him. Tuberculosis took him the winter I turned five. I want to be to your sons what your father has been to me." He tried without success to cover the gravel in his tone. She gave his arm a slight squeeze of comfort, and he continued. "I also hope to be there for you in a way my momma needed when she was trying to raise me alone. It was a hard life. One I hope to spare you from." He cleared his throat and snapped the reins, effectively ending the conversation. "Get up, Mack. We need to get to town."

His mother had done her best but life without a father had been difficult.

Daisy's dad had raised his daughters with the help of a housekeeper who came during the daytime. Mr. Warren had made it seem so simple. Tucker knew that wasn't true. Parenting was a difficult job for two parents. It was more than double the work when one parent was left to do the task alone.

He knew Daisy was strong. She'd managed to care for her boys and the farm since her husband's death. The spiritual comfort of God and those precious boys had probably bolstered her courage. But she couldn't survive on courage alone.

He stole a glance at her. He knew in his heart that she still loved the man in the grave at the top of the hill behind her cabin. Tucker had been her friend all those years ago. He'd come here as her friend. Would she ever see him as more that?

Chapter Two

Tucker pulled the wagon to a stop and set the brake in front of the general store. He called to the boys. "James and John, come with me. How would you like some candy?" Sleepiness evaporated at the promise of the treat, and the boys tumbled from the wagon.

Walking to the side of the wagon, Tucker offered his hand to Daisy. She moved to accept his help, and he could see she was surprised when he grabbed her by the waist and set her on the ground. He wondered if it was because he lifted her. Did he make her skittish? He'd have to be careful not to make her uncomfortable.

Tucker leaned close so the boys wouldn't hear. "Do you want a few minutes to speak to the pastor before I come to the church? I can take the boys into the store and meet you later." He knew she must be overwhelmed with the day's events. He could see the strain on her face ease at his suggestion.

"Thank you." Daisy gave him a slight smile. "I'll go there now and meet you at the parsonage in a half hour. That should give me plenty of time."

"Are you okay with all of this?" Mr. Warren had insisted the wedding take place on the day of his arrival, but Tucker was concerned about Daisy's peace of mind.

She didn't look at him when she answered. "Papa's right. This really is for the best." Was she trying to reassure him or convince herself?

"I think so, too, but I could get a room in town and stay for a few days. If that would make you more comfortable." It would delay his start on the work he needed to do at the farm, but if it helped Daisy, he could make that small sacrifice.

"No. Thank you, but that won't be necessary." She shook her head, and he saw the resignation in her eyes. "There's no need to spend money on a hotel when you'd just be coming to the farm in a few days."

The sadness of her circumstances struck him anew. Thinking of the weight she must be under had been a driving force in his agreement to this arrangement. Her face was thin and pale. She lacked the vitality that was such a part of her personality. The sooner her life was settled, the sooner she could start to heal from her pain.

Tucker knew her sons would help to heal her heart. He hoped he could give her mind rest from the pressure of running the farm alone.

"I'll meet you in a few minutes, then." He nodded and looked over his shoulder to see the boys staring into the large storefront window.

"The boys can show you the way." Daisy turned, and the heels of her shoes clicked a rhythm on the boarded sidewalk as she hurried away.

Tucker watched her go, thanking God for the opportunity to have her in his life. In the years after she'd left her father's ranch, Tucker had kept busy with work.

He'd focused on being a successful rancher and put all thoughts of love out of his mind.

He knew in his heart Daisy would never love him as she'd loved Murdock. And he certainly wasn't interested in being a second-best husband. But he did hope her friendship would fill the aching loneliness he suffered.

"Daisy, what a lovely surprise!" Peggy greeted Daisy and ushered her into the parsonage. "David, come into the parlor. Daisy Mosley is here." Peggy offered Daisy one of the two chairs by the front window. "Sit down and tell me how you're doing." Peggy sat in the other chair.

"I'm doing better. As a matter of fact, that's why I've come to town today. I have news." Daisy was interrupted when Reverend Dismuke entered the room.

"Mrs. Mosley, to what do we owe the honor of your visit?"

"I was just about to tell Peggy. I've received a letter from my father."

"Does he want you to move back home?" Peggy asked anxiously.

"No." Daisy looked from Peggy to Reverend Dismuke. "He sent Tucker Barlow. Tucker came to work for him when I was still in school. He's been a dear friend to me and my sisters."

"That's seems a sound idea," the reverend approved. "You'll be needing a man's help with the farm."

"And the boys," Peggy added.

Daisy bit her lower lip before continuing. "Papa wants me to marry Tucker. He doesn't think it would be proper for a Christian woman to have a man on her property unless they've been wed. He wants to protect the boys and me from gossip."

"Also a wise consideration," Reverend Dismuke agreed. "People can be cruel. Children are especially vulnerable to be hurt."

"What about you? Are you okay with this idea?" Peggy asked.

"I won't lie and tell you it'll be easy. I miss Murdock terribly." Daisy reached and covered Peggy's hand with one of her own. "But I don't think I have a choice. Papa's right about the boys needing a father in their lives. There's also the question of the land."

"You can own the land now. There's a new law," Peggy offered.

"It's not been tested. I can't risk losing everything Murdock worked so hard to give to James and John."

"But what about…love?" Peggy wanted to know. "You can't just marry someone to save the farm. You've got to consider your heart, as well."

"Tucker's a good man. And my father picked him. Besides, there's more to think about than love." Daisy tried to hide the uncertainty in her voice.

"Mrs. Mosley, may I speak frankly?" Reverend Dismuke asked.

"Of course. I trust your counsel." Daisy waited for his next words.

"As the shepherd of this flock I've seen many women go through what you're facing. Their husbands die or are killed suddenly, leaving them as widows with land and children. Many with little or no money. I have yet to see one survive without help. This is not the kind of country a woman alone can conquer safely. What if you find a way to handle everything about the farm and the boys, and then one day those thieves come back?"

"David! Don't frighten her!" Peggy gasped.

"I'm not trying to frighten her," he assured, "but I saw Sheriff Collins yesterday, and he still hasn't had any success in tracking down Murdock's killers."

Peggy clicked her tongue in disapproval. "I'm not sure why we trust that man to protect this county."

"He's a good sheriff, Peggy. He's just not much for decorum," Reverend Dismuke disagreed.

"Well, he always looks as if he's just rolled out of bed," Peggy insisted. "How do we know he's done all that can be done to find those thieves?"

"I've talked with him at length, and I assure you he's doing his job. It's just not an easy one." To Daisy he said, "I'm sorry. I know this is very difficult for you."

"I've wished a thousand times that I'd been home that day. Maybe I could have saved him." Daisy's remorse was palpable.

"Oh, Daisy, you can't torture yourself like that. You and the boys could have been hurt—or worse—if you'd been there," Peggy lamented.

"My wife is right. God was protecting you and your sons that day. I don't pretend to understand all He does or why, but I know He had a purpose for you to be spared." They all sat in silence for a moment.

Daisy couldn't bear the thought of those murderous thieves returning and harming her sons. She hoped each day to hear news of their capture. Would she always have one eye on the lane while she worked? Would she be able to let the boys return to school? She wondered if they'd ever be safe again.

Reverend Dismuke was the first to speak. "I think you should accept Mr. Barlow's offer of marriage."

Daisy nodded her agreement. She hadn't been able to save Murdock, but at least she could protect his sons.

"Are you sure, Daisy?" Peggy leaned over and grasped both of Daisy's hands.

"I've prayed, Peggy, and I feel this is what the Lord would have me do." The resolve in Daisy's voice won her friend's agreement.

"Okay, then." Peggy sat back up straight and smoothed her dress. "Well, when do we meet this Mr. Barlow, and when is the wedding?" Peggy asked.

A knock sounded at the door.

"Now. And now," Daisy sputtered with a laugh.

"What?" Peggy exclaimed.

"I'll answer that. You calm down," Reverend Dismuke teased his wife as he went to the door.

Both ladies stood as Tucker and the twins entered the room. The boys stood on either side of Tucker, making an obvious effort to stand at their full height, so much so that their small necks stretched to achieve full advantage of their stature. Small grins tugged at their matching faces, but she saw the restraint to prevent pride from bursting forth. Then she noticed the reason for this new posture. Tucker stood, hat in hand, and each boy had a smaller, though very similar hat, held in the exact way. John stole a look at Tucker to confirm he had the stance correct.

James could hold his peace no longer. "Momma! How do you like our hats? Mr. Tucker helped us pick 'em out!" He offered her a closer look without moving from Tucker's side. "These are real Stetsons just like Mr. Tucker's! Only they're different 'cause everyone can make his Stetson how he wants. I like mine with the brim down, like Mr. Tucker. John likes his with the top pushed in just so. They're great, aren't they Momma?"

"That's very nice, James." Daisy touched the felt

brim. "What about yours, John?" She moved to stand in front of the youngest twin.

"I like mine just fine, Momma. They were expensive, but Mr. Tucker said we needed them." He didn't meet her gaze. John was always cautious, and a matter was never settled for him as quickly as it was for James.

Daisy turned to Tucker, tilting her head to see into his eyes. She saw the mirth there. He was enjoying the happiness of her sons. She was grateful to see them excited. They hadn't had a treat in a long time, and certainly nothing so grand.

"Need them?" She raised her eyebrows and waited for an explanation from Tucker. Surely he understood they didn't have that kind of money.

Tucker stretched his neck to pronounce his height and tilted his head to one side ever so slightly. "Yes, ma'am. Every working farmer needs a good hat. These young men are no exception. It wouldn't be proper for me to expect them to work without the tools they need." His barely suppressed grin reminded her of the twins forced restraint. They'd only met a few hours ago, and already these males were forming an alliance she was certain she'd have to confront on a regular basis.

Looking from one to the other she addressed all three at once. "Well, I see you had a successful trip to the general store. Now it's time for us to go to the church."

Everyone made their way to the front door and down the steps to walk toward the church. Daisy looped her arm in Tucker's, easing back into the friendship they'd shared for years. In a voice for his ears only, she leaned in and said, "When I said they could have a treat, I meant something like a piece of candy or fruit. I don't know how you thought we could afford something like that."

"Oh, they got candy, too."

Daisy looked ahead to see both boys pulling a handful of candy from their pockets to compare.

"In the future we need to talk about things like this before they happen. And why are they calling you Mr. Tucker?" Daisy almost sounded as if she was scolding Tucker.

Leaning closer to her, without losing his grin, Tucker spoke. "There are a lot of things we'll talk about in the future, but buying those hats was my decision, and I stand by it. And they're calling me Mr. Tucker because I prefer it to Mr. Barlow. We're going to be family in just a few minutes."

"Well…" she interrupted.

He held up his free hand. "Well, nothing. You said you wanted us to stay focused on the events of today. We'll talk about other things later, but right now…" Tucker gestured to the door of the small church that John held open for them. The others had walked ahead and were already inside. "Right now, we're going to a wedding. And I think we both need to concentrate on that." His fingers brushed the length of her jawline, and he smiled.

Daisy drew in a breath to calm herself. "Okay. I'll focus." She lifted her skirt just enough to keep from stepping on it as she climbed the steps. "But we have a lot to talk about, Tucker. And we will talk about it." She dropped her hem and smoothed her skirt as they passed through the doorway.

"I'm sure we will, Daisy." Tucker removed his hat and handed it to John for safekeeping during the ceremony. "I'm sure we will." He offered her his hand, and they proceeded up the aisle.

Daisy stood beside Tucker at the altar of Pine Haven

Church. She took advantage of the opportunity to study him in what must be his best shirt and trousers. The red hair had been tamed with a fresh combing. He was every inch a man—and a tall one at that. He stood a good foot taller than she did with strong shoulders and a broad chest. His boots wore a fresh shine.

James and John sat on the first bench, watching as Reverend Dismuke performed the wedding ceremony, their new hats carefully resting beside them, Tucker's much larger hat on John's farside. They giggled a little at first, but Tucker silenced them with a look. Daisy was surprised by how quickly he'd taken command of the boys' behavior. She'd been prone to leniency since their father's death. Truly things were changing today. Daisy would do her best to keep the changes at a manageable pace. The twins would need time to adjust to Tucker's authority.

Reverend Dismuke went through the vows with great reverence, explaining the weight of the commitment of the marriage ceremony in the eyes of God.

"Tucker, wilt thou have this woman to thy wedded wife, to live together after God's ordinance, in the holy estate of matrimony? Wilt thou love her, comfort her, honor, and keep her, in sickness and in health, and, forsaking all others, keep thee only unto her, so long as ye both shall live?"

Tucker looked at her and answered, "I will."

Daisy, in turn, promised herself to him. With each word spoken a heaviness settled on her soul. She knew she had no choice—knew she was doing the right thing. But could she find the inner strength to build a relationship with an old friend into a marriage? Her first husband had captivated her fancy, and she'd fallen deeply in love with him. Now she stood in her church before God and witnesses and pledged to give Tucker the same commitment she'd shared with Murdock. Tucker had been a dear friend. But her husband? Never had the thought crossed her mind. Daisy was surprised by how quickly the ceremony progressed. Before she realized it the reverend asked if there was a ring. Something she hadn't thought about.

"Oh, we don't—" Daisy shook her head, only to be stunned into silence when Tucker pulled a ring from his shirt pocket and handed it to the preacher.

"Let us pray." Reverend Dismuke bowed his head and spoke. "Loving God, we ask You to bless this union. Help Tucker and Daisy to grow together as husband and wife. Build a strong bond between these two souls." Daisy felt the heat rush to her face and prayed her own prayer that she hadn't blushed as deeply as she felt. "God help these two fine young men, James and John, to bring You honor by the way they respect their momma and their new papa." The boys both opened their eyes at this point. "And most of all, God, we thank You for bringing these folks together as a family. May they live, as this ring represents, an endless circle of love that shines with beauty and strength. Amen."

"Amen." Tucker and Daisy spoke softly in unison. James and John sat in silence. Peggy wiped a tear away with her handkerchief.

Reverend Dismuke returned the ring to Tucker, who reached for Daisy's hand. She stared at him, unbelieving, as he slipped the delicate ring on her finger. Intricately carved leaves and vines wrapped around the gold band. Tucker repeated after the minister, "With this ring

I thee wed, with my body I thee worship and with all my worldly goods I thee endow."

Reverend Dismuke finalized their commitment by saying, "I now pronounce you man and wife. You may kiss the bride."

Tucker looked to Daisy, asking permission with his eyes. Feeling it would be unfair to deny Tucker this right after all he was sacrificing for her and her children, Daisy nodded her assent with the slightest tip of her head, lowered her gaze and waited. He gently took her face in his large hands and tenderly brushed a kiss across her cheek. She opened her eyes wide and thanked him from her soul without speaking a word. His smile acknowledged his understanding of her gratitude.

As the small group left the church, Reverend Dismuke pulled Tucker and Daisy aside. "Sheriff Collins has been trying to find the men who killed Murdock. He sent word of the killing to sheriffs in the neighboring counties. I'm sure he'd be glad to meet you, Tucker. He's been concerned for the safety of your wife and the boys."

"Thanks," Tucker said. "I'll stop by his office and introduce myself."

"He's a bit rough around the edges, but I think he's doing all he can."

"I'll see if there's anything I can do to help him." Tucker settled his hat back on his head. "Right now, though, I'm going to take my new family to supper. Thanks, Reverend, for your time today."

Tucker's words rang in her head as she walked with him to the wagon. They were a family on their way to supper. Only they weren't an ordinary family. Nothing about this day had been ordinary.

* * *

"Boys, put your hats on the rack here by the door." Daisy noticed Tucker hung his hat up high so the twins could use the lower pegs.

"Are we really gonna eat in the hotel, Momma?" the ever-curious James wanted to know.

"She already said so, James." John was losing patience with his brother today.

"Yes, we're eating here. I want both of you on your best behavior," Daisy admonished as she pulled her gloves off and tucked them into her reticule. "Papa Warren is giving us this wedding supper as a gift. I want everyone to enjoy it. So mind your manners."

The hostess escorted them to a table set with linen and glassware. The smell of freshly baked bread filled the room.

Tucker held a chair for Daisy, signaling the twins to wait until their mother sat. When they were all seated, a young girl wearing a starched white apron over a simple brown dress offered them menus.

Daisy skimmed the choices before looking to Tucker. "Roast beef for everyone? With creamed potatoes and carrots and some of that delicious-smelling bread?"

"Sounds wonderful to me." Tucker closed his menu. "I think this is just the kind of place your papa had in mind for our wedding supper."

"I wish he could be here." Daisy's heart ached for the comfort of her father's love. She sniffed and straightened in her chair, neatly folding her hands in her lap. Her voice went up just a notch in tone, but not volume. "But that's not possible, so we'll make the most of the occasion he's provided for us. I'll write him a letter tonight and tell him how much we appreciate his gift."

Her head was still spinning with the knowledge that she was married again. Table conversation was a great effort, but she did want to honor her father by enjoying this meal. It was a great luxury that wouldn't likely come their way again soon.

"I'm sure he would like to know things have worked out like he hoped. Let's send him a telegraph on the way home. Then you can write a letter with all the details, and we can post it the next time we're in town," Tucker suggested.

"That's a fine idea. Then he'll know everything is settled, and the boys and I are safe," Daisy agreed.

The boys grew fidgety at the table, most likely in response to all the candy they'd managed to eat by sneaking pieces whenever they thought no one was looking. Now they both had empty pockets.

"Stop kicking me." John sent James a glare.

"I'm not kicking you." James spoke just a little louder than John.

"That's enough." Tucker's voice was even, but serious. "James, stop swinging your legs under the table. John sit up straight in your chair, and you won't be close enough for James to accidentally kick you." The twins immediately obeyed, looking to Daisy as their eyes worked to conceal their displeasure at his command.

Daisy was again taken aback when Tucker corrected James and John. Murdock had always left the day-to-day manners and attitudes for her to deal with. She wasn't accustomed to someone taking over her responsibilities, and she was certain she didn't like it.

Tucker spoke again before she could decide how to address the matter with him. "I need to take care of some business before we leave town." The young waitress approached and filled his glass with tea. "If you need anything from the general store, I can drop you there, and you can shop. I'll pick you up when I'm finished." The waitress circled the table to serve the boys and Daisy before leaving.

"What kind of business can you possibly have? You just arrived today," Daisy said, picking up her glass. James had inherited his curiosity from his mother. She'd always had a deep-seated desire to know everything that was going on around her at all times. Constant observation and well-placed questions kept her from feeling uninformed. She never liked to be caught unaware.

"Just some business matters I need to handle." Tucker answered vaguely. "I won't be long."

The door to the kitchen swung open as the waitress backed through it carrying a large round tray with their food. James and John sat up eagerly to watch each plate be set on the fancy table. Daisy had instructed them on the flatware, but she knew they'd be hard-pressed to muzzle their excitement over this new experience. The waitress left after placing a large basket of bread in the center of the table next to a silver dish of fresh butter.

Daisy leaned forward and reached across the corners of the square table to take the twins by the hand. They looked at one another and then at her. She raised her eyebrows toward Tucker before they reluctantly reached their other hands to him. This was the kind of reluctance she expected from her sons today. It was a wonder they'd been as agreeable as they had for much of the day. Accepting a new hat from an old friend of hers was one thing. It was another thing entirely to include the same friend in their family traditions—like prayer over a meal.

* * *

Tucker had been leaning back with one leg crossing the opposite knee before the food arrived. He'd pulled his chair closer to the table as the waitress retreated behind the still-swinging door. His hands held the edges of his chair. Looking up, he met Daisy's gaze and saw her intent. Unfamiliar with his new family's mealtime expectations, the cowboy turned to each boy and took the offered hand.

"Will you give thanks, Tucker?" Daisy asked.

"Hmm-hmm." Tucker cleared his throat. He wasn't accustomed to praying aloud. "Dear, Lord. Thank You for this bountiful supper. We thank You for Your protection and guidance. Help us all to follow You in everything we do and to be good examples of Your love. Amen."

"Amen," Daisy said with the boys before they all tucked into the delicious food.

"This is a fine supper. I didn't realize how hungry I was." Tucker put a bite of bread in his mouth.

Daisy agreed with him. "The roast is so tender. I would never have had time to cook something this nice for us tonight. Not starting so late in the day."

He was glad to see her enjoying the meal and kept the conversation away from anything that would spoil it for her.

Careful of Daisy's admonishment to mind their manners, the boys didn't talk because they were too busy eating. Only after John finished the meal and put his fork down, did he speak.

"That was good!"

"I really liked it, too. But I like Momma's best." James joined the conversation.

"That's very sweet of you, James. Thank you. It was a fine supper." Daisy took her napkin from her lap and folded it neatly before laying it on the table. "Now let's go see what we need from the general store before we head back home." She moved to push her chair back.

"We haven't had dessert yet." Tucker had watched her speech and knew she was trying to set the agenda again. He knew she liked to know all the details beforehand, but he wanted to surprise her.

"Dessert?" two boys chimed in unison.

"Cake, actually." Tucker caught the attention of the waitress by lifting one hand.

"Yes, sir? Are you ready now?" she asked as she approached the table.

"I believe we are. Thank you."

The waitress cleared away their plates and disappeared into the kitchen.

Tucker watched Daisy as the door opened again, and the girl turned toward their table.

"It's the most beautiful cake I've ever seen." Smooth white icing with intricate layers of piping created a look of lace. "I've heard of the hotel's reputation for great desserts, but never seen one." Her face glowed with admiration for the unexpected treat.

"Would you like me to serve you, or would you prefer to cut it, ma'am?" the waitress asked while setting dessert plates on the table.

"I think we can manage, thank you." Daisy reached for the knife and hesitated. The waitress left them. The boys were wide-eyed at the cake. Tucker sat leaning back with his arms folded across his chest, smiling.

"You did this," she accused. "How?"

"I confess. I stopped in on my way through town and

asked about a special dessert before I went to your place to propose. I thought it would make a nice ending to the day." He was pleased by their reactions.

"What if I'd said 'no'?" Daisy pointed the knife at him teasingly.

"Oh, I thought you'd come around to your papa's way of seeing things." He couldn't stop the grin that pulled at the corners of his mouth.

"I see," Daisy said before slicing a substantial slab of cake. "We'll just have to see about how well you can predict my thinking in the future." He heard the taunting tone in her statement as she passed a dessert plate to him.

Tucker smiled. "I fully expect to be challenged on a regular basis. And I expect to rise to the occasion." Using the side of his fork, he cut off a large bite of cake and paused before putting it in his mouth. "Don't forget I've known you for a long time. I know a lot about how you can be." His smile almost became a smirk, effectively returning her challenge and making her smile.

"I'll keep that in mind." She cut practically identical pieces of cake for the boys. Tucker imagined equality was the only road to peace between them.

Daisy served herself, and Tucker watched her savor the sweet dessert with all the fervor of the twins. While they ate, he remembered how he'd once hoped for a strong and healthy marriage with this beautiful woman. If she'd been older, he would have told her how he felt. Before she had ever met Murdock. Now he knew that even after she had time to grieve the loss of her first husband, Murdock would always be her one true love.

Falling for Daisy all those years ago was the last time he'd risked trying to find lasting love. As a boy, he'd seen his mother never recover from the loss of his father. He also watched Daisy's father choose to live alone after losing his wife. He wouldn't let himself dwell on how he'd learned firsthand the power of someone's first love. Rejection was hard to live with. It was harder to leave behind. He vowed never to put himself in that position again. He would be Daisy's friend—but nothing more.

Chapter Three

Daisy held the edge of the seat as Tucker pulled the reins and stopped the wagon in front of the general store. James and John leaped to the dirt and assisted their mother from the wagon.

"Good job, boys. I'll be back as soon as I've taken care of a few errands." To Daisy he said, "Get whatever you need. I'll stop in and settle up when I get back." Tucker signaled Mack, and the wagon lurched forward.

James and John each grabbed one of Daisy's hands and tried to pull her into the store. "Come on, Momma. We can help you shop. Mr. Tucker says we're good shoppers. He says we got good taste." James rattled away as usual.

Daisy resisted their pull long enough to see her wagon turn right at the corner. Tucker could be going almost anywhere. Pine Haven consisted of two intersecting streets lined with businesses that served the small, growing community. Pine Haven Church sat at the opposite end of the street Tucker had turned on, and the livery was at the other end. The general store was just shy of the main crossroads.

Standing on the porch of the general store, Daisy wondered what business Tucker could be conducting. He'd turned in the direction of the bank and the lumber mill. There was also a post office and a blacksmith in that area. Or could he be going to the livery? He'd mentioned wanting to purchase horses. They hadn't discussed money yet. Daisy hoped he wasn't going to take on too much without at least talking to her. She'd always known what Murdock was doing with their money. Was Tucker a man who considered their money to be his money? Did he think a woman should leave matters of business to the man? Murdock had taught Daisy how to keep the financial records for their cotton crop. She was well versed in the costs of farming, how to balance the funds to make it from one harvest to the next and how to survive lean times.

Feeling a tug on each hand, Daisy followed James and John into the store, still thinking about Tucker's errands. For all their past friendship, there was a lot Daisy didn't know about the man who was now her husband.

Tucker opened the door of the sheriff's office and stepped into the dank atmosphere. The two small cells on the back wall each had a tiny window lined with bars to prevent escape. Minimal light came through the dirty front window. The smell of gun oil and dust assailed his nostrils. A man sporting a heavy mustache and several days' growth of beard dozed behind the massive wooden desk. The tarnished star on his vest was the only clue the unkempt man was indeed the sheriff. He was of an indiscernible age somewhere between thirty and fifty. The chair creaked under his weight as he shook himself and lowered the front legs to the floor at Tucker's appearance.

"Sheriff Collins?" Tucker extended his hand. "I'm Tucker Barlow."

The sheriff fumbled to his feet and squinted at Tucker from beneath scraggly eyebrows. "What can I do for ya?" His face remained wrinkled as he stirred himself from sleep.

"I'm new in town. Just wanted to stop by and introduce myself. I married Daisy Mosley earlier today. I understand you've been searching for the men who killed her first husband."

"Yep." Sheriff Collins sat back in his chair. "Wanna sit? Sorry you caught me nappin'. I've been up late most nights trying to keep an eye on things in case those thieves head back this way."

Tucker took the offered seat. "Have you had any success?"

"Not much to go on. The sheriffs from the counties around us haven't been able to help me, either. Nobody's seen nothin'. I sent out flyers and telegraphed everybody I figured would know something. Even got the Rangers lookin' into it for us. Only know more horses were taken from a county south of here. Owners weren't home so nobody got hurt."

"What about clues from the Mosley farm? Did they leave any signs of who they were?"

"We know for sure there's two of 'em. Know that from the horseshoe prints they left. Murdock's horses was shoed here in town. Blacksmith here knew which marks was from Murdock's horses and which ones wasn't. Tracked 'em to the creek at the edge of the property, but lost 'em. They knew to get in the water and ride.

Smart thieves, too. Murdock had some good horseflesh. I want you to know we've done all we could. It's hard when nobody saw or heard what happened. The little missus was in town with her boys."

"Will you let us know if you hear anything? I'd like to see these men brought to justice. I hate to think of them hurting other people like they did the Mosley family." Tucker stood and put his hat back on his head.

"I'll sure do it, Mr. Barlow. You take care out there. Don't like them fellas being on the loose myself." Sheriff Collins leaned the chair back and propped his feet on the desk again. "I been especially worried 'bout the missus and those cute little boys. Didn't want no more harm to come to 'em."

"I'll be protecting them now. By the good Lord's help, we'll be fine."

An hour later Tucker returned to the general store. Daisy stood at the porch railing, her toe tapping the boards, impatience growing by the minute. She and the boys had finished their shopping within twenty minutes. The twins' restlessness with waiting caused her to send them across the street to the Ledford Dressmaker Shop. Milly Ledford had a son, Reilly, who was a year younger than her boys. They were playing upstairs in the Ledfords' living quarters.

"Ahh, you're ready. I'm glad. It's going to be dark soon. I didn't want to have to wait long." Tucker pulled the large brake handle and vaulted from the wagon to the ground in front of her, smiling. "What do I need to load up?" He was looking around for her purchases. "And where are James and John?"

"Ready?" The word came out slowly. Daisy took a

deep breath. "Yes, you could say we're ready. We have been for the better part of an hour." She indicated a small package wrapped in brown paper and tied with twine. There was also a crate with a few grocery staples. "The boys could only be still so long. I sent them across the street to play with a friend."

"Will you get them while I go in and settle the bill?" Tucker set the crate over the side of the wagon and brushed his hands together to remove the dust.

"I'll get them now." Daisy descended the two front steps, pretending she didn't see his offered hand. "But the bill is already settled." Daisy kept walking without looking back. She disappeared inside the dress shop for the briefest moment and then returned to the wagon.

Tucker reached out a hand to help her, leaning in closely to speak softly against her golden hair so only she could hear. "I told you I'd settle the bill."

"I already had it covered." Caught off guard by his sudden nearness and not wanting to fall and embarrass herself, she was forced to accept his hand to climb up and take her seat.

"It's my responsibility to provide for the family. I can pay for the things we need." Tucker climbed into his seat and took the reins.

"I have already made provision for the things we will need until next year's harvest. You don't have to spend your money on us." Daisy's stubborn streak refused to allow her to relinquish complete responsibility for her family.

"We're in this together now, Daisy. I know your stubbornness has helped you survive all you've been through. I admire your strength and spirit, but we've got to work together now. We can't build a future if you refuse to let me help. I didn't sign up to be a farmhand. I signed up to be your husband."

Daisy sat with her back straight in stony silence. Part of her knew he was right. She finally looked at him. "I've had to do everything on my own since Murdock died."

"I understand that. I'm only saying you're not alone anymore. I'm here to help."

The boys sprinted out of the dress shop, yelling their goodbyes to Reilly and Mrs. Ledford, before jumping into the back of the wagon.

"Whoa, there, boys. Be careful. Your momma has her packages back there. And there's a crate of mine that I don't want you to get hurt on." Tucker admonished the twins and released the brake. Once again he took the lead in instructing the boys.

"What did you get, Mr. Tucker?" James couldn't resist being nosy.

"Just some things I'll be needing at the house, James, nothing for you to concern yourself about. You boys have a seat. I'm going to press Mack to get us home before dark. Hang on." With a crack of the reins they were soon leaving town in the distance.

The sun was just visible on the horizon when Tucker turned the wagon onto the lane that led to their cabin. The boys had again fallen asleep. This time they'd covered their faces with the new hats. Daisy smiled at their attempts to appear grown as she roused them before Tucker had a chance to speak.

"James and John, we're home. I need you to wake up and help with the wagon."

Sleepy boys in rumpled clothes leaned over the back of the seat to collapse on Daisy's shoulders. "Momma, do we have to help? I'm tired." James buried his head in her sleeve.

"Yes, you do. Mr. Tucker is tired, too. He's been traveling for several days. You can help with the wagon and see to the animals. Then you can go to bed. If you hurry, I'll have milk and another piece of cake waiting for a snack."

Everyone carried something into the house when the wagon came to a stop. The waitress had boxed the remainder of the cake before they left the restaurant, and Tucker had stowed it safely under Daisy's seat.

"Boys, I'll unhitch the wagon while you see to your regular nightly chores. Let's see who can get to the cake the fastest." Tucker challenged the twins, who responded more for the cake than the challenge. He laughed when they stirred up a trail of dust in the evening twilight as they ran to check their animals.

Tucker turned to Daisy as she moved to close the door from inside the cabin. "I'll be a few minutes. I'd like another slice of cake, too. After the boys are in bed, I'd appreciate it if you and I could visit for a bit."

Daisy stood in the doorway framed in the glow of the lamp she'd lit on the table behind her. "Okay. We certainly have a lot of catching up to do." She closed the door softly. Leaning her forehead against the door, she heard him whistling a happy tune as he stepped off the porch.

Icing on the tip of John's nose let Tucker know the boys started eating their cake before he finished his chores. James was putting his empty plate and cup in the dishpan on the cabinet under the front window. Tucker hung his hat on the highest peg inside the front door.

"That's papa's peg," James spouted. "No one hangs their hat there but my papa."

Tucker stood still, assessing the situation. Daisy turned from where she was stoking the fire and put the poker aside.

"James. Be quiet," Daisy cautioned her eldest.

"But it's Papa's peg. Not Mr. Tucker's. He can't take Papa's place." The youngster was working himself into a panic. His breathing was starting to come in short rasps, and his shoulders started to shake.

"James, I'm not trying to take your papa's place." Tucker said, as Daisy put an arm around James's shoulder.

John started to whimper at the table. He put his head down on crossed arms and began to cry in earnest.

"Oh, boys, don't cry. Tucker is here to help us. Not to take your papa's place." Daisy steered James to the table and sat on the bench between them, gently rocking with an arm of comfort around each son.

Tucker sat at the head of the table. "Your momma's right. I'm not here to take anyone's place. Only to help."

"But now you're sitting in Papa's chair," James wailed. "And you whispered in Momma's ear while we were in town. You're doing all the things our papa did!" John continued to weep, but didn't say anything. Daisy looked at Tucker over the tops of their small heads. He saw the pain in her eyes.

"Look at me, boys." Tucker's tone was gentle, but firm. Two blond heads tilted upward. Tears still flowed, but they were silent now. "No one can take your papa's place. He was a fine man." James sniffed loudly and wiped his face with the sleeve of his nightshirt. "I knew your papa. I met him years ago when he started courting your momma." John dried his eyes. Tucker had their complete attention.

"You did?" This quiet question came from John.

"I did." Tucker nodded. "I remember the first day he came to see your papa Warren and ask if he could come calling on your momma. He was tall and lean. A handsome young fellow, about twice your age, I'd say." The twins sat up to listen. Daisy's arms fell to her sides, and her eyes misted over as he continued telling his story.

"He was wiry, but strong. Went right up the front steps, took off his hat and rapped with the knocker. Your momma came to the door, all shy and sweet. Her hair was down and full of curls. She was wearing a blue dress the color of the sky in springtime. Her eyes sparkled, and her face went all pretty and pink when she saw it was your papa on the porch." Daisy's eyes widened in wonder. Tucker knew she'd been unaware he'd stood just inside the barn door watching the events unfold that day. She only had eyes for Murdock then.

"Really? Tell us more!" James was intrigued.

"Well, I couldn't hear what he said, but I saw your momma go inside and come back with your papa Warren. He walked outside, and him and your papa took a walk down by a stream that runs by your momma's old home place. They were only gone a few minutes. I could see your momma peeking through the parlor curtains trying to see what they were doing. She was trying to be all sneaky and hide, but I could see her. She never has been much for waitin' and seein'. She always wants to know what's happening right when it's going on."

Daisy's mouth dropped open as if to refute him, but closed when he met her stare and raised his eyebrows.

The twins chuckled. Tucker figured they knew this first-hand, but that no one had ever described her like this.

"What happened next?" John asked quietly.

"Seems like I remember your papa whooping out loud and slapping his hat against his leg. Then he turned and started to trot up the hill back to the house. But he stopped real sudden like and hollered down the bank at your papa Warren. 'Thank you, sir!' he said. Then he broke out in a run and took the porch steps two at a time. You would've thought the knocker was gonna break right off the hinge the way he beat on that door." Everyone laughed at that.

"What did Momma do?" James interrupted, again showing his inherited impatience.

"James, your momma's a lot like you, I think. She'd seen your papa celebrating and must have figured out her papa had permitted their courting. She was at that door swinging it open so fast your papa almost fell in when she opened it. She was grinning from ear to ear. I've never seen her look happier. Except on the day she married your papa." Silence settled over the small group as they each absorbed the sweet memory he'd shared.

"So you see, I know how special your papa was to your momma. And I know what a good man he was, or your papa Warren would never have let him court your momma. I watched them court and saw their relationship grow into a deep love. That's something special. Not everybody gets to love, or be loved, like that. Your papa was always good and kind to your momma. It was obvious to me, and anyone else who took the time to notice, that your momma and papa were meant for each other."

Seeing her true love for Murdock had prevented Tucker from declaring his own love for Daisy back then.

He had loved her so much he wanted her to be happy. Even if that happiness came from her being with Murdock. He remembered the ache in his chest that day. His heart had started to grow a protective shell as his hope of having Daisy for his wife had been extinguished.

"Out of respect for their relationship, I promise I won't try to take your papa's place. But I'm your momma's friend—have been for many long years. I came here because I care about her, and I care about you boys. Do you think you could grow to respect me as your momma's friend and someone who cares about all of you?" Tucker waited while the boys thought. He looked at Daisy. Tears slid down her cheeks.

"Yes, sir. I believe we can." James answered for both twins. John nodded his agreement. "But what about Papa's hat peg and his chair at the table?"

"Well…" Daisy spoke for the first time since Tucker had started his story. "Since Mr. Tucker and your papa were friends, do you think Papa would be okay with letting Mr. Tucker use things that he used, since Papa's in heaven and won't be needing them for himself?"

"It hurts so much that he's never coming back, Momma." John's broken heart seemed to cry out for the papa he could no longer see and touch.

"I know, John." Daisy pulled him close. "Papa didn't leave because he wanted to, but we know he's safe with Jesus. He'd want us to be happy and make new friends and build new relationships. Mr. Tucker has been my friend for a long time. I'm sure your papa's glad he's come to help us. I think it would be okay with your papa for us to share his things with Mr. Tucker."

"If you're sure," James said.

"I'm sure." Daisy hugged both boys close.

"Okay," John added.

Daisy stood up and patted her hair smooth. "I think it's time for the two of you to get to bed. Tell Mr. Tucker good-night."

Watching the three of them go into the boys' room, Tucker almost wished his heart hadn't frozen over when Daisy married Murdock. But experience taught him that Daisy would never love anyone the way she had loved Murdock. His heart was better left cold, rather than warming only to be rejected yet again.

Chapter Four

Daisy joined Tucker in the front room after settling the boys for the night. She sat in her rocking chair near the fire. The night had cooled to a chilly temperature. Tucker sat on the other side of the fireplace in Murdock's chair. The warm glow of a lamp cast the room in shadows.

Her family had happily shared this small space for many years. This morning it had seemed cavernous without Murdock. Tonight it felt suddenly cramped. Tucker was a big man. His presence and person would be impossible to ignore in the confines of the room.

"They are finally asleep. It was quite a day for them." Daisy stared into the fire. She noticed Tucker had added more wood to it and stacked several logs on the hearth to be used during the night, if necessary. His act of kindness made her realize how bone tired she was. Carrying the load alone for almost a month had taken a toll on her body and mind.

"It was quite a day for all of us, Daisy." Tucker leaned forward and placed his elbows on the arms of the rocker. "You've got to be as exhausted as those boys."

"I am tired." Daisy leaned her head back against the

chair and closed her eyes while still rocking the chair. Moments later she started slightly. Tucker stood over her with a hand on her shoulder.

"I'm sorry. I must have drifted off." Daisy shook her head. "Please forgive me. I can make us some coffee." She moved to get up from her chair.

"No need." Tucker took his hat from the peg by the door. "I enjoyed the evening with you and the boys. I'll leave you to get some rest."

"Oh, I hadn't thought. Where will you sleep?" Daisy said in a small rush. "I can fix a place for you here between the fireplace and the front door. Or you can take the bed, and I can make a pallet with the boys." She started to chatter nervously, having only now thought about sleeping arrangements and what Tucker might expect.

"Relax, Daisy. I've already fixed a place in the barn. I'll stay there for now. You go to bed."

"You can't sleep there. It's cold, and the animals are there. It's not right."

"I'll be fine. I've slept with animals more times than I can count. They'll help keep the barn warm. It's not too cold out tonight. We'll get something more permanent figured out soon. Now get to bed. Bolt this door after I go. I don't want to take any chances with your safety." Tucker opened the door. The night breeze found the opening and stirred the flame of the lamp on the table.

"Tucker?" Daisy stopped him with a hand on his sleeve as he put his hat on.

He turned and looked down on her with green eyes. "Yes, Daisy?"

"Thank you for what you told the boys about their papa."

"Glad to do it. Their papa was a good man. They need to know I'm not trying to take his place." He patted her hand and lifted it from his sleeve.

"I didn't know you'd seen all that, much less that you'd remember." Daisy spoke quietly.

"I remember a lot of things from back then, Daisy." He touched her cheek with the back of his hand. "Sleep well." Tucker stepped onto the porch and pulled the door closed behind him.

After she slid the bolt in place, Daisy heard his boots descend the steps. The lonely strains of his whistled tune barely reached her ears.

How could she have fallen asleep on her wedding night? Of course, it wasn't a real wedding night, but it was still an important day for both her and Tucker. She knew his life had changed today in ways he could not have imagined. He'd never been married. He didn't know firsthand about the responsibilities of a family. This wasn't like signing on for a cattle drive that ended with a sale and profits. Would he be sorry when he found out that the work never ended and the goals were so long-term, they seemed illusive in the good times and unattainable during the hard times?

"Anybody awake in there?" Tucker called out the next morning and knocked again on the front door of the cabin.

"We're up." He heard Daisy's muffled voice. "John, open the door for Mr. Tucker."

The bolt slid and John pulled the heavy door open. Tucker watched in amusement at the flurry of activity inside.

Daisy set the coffeepot on the stove. "James, run

down to the smokehouse and bring me a slab of bacon. John, you get us some eggs." She was grabbing a bowl from the shelf when James grumbled.

She pointed a wooden spoon at the oldest twin. "We're running late today. Skedaddle."

Tucker entered the cabin and took off his hat. He hesitated before he hung it on the controversial peg. "Morning, James. John." The boys watched and looked at each other and then their mom. Silent agreement passed among them all. The issue of Tucker using their papa's things was settled.

Both boys headed for the door. "Morning, Mr. Tucker!" they shouted in unison as they raced to see who could get to the outhouse first before retrieving the items Daisy needed for breakfast.

Tucker laughed and reached for a mug on the shelf above the stove. He grabbed a towel to protect his hand and poured himself a cup of coffee before going to look out the back window.

"Sorry to wake you by chopping wood so early, but daylight is limited this time of year, and there's a lot of work to be done."

He turned from the window near the foot of her bed, noticing she hadn't taken the time to straighten the quilt. He could see the imprint where her head had rested on the pillow. He stepped around the chest that held her most precious possessions, remembering the day he'd gone to town for her father and picked it up from the general store. Mr. Warren had ordered it for her sixteenth birthday. The same year she'd met Murdock.

How ironic that God had brought him to this place. After giving up hope of ever having Daisy for his wife, he'd resigned himself to live life alone. Now God had put him in a place where he and Daisy were together, but neither of them could love the other. He'd proposed to a young woman long ago. Alice Fields's abrupt dismissal of his heart in favor of a former beau had shown him the depth of a woman's first love. Then he'd allowed himself to grow fond of Daisy, but never told her. Now her heart would always belong to Murdock, and his had long since retreated into the hollow of his soul—never to risk rejection again.

Daisy's voice broke into his thoughts. "I'm sorry things are so behind. I've done the best I could, but it's really more than one person can keep up with. James and John do their best, but they're so young." She opened the oven and put a pan of biscuits inside.

The front door blew open, and James dropped the bacon on the cabinet beside the dishpan. Just as quickly, he trotted back outside.

"Eager, isn't he?" Tucker observed.

"He knows he has to do his chores and lessons before he gets any free time. He likes to get as much done before breakfast as possible. It makes him feel like he's got some say in the latter part of his day." Daisy was slicing the bacon and laying it in the bottom of a hot skillet. The sizzling sound promised to become a delicious smell soon.

"He's a lot like you." Tucker had removed the ashes from the fireplace and put in fresh wood for the evening. He took the ash bucket to the front porch to empty later. John came in with a basket of eggs and left to help his brother in the barn.

"What makes you say that?"

"He's always asking questions, always seems to be taking charge, and just a little impatient." Tucker teased her with his observations about James. "Not that those are bad things."

Daisy turned with one hand on her hip and the butter dish in the other. "If you mean he's constantly aware of what's going on around him, learning by inquiring, has good leadership skills and doesn't like to waste time, then, yes, he is like me." Daisy set the butter down on the table with a thud to punctuate her speech.

"See. My point exactly. He's a lot like you." Tucker opened the door when he heard James coming up the steps with a fresh pail of milk. James set the pail on the cabinet and went to wash his hands behind the screen. John was only steps behind his brother.

Tucker poured milk for both boys and coffee for Daisy. Then he refilled his own mug. The boys sat on their bench, and Daisy put the last of the food on the table and took her place on the end, by James. The twins and Daisy joined hands. John was seated next to Tucker and reached for him. Tucker couldn't resist smiling at the quiet child and took his hand. Daisy and the boys bowed their heads.

Tucker took the opportunity to study her. Tresses of golden hair escaped the bun twisted at the nape of her neck. Her face was hollow from the grief she'd suffered. Her freckles stood out against pale skin. One small hand held the hand of James. The other lay on the table, and his mother's ring caught the shaft of morning sun that peeked through the window. The whole picture painted a stark reminder of the toll a person suffered on losing their true love.

Daisy lifted her head and caught him staring. She indicated that he should pray. Raising her eyebrows higher and leaning her head toward the boys, she let him know she was asking for the sake of the twins. Tucker bowed his head.

"Lord, we thank You for all Your blessings. Thank You for the food, and help us to make the most of this day You've given us. Amen."

Daisy and the boys added, "Amen." She was looking his way when Tucker reached for the biscuits, and she smiled her thanks.

It might take Tucker a while to adjust to the day-to-day workings of family life, but that's what he'd come here to do. Would Daisy be willing to adjust to him? He could see them beginning to rebuild their friendship from the past. He hoped she never expected more than that, because that's all he had left to give.

After breakfast Tucker disappeared into the barn. Between breakfast and lunch during the week, Daisy did lessons with the boys. When Murdock had been killed, the twins were terrified of leaving her alone. She'd agreed to let them school at home until after Christmas. In just over two months they would head to the town school every morning. She hoped the thieves would be found by then.

She cleared away the dishes while James and John brought their books to the table. Watching out the window while she washed the last of the dishes, Daisy caught sight of Tucker riding out the back of the barn in the direction of the creek on the rear of the property.

"Did you boys tell Mr. Tucker where the creek is?" Daisy dried her hands, untied her apron and hung it on a peg to dry. She joined James and John at the table.

"Yes, ma'am. He asked us all kinds of questions yesterday on the porch while you were getting ready for the wedding." James climbed onto the bench and opened his speller. "We told him about the fence line from the ranch next to us, and about the pond where we go swimming in summer and even about how far the cotton fields go out toward the Dixon place."

"James told him lots of stuff. I still don't know how to talk to him much, Momma, but I'm trying real hard to like him because he's your friend." John had opened the Bible to find the place they would pick up their reading today.

Daisy pushed the curling edges of John's hair out of his face. "Thank you for trying, John. Mr. Tucker is a good man. I know you'll both grow to like him. It's okay to answer his questions. He has a lot to learn about our farm." Daisy added quietly to herself, "And us."

Tucker joined them for lunch. They ate the rest of the bacon and biscuits from breakfast. A piece of wedding cake prevented the lunch from being ordinary.

"We're going to miss this cake when it's gone." Daisy covered the remaining cake and put it on the cabinet under the window.

"You can make us something sweet, Momma. You're the best cook ever!" James licked icing from the corners of his mouth and headed for the door. "Can I go finish my chores now? I'm thinking I might want to go fishing later."

"Go ahead. Just don't leave to go fishing without coming to the house and letting me know first." Daisy poured water from a bucket into the dishpan. "John, you go with your brother. You've both studied enough for one day."

John stacked the books and carried them to the shelf

in their bedroom before joining James at the door. They both put on their new hats.

"Why don't you save those new hats for church and trips to town? Special occasions and such?" Daisy didn't want to see the hats come to harm during their everyday activities.

"Mr. Tucker told us these hats were for protecting our heads from the elements while we work. We're supposed to wear 'em every day." James adjusted his brim and looked to Tucker for confirmation. "I don't know what elements are, but I want to be protected."

Tucker chuckled. "I did say that. Elements are the weather. Rain, sun, heat and that sort of thing."

"Oh," the boys responded together.

"You'll need to wear a bandana, too," Tucker added. "Today's work is going to be hot work. You can tie it around your neck, or around your head and wear it under your hat, or you can just use it to wipe your brow when you think you might be getting too sweaty."

"That's a great idea!" James was eager.

"But we don't have any bandanas," John complained.

Tucker's gaze met Daisy's, and without looking away from her, he asked the boys, "Did your papa have any bandanas?" She searched his eyes and saw only tenderness for her sons there.

"He sure did!" from James.

John added, "My favorite was his red one."

"What about it, Momma? Do you think these boys can wear their papa's bandanas while they work?" Daisy saw the twins brighten at the thought and decided it would help keep Murdock's memory alive in their minds.

"That's a fine idea. I'll get them." Daisy went into

the boys' room and came back with two bandanas. She gave the red one to John and offered a blue one to James.

"We don't know how to tie 'em." James wrung the fabric in his hands while John lifted the red one to his nose.

"It still smells like Papa," John said.

Tucker approached the boys saying, "That's the smell of a hardworking man. You'll be smelling just like your papa before you know it." He took James's bandana and tied it around his neck with the knot in the back. "Working hard makes a man smell like a man." He tied John's bandana with the knot in the front. "What do you think?" Tucker backed away and let Daisy look her boys over.

"I think you look just like your papa. Both of you." This drew big smiles from both boys.

"Now head on over to the barn and start putting fresh straw in the stalls. I mucked them out before lunch. We've got to get the barn ready for some new animals." Tucker nudged the twins toward the front door. "I'll be along to help in a minute. I just need to talk to your momma first."

Happy boys bounced off the front porch, admiring each other and their new look. The hats were adjusted and the bandanas tugged until both were satisfied. Then the race for the barn ensued. Daisy smiled at them and turned to thank Tucker.

"Thank you. That was a wonderful idea." Daisy moved to start washing the dishes and watched the boys through the window.

"It's important for them to remember their papa. And to feel like they can be like him. I'm glad to do it. Thanks for agreeing and letting them have the bandanas."

"They were just in the drawer. I didn't know what

to do with them." Daisy put both hands on the cabinet and dropped her head to her chest, eyes closed, fighting back tears. Tucker came to stand behind her and put his hands on her shoulders.

"It'll get easier. I promise. I know it's hard right now. But you're doing the right things. You're letting them talk about their papa and reassuring them that he's with the Lord." His strong hands began to gently knead the tightness of her muscles. Daisy pulled her head to one shoulder and then the next trying to relax away her stress. Then suddenly she shrugged both shoulders to her ears and pulled away from Tucker. She went to stand on the other side of the room, putting the table between them. A shiver ran down her spine and she rubbed her arms to stop the tingling.

"I'm sorry. I just can't relax right now. I'm so tense all the time. I feel so much pressure to make sure the farm is a success and the twins are taken care of, and now I'm so obligated to you for all you're doing." She raised a hand to each temple and rubbed her fingers in small circles in an effort to release the pain.

"I'm the one who's sorry. I didn't mean to make you uncomfortable, Daisy. Please forgive me." Tucker made no move toward her. He actually took a step back.

"It's not that. I just hate that my emotions go from such grief and sadness one minute, to joy at seeing something make James or John smile the next." She picked up the remaining plates from the table and moved toward the dishpan. Tucker moved to the door, giving her plenty of space.

"You said you had something we needed to talk about." Daisy put the dishes in the water and began to work without looking at him. She heard him take his hat from the peg and knew he was spinning it in his hands. Daisy had noticed he often did this when he was choosing his words carefully.

"I'm getting the stalls ready for new horses. I know you said we'd have to talk about it later, but I feel we need to get things back on track as soon as possible."

"Okay. If you think that's best." She began stacking the clean dishes on the shelves above the cabinet. "We can go to the bank the next time we're in town and get the money out. I don't keep much money here. Murdock never thought it was a good idea to keep cash around. I finally understood why on the day he was robbed and killed. Those men took a lot of things from us, but most of our money was safe in the bank." A tear ran down her cheek. Turning her back to Tucker, she caught it with the dish towel and sniffed. Raising up to her full height, Daisy pivoted to face him again. It surprised her to see that anger virtually oozed from every fiber of the man. His red hair seemed aflame on his scalp. His nostrils flared, and he took deep breaths. She couldn't ever remember seeing him so mad. Not even the day she shot him when her papa was teaching her to shoot.

"I will pay for the horses." Tucker rammed his hat on his head. "And if those murderous thieves ever come near here again, I'll see that they pay, too." The force of the slamming door caused it to bounce open again as she watched him stomp across the yard. It took a moment for her to realize she was holding her breath.

Daisy hadn't meant to upset him. Her papa was right. Being married to each other was definitely going to be a major adjustment for both of them. She knew he was just being friendly when he touched her, but she wasn't ready to be touched. It was too soon. And she couldn't let him pay for those horses. The farm expenses were her responsibility. And that temper!

Help us, Lord, or this is going to be a rough road.

Chapter Five

Tucker entered the barn and saw the boys had finished two of the stalls. Calming himself with great restraint he said, "Good job, men. I need to ask you something." He stood in the middle of the barn. James and John stilled their pitchforks. "Are you good fishermen?"

"We sure are!" James bragged. "We catch something every time we go!"

"Almost every time, James," John added. "Sometimes the fish don't bite."

"But that's not our fault, so I say we catch something every time. If the fish are biting, we're bringing 'em home." James hesitated and looked at Tucker. "Why? You want us to teach you how to fish, Mr. Tucker? We can. I just thought you might already know since you're so old and all." The boy spoke with youthful sincerity. On any other day Tucker would have laughed, but right now, he just needed some time alone.

"That's a mighty fine offer, James, but not today. I may let you give me some pointers next time. For today, though, I'd like the two of you to go see if you can bring home some supper. Part of a man's job is to put food on the table. Think you're up for the challenge?" He looked from one boy to the other.

"Yes, sir! We can do it." John turned to his brother. "Come on, James, let's get our gear. I'll race you." Pitchforks fell to the ground as eager boys headed to the other side of the barn for poles.

"Whoa, just a minute. There's another important thing a man does. He takes care of his tools. Put these pitchforks away, then get your gear and don't forget to tell your momma where you're going. Make sure she knows I'm sending you to get our supper."

"Yes, sir!" they said in unison. Within seconds Tucker had the barn to himself. He was so angry he knew he needed to be alone. Hoping some hard work would relieve his stress, Tucker rolled up his sleeves and finished spreading straw.

Enough bad things had happened to Daisy lately without him adding to it by showing her his anger. He didn't know why those men came and took her husband from her and the papa from those fine boys. He couldn't bear to see her in pain. He came here because her father asked him to, but the good Lord knew no real man could stand by quietlike while a woman suffered.

Marrying Daisy was supposed to alleviate his loneliness, not confuse him. He gained a sense of accomplishment when he helped her or the twins do something. Just being on the property to protect them brought him peace. More than once last night he'd looked out the barn door and checked to be certain everything was as it should be at the cabin. It was his duty as her friend.

But watching Daisy cry tugged at the edges of his hardened heart. That was not part of his bargain with Daisy or her father. Or God. Tucker was trying to be patient and not make her uncomfortable, but he wasn't accustomed to a woman's tears. It was a hard thing to watch without offering comfort. Yet she rejected his attempt to comfort her when he touched her shoulders. He'd need to remember not to do that again.

And he certainly didn't know how to deal with a woman who wanted to handle the money! His heart broke for her over all her suffering. At the same time he wanted to grab her and kiss her senseless when she wanted to take charge of everything.

Where had that thought come from? If she didn't want him to touch her, she sure wouldn't want him to kiss her. And he wasn't about to open himself up to more rejection. Better to keep a safe distance. Keep things friendly. Just not too friendly.

Lord, give me patience! And I think You better hurry.

Needing to steer clear of Daisy for a while, he tackled the broken boards on the stall in the corner because he felt the need to swing a hammer. Then he moved outside and repaired the chicken coop. He even moved the outhouse.

He worked until he was exhausted, but nothing could erase the memory of a single tear trailing down her face when she turned her back on him and refused his comfort.

Supper was fish, grits and hush puppies. James and John were praised for their success. They celebrated by finishing off the rest of the cake before the boys went to bed.

When Daisy came out of their room Tucker was on his way out the front door. She noticed he had stoked the fire and hauled in more wood.

"Wait, Tucker." Daisy spoke softly.

Hand on the door, Tucker shook his head without looking back, put his hat on and took a step onto the porch.

"Please." That stopped him. She'd hoped it would. "I want to apologize. I didn't mean to be so sensitive this afternoon. Please stay and sit in the warmth for a while. Have a cup of coffee." The last was almost a question.

Tucker turned and stepped back inside, closing the door to keep out the night chill. "You don't owe me an apology, Daisy." His hat once again was spinning in his hands. He stared into the fire instead of looking at her. "I didn't mean to make you uncomfortable. I promise to be more careful." He glanced up then.

Daisy smiled and reached for his arm. "You were being a kind friend, Tucker. I'm truly sorry. Please forgive me."

He patted her hand briefly and withdrew his arm. "If you'll forgive me," he said with a smile.

"Okay." Daisy went to pour the coffee. She added honey to her delicate cup and stirred it gently.

"Okay, then." Tucker hung his hat on the peg and took a seat by the fire. He moved the rocker back from the hearth, then slid low in the seat and stretched his legs. He propped his arms on the sides of the chair, moaning a little. "We sure do seem to be apologizing to each other a lot." She heard the effort he made to keep his tone light.

Daisy put a heavy mug of rich black brew in his hand. "Well, there's one thing for sure—" She untied her apron with one hand, pulled it loose, and took her seat. She draped the apron across the chair arm. "If we keep having these disagreements, you'll have this place in fine order in no time." She grinned and took a sip of the sweet liquid.

Tucker laughed and immediately grabbed at his stomach. "Don't make me laugh so much! It hurts!" This sent her into giggles.

"Are you very sore?" At his nod she added, "That's what you get for being so hot-blooded." She couldn't stop laughing. Catching glimpses of him working that afternoon, she had worried he might be trying to do too much at once. He'd moved from one project to another without so much as a break to rest.

"Me? Hot-blooded? You have no idea." He chuckled, only to stop and grab his side again.

"I've heard about you redheads." She teased him mercilessly, knowing it hurt him but enjoying watching him squirm. "I'm trying to think what I need to do tomorrow to get the smokehouse door fixed. It's awful hard to close. I've been afraid some animal might get in there and get our winter stores. I might have to sleep late or burn the flapjacks or something."

"Is that what you're thinking?" he asked still smiling. "Let's just see if your little plan works. Next time I may ride off just to see the lay of the land."

"You wouldn't!" She tossed her apron at him.

"I heard in town that the neighboring ranch was really nice. Might come up for sale soon. Who knows? I may surprise you and ride over there and buy it." He chuckled, but she immediately sobered.

"The Thornton place?" Daisy stopped rocking and leaned forward, eyes wide.

"I think that's what they said." Tucker's tone was serious now. "Seems her folks are real sick. Want them to come take care of them and their home place. When they pass, the Thorntons will inherit the land."

"Oh, how sad. Judy has been a dear friend for years. I'll surely miss her." Daisy leaned back and set her chair in motion. She stared into the fire, her coffee forgotten on the small table between the chairs. "Nothing stays the same, does it, Tucker?"

"No, Daisy, it doesn't. That's the thing about life. You just have to keep moving forward. Sometimes you walk, sometimes you run and sometimes you soar like the eagles. I've tried to live by that Scripture. It keeps me from giving up."

"'But they that wait upon the Lord shall renew their strength; they shall mount up with wings as eagles; they shall run, and not be weary; and they shall walk, and not faint.'" Daisy quoted the verse from memory, still staring into the fire. "I've been walking for the last little while. I'd be lying if I said I haven't grown weary."

"I understand. I've been through long times when I had to keep walking the path God laid out for me, even though I didn't understand why life couldn't be another way. I've learned He's faithful." Tucker took a drink of his coffee and continued. "I spent most of my childhood growing up in a hotel, watching my sweet momma work herself to death. She taught me that verse to help me when times were hard."

"I never knew you grew up in a hotel, Tucker."

"Momma went to work in a hotel after my father died. Those were hard years, but I learned a lot from her about how faithful God is."

Tucker turned up his mug and drained the rest of the coffee. "I best be getting to bed. I've got a lot of soreness to sleep off tonight." He pushed up on the chair arms and gave an exaggerated groan.

Daisy looked at him and smiled. "You've done it again, my friend."

"What's that?" Tucker stood over her, and she had to tip the chair backward to see his face.

"Made me smile when I feel like crying." She stood and followed him to the door as he set his hat in place. "Thanks for being such a good friend to me."

Tucker tipped his hat to her. "Anytime, ma'am, anytime." With a smile he was gone, into the darkness.

Daisy bolted the door and leaned against it wearily. She wondered why more sad news had come. She would miss her friend Judy. She hoped the Thorntons would be able to help her parents recover. Daisy made a mental note to pray for them. She placed the cups in the dishpan and put out the lamp on the table.

She smiled again at Tucker's exaggerated movements and groaning when he'd got up from the chair. Years before she would laugh at the way he teased her. Many times as a young woman, she'd become frustrated or upset with some situation or another. She could count on Tucker to lighten her mood if he was around. Now it seemed he was able to lighten her heart.

After changing to her gown and climbing beneath the chilly quilt, Daisy suddenly realized what Tucker had said. *I may surprise you and ride over there and buy it.* She sat up in bed. Surely he wouldn't buy the land next to hers! Not without talking to her. After all, the Thorntons had a ranch. Daisy grew cotton. He must have been teasing. No. She refused to believe he would make such a major decision without her knowledge. Daisy thumped her pillow and buried her head in it, determined to get a good night's rest. She had a feeling she was going to need it.

After a few minutes she rolled over to face the wall. Had it really only been two days since Tucker arrived? A month ago she would have been snuggled close to Murdock.

Tonight she lay alone, after telling Tucker good-night and sending him to the barn to sleep with the animals. Tucker was her husband now.

Lord, let him be satisfied with friendship. I just can't love another man. It's too painful.

For years Murdock had been such a presence—the heart and soul of the farm and family. There were reminders of him everywhere. But in just a matter of weeks, his essence was fading away. She tried to hang on to it, but it was evaporating. Daisy pulled Murdock's pillow close and realized even his scent was gone. Silent tears wet the pillow. How long would she cry for Murdock?

Chapter Six

Breakfast was over, and Daisy got the twins set up to study on their own. She hung up her apron and headed out the door in search of Tucker. She needed him to confirm he was only joking about buying the Thornton ranch.

The barn door opened, and he appeared. At that same moment the sound of an approaching wagon reached them. They both turned to look up the lane, and Daisy realized it was two wagons.

"Aha. They made it." Tucker pulled heavy leather gloves from his belt and tugged them on as he headed to meet the wagons. Daisy recognized Will Thomas, owner of the lumber mill, driving the first team of horses. The wagons were loaded with fresh boards, boxes with nails and hardware, and what looked to be two windows wrapped and tied in brown paper. She followed Tucker, trotting a little to keep up with his pace.

"What is this?" Daisy demanded.

Tucker didn't slow his speed, but spoke over his shoulder. "It's lumber, Daisy."

"I can see that." Exasperation began to boil to the

surface. She'd been none too happy coming to see him in the barn, and now here was another surprise. A big surprise. And so far, no explanation. Daisy heard the boys come onto the front porch. They were both wearing the now ever-present Stetsons.

"Can we help?" James eagerly approached Tucker.

"Do you think we can, Momma?" John came more cautiously.

"Sure," Tucker said.

At the same time, "No!" Daisy snapped.

Tucker stopped so abruptly that Daisy bumped into him. Confused boys looked at one another and shrugged their shoulders.

"They are big enough to help unload a lumber wagon, Daisy." Tucker turned to speak to Will Thomas. "Can you pull around to the back of the house and let us unload there?"

"Wherever you want it, Mr. Barlow. What about stowing the windows in the barn till you're ready for them? Might be safer."

"Good idea," Tucker said. "James, show Mr. Thomas the first empty stall, the one with no straw."

Will Thomas urged his horses toward the barn and directed the other driver to the back of the house.

Daisy stopped, put both hands on her hips and patted one foot repeatedly. "Tucker Barlow, what is going on here?" Her voice brooked no argument.

"We're about to unload a wagon. Now if you don't mind, it's mighty hard work. Do you think you could make us a refreshing drink for when we've finished? With five men working, we should be done in about half an hour." Tucker signaled John to follow him. John adjusted his hat and puffed out his chest to rise to the title of "man."

"John, you go ahead. Tucker, I need to speak with you for a minute." At Tucker's raised eyebrows, she added, "Please."

"Go show the driver where we need to stack the wood, John. I'll be right there." John started up the hill, and Tucker walked close to Daisy. James jumped on the back of Mr. Thomas's wagon and rode around the house to join his brother.

"What's the matter, Daisy?" Tucker stifled a grin.

"Is something funny, Tucker? Obviously I'm missing something." She pointed up the hill to the working men. "Everyone seems to know what's going on around here—except me."

"Oh, that." Tucker followed the direction of her finger with his eyes, before turning back to her, his back to the others. Speaking so only she could hear, Tucker asked, "Do you really want me to sleep in the barn all winter?" A teasing grin punctuated the question. "Would you do that to me, Daisy? I thought we agreed to be friends."

"Friends share secrets. They don't keep them from each other." Her foot began to tap again. Her appreciation for his lightheartedness was completely forgotten for the moment. It was being overridden by the feeling she no longer had control over anything in her life.

Tucker quietly explained. "I knew it wouldn't work for me to sleep in the barn when winter hits full force. I anticipate some issues with the boys, too."

"Of course I don't expect you to sleep in the barn in the winter. I'm not heartless. What issues?" Daisy was growing more frustrated by the second. He had yet to answer a single question.

"I don't have time to go into everything right now, but I promise we can talk as soon as Mr. Thomas and his helper leave." Tucker put a hand on each of her shoulders. "Please let me go to work now, before they think you want them to unload everything without me." He released her and walked away, calling over his shoulder. "Do you think you could fix those drinks?"

"Of course, Tucker. Be glad to," Daisy called bittersweetly. "Ooh, the nerve of that man! We will talk before this day is done." Daisy muttered under her breath while going up the steps. "And it won't just be questions. There will be answers."

A full hour later, Will Thomas and his two wagons rode off the property while Daisy watched.

"Boys, go back to your lessons now. I'll be busy for a bit, so don't interrupt me."

"Oh, Momma, can't we help Mr. Tucker?" James was reluctant to end the excitement.

"You heard your momma. Get back to your studies. There'll be plenty of work for everybody." Tucker looked at Daisy. "I'm not going to be getting started right away. Your momma and I have some things to take care of first."

"Yes, sir." A dejected James followed John into the cabin and closed the door.

"Want to walk down to the creek with me?" Tucker offered.

"That will be good. I don't want the boys to hear us." Daisy huffed along ahead of Tucker for a short distance.

"We could probably talk better if you slow down and walk beside me, Daisy." The teasing began anew.

"I'm not in the mood for your joking, Tucker." Daisy

stopped and turned in a split second. He had to grab her arms to keep her from falling as he plowed into her.

"You okay?" he asked.

"Yes." Daisy brushed her sleeves to straighten them and turned to walk beside him. "Tucker, you've only been here two days. And I don't know how you've managed to do it, but you've completely turned my world upside down." She pulled at the tall dry grass that bent in the breeze, tearing a stalk loose to peel into layers while she walked.

"I didn't mean to upset you, Daisy."

"There you go apologizing again. Can't we get beyond that and lay some kind of ground rules to help us communicate better?"

"What do you have in mind?" Tucker adjusted his hat as the late-morning sun climbed higher.

"Well, for starters, how about you stop asking questions and start answering some?"

"What questions?" Tucker asked innocently.

"See! That's what I mean!" Daisy walked ahead of him and took several deep breaths. She was beginning to wonder if he just enjoyed teasing her or if he wanted to provoke her outright.

"Tell me what you want to know. I'll answer." He stopped and waited.

She turned to face him. "Several things." Rolling her eyes toward the sky, Daisy thought about the order to proceed. If he suddenly clammed up, she needed the answers to the most pressing questions first. "First, what is the lumber for?"

"I'm going to build another bedroom onto the cabin— a large one with a private dressing area for you. It's my wedding gift to you." Tucker's mouth turned up slightly at the corners. "Surprise." His eyebrows climbed, and his grin grew to full size. He asked, "Do you like it?"

"Oh, Tucker," Daisy spoke breathlessly. "What on earth?"

"After I saw the cabin, well...the boys are small now, but they'll be young men before you know it. You need privacy. Remember, I grew up with my mother. There were times she needed privacy, and it wasn't possible. I couldn't do anything then, but this is something I can do for you. I wanted to surprise you." He paused. "Did it work?"

Daisy was flabbergasted. "You! That's another question." They both laughed. Daisy's face grew serious again. "That's very sweet, Tucker, but you don't have to do that for me. It's too extravagant. We don't have a lot of money. We've got to pay for more horses, and our money has to last until next harvest. I budgeted it all out. There's not a lot of extra."

"This is my wedding gift to you, Daisy. It's not coming out of the money you have in the bank. I used my own money for this." Tucker tilted his head to one side and held out his arms. "Say you like it...please." Green eyes sparkled. She'd forgotten how much he made her laugh.

"Okay. I like it." She gave him a friendly hug and backed away. "But I wish you hadn't done it."

"Really?" He lifted his hat and ran his hand through his hair.

"Stop with the questions. I'm asking them today." She smiled back at him.

"There's more?" he teased.

Daisy blew out a quick breath. "What did you mean about the boys having issues?"

Tucker sobered. "You saw how they reacted when I put my hat on their papa's peg and sat in his chair at the table?"

"Yes. But they're adjusting. They haven't said anything else have they?"

"No. But that doesn't mean they've accepted me. They haven't even seen me sit in their papa's chair by the fire." He paused and spun his hat by the brim several times while he thought. Putting the Stetson back in place he said, "I don't want them to be upset when I move into the cabin. Winter will be here before you know it. I think it will be easier for them if you have your own room. I can sleep in the main room."

"I hadn't thought of that at all." At his lowered gaze she rushed to reassure him. "Thank you for your consideration of their feelings. And for your patience with me. It means more than I can say."

A heavy silence hung between them.

Finally Tucker spoke. "Any more questions?" he chuckled.

She smiled. "No. I think I've asked quite enough questions today. Don't you?" She laughed in earnest. Daring to look at him as he raised his head in her direction, Daisy saw something in Tucker's eyes she'd never seen before. There was a depth she hadn't contemplated, an intensity she wasn't expecting, a pull she found magnetic. She blinked quickly and looked away. "Well," she said, looking over her shoulder at the house. "I better go see what those two are up to." She cleared her throat and took one hesitant step before pausing to look at him again.

"Thank you, Tucker. It's a lovely gift."

"You're welcome, Daisy." Tucker turned and walked to the creek.

She watched him squat and draw handfuls of the cool water to splash his face.

How could she ever repay him for his kindness? He wasn't just protecting her and her sons physically. He was guarding their wounded emotions. Tucker was once again proving himself to be a dear friend. A generous friend at that.

If only she could discern the look she'd seen in his eyes.

Lunch was a lively meal. Tucker listened as everyone gave their opinion on the big surprise.

"You really were surprised, weren't you, Momma?" James had been thrilled to keep such a big secret from her. At her nod, he said, "Mr. Tucker told us in the barn this morning. We knew and didn't say anything! We're good at secrets." He beamed at this accomplishment.

"I didn't want to tell you and ruin the surprise. I'm glad you like it." John was much calmer.

Daisy laughed and told them how pleased she was with the surprise. "I was very impressed with how hard both of you worked this morning unloading those wagons. Weren't you, Tucker?"

He nodded in agreement. "Very impressed, indeed. Not just with the work but also with the ability to keep a confidence. It's important for a man to have a good reputation. Once you give your word about a matter, you have to keep it. No matter how difficult that is. I'm proud of both of you."

"Does that mean you'll trust us again, Mr. Tucker?" John wanted to know.

"It does, John. You've both proved yourselves to be trustworthy men." His praise brought big smiles to the two young faces. He hoped to win their confidence and respect, too. Losing his dad at such a young age and never having siblings had caused an emptiness in Tucker.

He'd often been jealous of the families he'd seen come and go at the hotel where he and his mother had lived. The closest he'd come to being part of a family after his father died was when Daisy and her sisters were young and had looked to him for advice and friendship. He'd longed for a real family most of his life. One complete with a father, a mother and several children. Now he had all the pieces. Could God help them grow the love that would make them become a true family?

"It's time to get after the chores now." Daisy started clearing the table. "There's still plenty to be done before dark."

"Your mother's right. The two of you get the chores done, and I'll go get the drawing for how we're going to build this room." Tucker's chair scraped across the floor as he pushed it back and stood.

"We?" James didn't miss a lick.

"We," Tucker confirmed. "I bought some extra tools so you can work side by side with me. So let's get to it."

Hats came off pegs, and whoops of excitement echoed in the afternoon air as the boys jumped from the porch, skipping the steps entirely.

Daisy expressed concern. "Tucker, I'm not sure they're old enough for tools of their own."

"I think they're ready. Boys grow up faster than you'd think," he assured.

"I just don't want them to get hurt."

"I promise to teach them to be careful." Tucker continued cautiously. "But getting hurt is part of growing up."

"They already know more about pain than any boy their age should!" Daisy was visibly upset now.

"I know." Tucker kept his tone gentle. "Remember I was in the same place at an even younger age."

Daisy's anger deflated. "I guess you're right." Was that apprehension in her gaze? "But do be careful."

He smiled his promise. "We will."

Daisy turned to wipe the table with a cloth. "Thank you for teaching them lessons about character and such. A lot of men overlook that in an effort to make boys tough."

"A man is more than a strong back and provider. He needs to be reliable in spirit and heart, as well." Tucker put his hat on. "I'll see you after a while. Thanks for the meal."

He left the cabin and headed to retrieve his tools from the barn. Daisy's reluctant acceptance of his wedding gift affirmed his need to guard his heart. She'd been so determined to persevere on her own that she greeted any effort he made at easing her load with suspicion. She'd agreed to let him stay, but he knew she hadn't abandoned her refusal to need him.

It might be easier for both of them if he gave her wide berth. If only the sight of her didn't threaten to ignite something inside of him—like an ember in a long extinguished fire searching for a rekindling spark.

While Daisy washed clothes later that day, she pondered Tucker's words about a man having a strong back and being a provider. For years at her father's home, she'd seen him work as hard as a man could. When she turned to hang clothes on the line, she had an unobstructed view of Tucker across the yard moving lumber and sawing boards to provide shelter for her. His dependability was never in question.

But she was just beginning to realize the value of his spirit and heart. His faithful character was a good example to her sons. She was grateful to God and her father for sending Tucker to her family.

Daisy stretched up to hang one of his shirts on the line. Tucker looked up at the same time and caught her gaze. She couldn't deny she was drawn to the sight of him as he worked in the afternoon sun. He was different from Murdock in so many ways. She had never imagined herself with anyone other than Murdock. Until now. Guilt flooded her at the thought.

Daisy turned her full attention to the washtub and continued scrubbing the barn dirt from his shirts, only to catch a glimpse of him watching her again as he wiped his brow with his forearm. He set his hat back on his head and acknowledged her with a nod. When she blushed, he chuckled and went back to work. She watched him take his time instructing the twins.

She hung the next shirt to block the line of sight between them. Could she really move forward with her life? Tucker had sacrificed a lot to move here and marry her. Now he was building a room for her—for them. But he was attaching it to the house Murdock had built. Was it possible to make the home that was hers with Murdock into a home and family for her and Tucker?

Chapter Seven

The next day saw a new pattern emerge. Chores were eagerly done before breakfast. Schoolwork was exchanged for life skill lessons as James and John learned basic carpentry. By supper all the menfolk were exhausted. No argument over going to bed occurred. Tucker only stayed long enough to bring in firewood and stoke the fire before heading to the barn.

On Saturday the rooster crowed, but it was too late to wake Tucker's new family. Both boys were already dressed and doing their chores. Watching Daisy slice bread for their breakfast, Tucker decided they probably woke the rooster. Ham sizzled on the stove. John brought in a basket of eggs, and Daisy prepared to scramble them.

"Boy, it smells good in here." Tucker closed the door against the morning chill and went to stand with his face to the fire. He extended his hands and rubbed them together before turning to warm the other side of himself. "We may have an early winter. We're going to have to keep a steady pace to get everything done before the cold weather comes in earnest."

"How much longer will you be staying in the barn?" Daisy kept her back to him as she cooked. When he didn't answer she turned around. Her brown eyes met his as if searching for something. Neither of them moved nor spoke. Her cheeks flushed, and she turned to the stove. Was she as confounded as he was by their new relationship? Friends? Yes. Husband and wife? Yes. And no.

Daisy asked again, "Do you know how much longer?" She set the plate of ham on the table.

"What?" Tucker cleared his throat and pulled his attention to the day at hand.

"How long will it take to finish the room? When will you be able to stay in the cabin and not in the barn?" She placed the eggs and bread beside the ham.

James brought in the milk and poured a cup for John and himself.

"Shouldn't take too long. The basic frame will be finished in a couple of days. Then the roof. That'll be the hardest part because of having to climb up and down so much. I thought I'd see if Will Thomas knows someone I could hire to help me for a couple of days." Tucker got a mug for his coffee and poured a cup for Daisy, too.

"When are we going to town?" James was always ready for an adventure.

"First thing after breakfast." Tucker took his seat at the table and extended a hand to John for the now-familiar blessing over their meal. It was John's turn to pray. Then they all served themselves.

"I didn't know you wanted to go to town today," Daisy said to Tucker.

"We need to get the horses. I need them for clearing the next section of land before Christmas. That only gives me a couple of months. I want it to be ready for next spring. There are a couple of other things that need to be taken care of." Tucker tore his bread and put a large bite in his mouth, cutting his ham while he chewed.

"You're planning on clearing more land? I thought we might talk about the finances and this year's harvest, and plan next year's planting before you actually started any work like that." She spread butter on her bread and waited for him to speak.

"The boys told me where the land lines are. I've ridden over everything and think clearing about ten more acres on the northernmost field would add nicely to the profit next season." He'd scoped out the land the morning after their wedding. Expanding the cultivated acreage every year was vital to his plan for the success and growth of the farm.

"I really think we need to talk before you make a lot of plans, Tucker. It's not like the ranch. Cultivating ten more acres is harder than adding ten acres of pasture for increasing the herd size. Planting season and harvesting for cotton is a lot more labor than herding a bunch of cows."

Tucker pushed his plate away and ran a finger around the rim of his mug. "Is it now?" It was becoming crystal clear to him that he and Daisy had a lot to learn about who the other had become over the past ten years. She was no longer the owner's little girl, and he wasn't just a ranch hand.

"I'm sorry. I didn't mean that the way it sounded," Daisy gushed like James would in the same situation. "You know what I meant."

"I thought we were going to get past all this apologizing, Daisy. You can say what you mean. I can take it. You're not sure I can handle cotton farming." She squirmed in her chair at his words. He stood and moved for the door. "Tell you what. Tonight after supper you can teach me all I need to know about cotton farming. And since tomorrow is Sunday, if you don't think I've learned it all tonight, you can teach me the rest after church in the morning." He took his hat from the peg and turned to the twins. "Want to help me hitch up the wagon?" Before Daisy could say anything they were all out the door, leaving her to do the dishes and prepare to go into town.

It felt awkward for Daisy to go into town with Tucker as her husband. Their trip on Monday had seemed almost surreal at the time. He'd been a friend from the past helping to preserve a future for her and her sons. Today they looked like any other family. She and Tucker knew it wasn't true, but others would see them and assume it was. In the hotel on their wedding day, Daisy didn't see anyone she knew well. Today they would encounter friends. Introductions would need to be made. Some people could ask questions. On the farm with just the family, they conducted themselves like the friends they were. In town, would people expect something else? And how many would judge them for marrying so quickly after Murdock's death? Feeling out of control again bothered Daisy.

"We need to go to the bank before we go to the livery," Daisy announced as they approached the edge of town. She chanced a glance at Tucker as he slowed the rig. He'd been quiet since breakfast, speaking only when necessary.

"The matter of the horses is settled, Daisy. I won't

go into it again." The muscles in Tucker's jaw worked as he clenched his teeth together.

"But, Tucker, we have money to take care of the farm. The horses are part of the cost of running the farm." Daisy didn't understand why he couldn't see her point. She pulled her shawl closer around her shoulders against the chilly morning breeze.

"I gave my word, and I won't back down. The matter is closed." Tucker's voice was even, but allowed for no argument. Daisy wouldn't risk undermining him in front of James and John, who stood up to hang on the back of the bench seat as they entered Pine Haven.

"Can we have candy, Momma?" James hoped for a treat from the general store.

"Not today. We've had a lot of special things this week. We'll wait for another time." Daisy's tone was tight and controlled. James knew better than to persist.

"I still need to go to the bank." Daisy turned to Tucker as they stopped in front of the general store. The boys jumped off the back of the wagon and headed inside. "And the land office."

"Now just why is that, Daisy?" Tucker set the brake and shifted toward her. He dropped one hand to rest on his knee, elbow bent upward, and waited. "What do you need to do at the bank and the land office?" His expression was clear and open, which surprised her. She expected to see storm clouds in his eyes. She had mistaken his silence during their ride to town for controlled anger. Now she realized it was his refusal to argue when he considered the matter of the purchase of horses to be resolved.

"Well…" Daisy lowered her eyes and twisted the drawstrings on her reticule between her fingers. She noticed how her new wedding ring caught in the sunlight. "I need to change my name on the accounts. And we need to add your name to the bank accounts and the deed for the farm."

"I see." Tucker was quiet for a moment and didn't take his eyes off of her. "So you're always planning and plotting in that mind of yours, aren't you?" He hopped to the ground and turned to help her from the wagon. "I'd be pleased to go with you to the bank and land office before we head back to the farm." He smiled up at Daisy and reached to take her by the hand.

Daisy stood and moved to the edge of the wagon without looking at Tucker. For the entire trip to town she'd considered how it would feel to acknowledge him publicly as her husband. Now she was taking the legal steps to prove his position in her life. Part of her felt disloyal to Murdock. Her mind knew that moving on was her only choice, but her heart wasn't ready to release the past. She was wrapped up in thought as she stepped from the wagon. Too late she looked up to put her hand in Tucker's. Her heel caught in the hem of her skirt, and she tumbled forward, missing his hand entirely. She let out a small squeal and felt her feet come out from under her.

Tucker's reflexes were quick. Strong hands encircled her waist to catch her in midair between the wagon and the ground. Daisy crushed against his chest with a thud, knocking the wind out of herself as he planted one leg backward to keep them both from falling.

"Got a lot on your mind, Daisy?" Tucker chuckled as he set her upright and released her.

"I just lost my balance," she harrumphed, stepping back to escape the fresh scent of his soap.

"Well, you nearly caused me to lose mine, too." Tucker teased and straightened his hat. "Are you okay?"

"Fine. Just fine." She turned to glare at him. How did he have the power to make her so uncomfortable? One minute he was her old friend laughing and teasing, and the next he was… The next minute she didn't know what he was. Daisy smoothed her skirt and pulled her shawl back into place before putting a hand to her hat and hair. Tucker stood blocking her path. Her gaze rose from the front of his broad shirt and climbed to his face. At his inquiring expression she added, "Thank you." Was everything about this man a question? She was much more comfortable in a world of absolutes. She'd easily read Murdock like the open book he was. She sensed Tucker held hidden layers she had no idea of, certain she held no experience to handle those many intricacies.

Making another attempt to peel away and discover something, Daisy asked. "Now exactly why are we at the general store? Aren't we buying horses today?" Taking a no-nonsense tone helped to restore her composure.

"More questions? Are you planning the morning in your mind?" Tucker teased her but only for a moment. She wondered what he'd think if he knew she was struggling internally to plan their entire relationship—not just the morning.

"There are some things I need to order. Will you help me choose?" Tucker took her by the elbow and escorted her into the store. The simple gesture sent a message of familiarity with a dash of possessiveness through Daisy. She was sure anyone seeing them would notice it, too. Once again she struggled to swallow the sense of betrayal she felt by allowing Tucker to hold her in ways only Murdock had.

A bell rang as Tucker pushed the door open, and the spring on the frame caused it to slam shut behind them. Daisy paused to allow her eyes to adjust to the dim interior. The smell of burlap and coffee beans assaulted her senses. Open barrels in the center of the floor boasted new merchandise. Worn wooden shelves against the walls held mundane, yet necessary, supplies. Bolts of fabric were stacked on two large tables under the front window. Tools hung on the back wall, and jars with brightly colored candy lined the counter by the cash register.

"Be right with you folks." Liza Croft called from behind the counter where she assisted a customer. Daisy saw James and John in the far corner looking through the small selection of toys. The swinging half doors, which separated the store from the storage room beyond, swung open and Liza's husband, Donald, came through.

"What can I do for you?" Donald Croft approached Tucker before he recognized Daisy. "Why, hello, Mrs. Mosley, how are you today?"

"I'm fine, thank you, Mr. Croft," Daisy answered and with one hand gestured toward Tucker. "I'd like you to meet Tucker Barlow." She took a slight breath as Mr. Croft reached to shake Tucker's extended hand. "My husband."

"Nice to meet you, Mr.—" Donald Croft stopped in midsentence still gripping Tucker's hand, and turned to look at Daisy. "Your husband?" He released his grip.

"Yes, Mr. Croft, Tucker and I got married on Monday." Daisy blushed slightly, quite uncomfortable with the explanation.

Tucker came to her rescue. "Tucker Barlow. It's nice to meet you, Mr. Croft."

"Call me Donald, Mr. Barlow. And congratulations on your nuptials." Donald turned to Daisy, "And you, too, Mrs. Mosley. I mean, Mrs. Barlow. Please forgive me. It might take me a time or two to adjust to your new name."

To Tucker he continued, "Welcome to Pine Haven. Now what can we do for you today?"

"We'd like to look at your furniture catalog. There are some things we need to order," Tucker explained.

"Right this way." Donald led them to the counter at the rear of the store. He lifted the hinged board at its side and stepped behind the large unit to retrieve the catalog. "What kind of furniture? I've got a couple of different companies. I can recommend what I know to be good quality if you'd like."

"That will be a great help. We need some bedroom furniture." Tucker answered because Daisy still had no idea what they were doing. She blushed again at the thought of discussing her bedroom with the store owner she knew only as a tradesman.

"I think this will be just what you need. The prices are marked, so I'll just leave you to browse until you see what you want. It takes about six weeks for most of these items to come, so bear that in mind when you're choosing. There are a couple of items the supplier keeps plenty of stock in, so those things come a mite sooner. The pages are marked. You can see the difference." Donald went to answer the clanging bell as yet another customer entered the store. He called, "Let me know when you decide," as he walked away.

Daisy stood close to Tucker and whispered, "Bedroom furniture?"

"Yes, bedroom furniture. Remember we talked about this." Tucker flipped the pages until he found something that suited his taste. "What do you think of this?" He pointed to a large bed with tall posts on each corner. The posts were carved with a curving scroll design. There was a matching dressing table with several drawers beneath a large mirror crowned with the same scroll design. Dark rich marble topped the drawers.

"It's lovely, Tucker, but I don't need anything fancy. We can just get a simple iron bed. I can use the chest I have now, and the mirror in the corner is more than adequate."

"I like it. This is what we'll get. Do you mind waiting the six weeks?" Tucker lifted his hand to signal Donald.

"Tucker, it's too much!" Daisy kept her voice low. "We can't afford it." Her eyes pleaded for him to understand before Mr. Croft came close enough to hear.

"It's part of the gift, Daisy." Tucker leaned close to her ear. His warm breath teased her neck and caused her flesh to tingle. "I never intended to build a room and not buy furniture. You said you'd accept the gift. This is part of it." Daisy was beginning to realize some battles with Tucker could not be won.

"If you insist," she finally acquiesced and stepped back, rubbing a gloved hand against the side of her neck to warm her skin.

"I insist." Tucker smiled down at her and leaned in close again. "Now that I know that works, I may have to insist on you not being so stubborn when I'm trying to be nice to you." He chuckled then, and Mr. Croft approached them, effectively cutting off any response from her.

Daisy watched Tucker place the order, wondering how he could afford such a purchase. The cost of the room and furniture was more than she could imagine, and he still insisted on paying for the horses. He was a mixture of what she needed and what she feared. She needed help with the farm and the twins, but she couldn't feel secure while he continued to spend so much money.

She prayed silently.

Lord, Tucker is a good and kind man. Help me. I'm so accustomed to handling everything in marriage the way Murdock and I did. I don't know how to deal with Tucker making decisions without discussing them with me. Give me patience. And give him wisdom. Please.

Chapter Eight

"Daisy!" Peggy Dismuke's voice drew Daisy's attention to the opening door of the general store. Peggy embraced her, then pulled away to look into her face. "How are you, dear?" Peggy smiled at Daisy.

"And you, Mr. Barlow, how are you?" Peggy included Tucker in her boisterous greeting.

"Well, Mrs. Dismuke, and you?" Tucker nodded a greeting to the reverend's wife.

"You must tell me how you are, Daisy. I noticed your wagon and hoped you'd still be here when I arrived. I came to pick up my order." Peggy's excitement required no comment from Tucker. He excused himself and went to check on the twins.

Peggy turned and looped arms with Daisy. Closing the space between them, she whispered, "How are you? Really? Is he kind? Are you and the boys all right?"

Daisy laughed gently at her friend, "Yes, Peggy, we're all fine. Remember Tucker and I have been friends for years."

"I know, but it's been a long time since you've seen each other. And Murdock's passing was so recent. I just don't think I could do what you've done if I lost my dear David." Peggy squeezed Daisy's arm. "It's just unimaginable to me that you've got another man in your home so suddenly. I mean, I know the boys need a father figure, but what about your own feelings?"

Daisy extricated herself from Peggy's pull. "Peggy, as my friend I must ask you to stop and think about what you're saying." Pain filled Daisy's eyes, and tears threatened to fall from her lashes.

"Oh, Daisy! I'm so sorry." Peggy hugged Daisy close before tugging her through the front door and around to the side of the building for a small semblance of privacy. "I could kick myself. What was I thinking running on like that and you having to live through it? Please forgive me? I didn't mean to be insensitive."

"Don't worry about it. I'm just a little prickly these days. It's been a lot to absorb, and I'm not sure I'm handling it all well. I seem to keep saying things that upset Tucker. I don't mean to. It just happens." Daisy stared at the dust at her feet. "I didn't think it would be so hard since Tucker and I are friends." She looked up then. "I don't think I truly considered what it would mean to be his wife. I know my father wanted the best for me and the boys, but it's not easy to lose a husband. Murdock and I were together for over ten years." *Ten years.*

Daisy shook her head slowly back and forth. "My emotions are so confused right now." She clung to Peggy's hand like it was a lifeline. "Yet Tucker has been so kind. And generous. He's very good with the twins, too."

Peggy patted her hand and offered, "Daisy. I'm sorry. I know this is difficult for you. I should never have spoken to you as I did."

"You only said the things I've been afraid to think

about. I feel like I'm being disloyal to Murdock if I don't
mourn him properly, but I feel like I'm not being appre-
ciative of all Tucker is doing if I hold back from building
a relationship with him," Daisy lamented. "Pray for me."

"I will. I'm here for you if you need me and I promise
to be a better friend from now on. I'll start by thinking
before I speak." Peggy hugged Daisy again. "If you're
okay, we'll go back into the store and see how your guys
are getting along."

The two stepped around the corner and onto the
wooden sidewalk. Daisy recognized Tucker's hat as he
disappeared into the lumber mill office. She collected
her sons and followed him, stopping briefly to post the
promised letter to her father. Papa Warren would really
be surprised the next time she wrote and told him all
Tucker had been doing. She was having a difficult time
absorbing it all herself.

Tucker had come onto the porch looking for Daisy. He
was about to round the corner when he'd heard her talking to Peggy. His scowl had twisted into a look of tor-
tured resolve as her words of pained confusion reached
his ears. Soundlessly he turned and walked away from
the corner, going in the direction of the lumber mill.

In his mind's eye he could see his mother wrestling
with her feelings for the owner of the hotel where she
worked when he was a boy. How often had he heard her
crying when she thought he was asleep? Loyalty to her
love for his deceased father had won. The owner's attempts to build a relationship with her were rebuffed,
and she worked and mourned until the day she died.
Alone—except for Tucker. He knew Daisy was struggling with the same emotions. He also knew her love for

Murdock would always be stronger than her friendship with him. It was a good thing he'd decided to keep his heart protected behind the barriers of his experience.

Tucker recalled the slicing anguish of separation he endured as a very young man when Alice Fields broke his heart. He'd surrendered it to her when he thought he'd won her love. How foolish he'd felt when she refused his proposal. She'd flitted away to her former sweetheart like a moth to a flame.

Pushing down the painful memories and focusing on the task at hand, Tucker entered the lumber mill looking for help to put the roof on the new addition.

Later, when Tucker exited the mill, Daisy and the twins were coming up the sidewalk.

"How did it go? Did you hire someone?" she asked.

"Two men for next Wednesday. We need to finish our business in town and get back to the farm so I can get to work. There's a lot to be done in a short time." Tucker tried to keep the gruffness out of his voice, but the echo of her conversation with Peggy still rang in his ears.

He wanted to get back to work on the cabin as soon as possible. Perhaps the exertion of swinging a hammer would relieve the tension building in the muscles between his shoulders.

Tucker set a brisk pace, and soon purchased two beautiful animals. He even asked James and John to give their opinions, assuring that each of them would be able to claim one of the horses for their own. They'd have to feed and care for the horse, but it would be theirs to ride. He stressed the primary purpose for needing the animals was to work the farm, so the boys would need to learn to work alongside him.

Not once at the livery did Tucker meet Daisy's gaze.

He knew she'd think him upset that she tried to discourage him from buying the bedroom furniture. Why couldn't she back down from being worried about their finances? She'd been reluctant to let him give her the house addition, and now the furniture, as a wedding gift. He'd come here to make her life easier, but she seemed resistant to his efforts. Her grief was the most obvious reason for her to hold back her approval.

Actually he hadn't given her much choice. He insisted on paying for the horses. After all, it was their farm now. She had ten years invested in it, and she'd just told him she was going to sign it over to him. What was the price of a couple of animals compared to all she'd already given?

Tucker assured Jim Robbins, the livery owner, they'd be back within the hour to get the horses. Then he led his family onto the sidewalk and headed for the bank.

"Are you upset with me?" Daisy asked quietly. James and John were skipping ahead of them to join a young boy playing in front of the dress shop.

"Why would you ask me that, Daisy?" He kept his focus forward as he moved swiftly up the boarded sidewalk.

"Let's see. For one thing, you're not looking at me." Daisy stopped and stood still. Tucker took two long strides before halting.

"We've got a lot to do," he spoke over his shoulder. "I don't have time for one of your question and answer interviews right now. It'll have to wait till later." He immediately started walking again, leaving her no alternative but to try to catch him.

"Obviously something is bothering you. If it's about the furniture, I was surprised. I'm not accustomed to spending so much money." She increased her pace to keep up with him.

"You didn't spend any money today, Daisy." Without varying his speed or his tone, he corrected her.

"True." Daisy paused as if seeking the right words. "What I mean is I'm uncomfortable having that kind of money spent, especially on me."

"Your wedding present was money I spent on us." Tucker stopped abruptly and turned to face her, catching her off guard. If he wasn't so hurt by her words to Peggy earlier, he would have chuckled at her startled expression.

Tucker looked at her with deep intensity, daring her to misinterpret his next words. "I spent the money on our future, Daisy. On our marriage. I know you're mourning right now. I made it clear from the beginning I wouldn't rush you into anything. But I do see the bigger picture here. We are married. Once you've had time to grieve for Murdock, and absorb the fact that I'm your husband now, we'll need all the things I've been doing." He took off his hat and raked his fingers roughly through his red mane in frustration and rammed the hat back into place.

Taking a deep breath he continued. "Don't worry about the money I've spent or the decisions I've made. I'm a grown man, and I know what I'm doing." He heaved a low sigh and put a hand on her sleeve. "By God's grace, I'm a patient man. I can wait." He opened the door to the land office and ushered her inside, whistling for the boys to join them.

Daisy squared her shoulders and took yet another step toward making her marriage to Tucker official.

The land agent looked over his wire glasses at her.

"May I help you, Mrs. Mosley?" he asked as he rose from his seat behind the massive mahogany desk. Its size lent an aura of power to the man whose stature was average at best.

"Good morning, Mr. Little. I'd like you to meet Mr. Tucker Barlow." Tucker moved to stand beside her, and the boys shared a chair by the front door. "My husband."

"Mr. Barlow, a pleasure to meet you. Please take a seat." Daisy and Tucker took the two seats facing Mr. Little's desk before he sank back into his chair. "What can I do for you today?"

Daisy spoke quickly. "Mr. Barlow and I married on Monday. I want to handle whatever paperwork needs to be done to make sure the deed to my farm is in proper order."

"I'm glad you came in. I was going to come see you myself next week. We usually give thirty days after the death of a husband before we call on the widow about the business of deeds." He took off his glasses and pulled a kerchief from his pocket to wipe the lenses. "Especially in a case like yours where there is no mortgage on the property. It gives more time for the business of death to be handled before a widow needs to move on with the business of life and the future," Mr. Little looped the temples of the glasses back over his ears. "My condolences on the loss of Mr. Mosley. He was a kind man. Must have been hard on you and the young ones—everything being so sudden and all."

"Thank you, sir." Daisy lowered her head to stare at the reticule in her lap, twisting the strings again. It was awkward to discuss her recently deceased husband with her new husband in the seat next to her. She'd have come alone to do this, but knew Tucker would have to sign the necessary papers. "We want to take care of the paper-work to transfer the deed, please."

Mr. Little reached for a dark accordion folder on the credenza behind his desk. He unwound the string and folded the large flap out of the way so he could retrieve two identical documents written on long thick parchment from inside. "I had this prepared for my visit to you next week, knowing you'd need to transfer the own-ership of the farm after Mr. Mosley passed away." He turned the papers and pushed them across the desk for Tucker and Daisy to read.

"Transfer of Deed?" Daisy asked. "You were going to bring me a transfer of deed next week?" Her voice rose slightly, and she moved to the front edge of her chair. "Mr. Little, why would you have thought I would be transferring ownership of my farm? You did not know I was married."

"Mrs. Mosley," he began but started over when Tucker cleared his throat. "Mrs. Barlow, I meant no disrespect. It's my job to make sure the deeds in this region of Texas stay current. As a widow the property ownership of your farm came into question. That's not anything of my doing, but it's the way of land ownership since Texas became a state. I'm only doing my job." Mr. Lit-tle's words struck Daisy as a feeble attempt to prevent her from becoming upset.

"Mr. Little," Tucker said calmly, "I'm sure you must be aware of the law that passed just this year allowing women to own property in their name. A man in your position must surely keep up with such things."

Mr. Little put a finger inside his shirt collar and stretched it away from his neck. "I've read about that law, Mr. Barlow, but it hasn't been tested by the courts yet. Most land offices are not willing to take the risk of titling the property to women. The law is just too new. Men like me would be at risk of our jobs if something were to be handled wrongly." He swallowed deeply. "I'm sure you can understand my position."

"I understand the citizens of this community expect you to uphold the laws of the State of Texas, Mr. Little," Daisy interjected.

"Mrs. Mos— I mean, Mrs. Barlow, I am only one man. I do my best. Please, Mr. Barlow." Mr. Little sought support from Tucker but none came. Sitting up behind the desk and straightening the few stacks of paper he'd been working on, Mr. Little changed course. "It's no matter for concern now, anyway. Mr. Barlow here will go on the deed. There'll be no problems. So you see, there's a good solution for your family right here. It's good you chose to move forward so quickly Mrs. Barlow. Your life will be much easier than that of a widow who chooses to go it alone and loses everything. You made a wise decision indeed."

Daisy's eyes grew dark and dangerous. Tucker placed a hand on hers to keep her from coming out of her seat. "Mr. Little, if you will please make the deed to Mr. Tucker Barlow and Mrs. Daisy Barlow, I believe we'll both be satisfied." Tucker's request fulfilled his promise to ensure the land was safely hers.

"Mr. Barlow, we normally make the deed to the man only." Mr. Little showed his discomfort with the turn in circumstances. He obviously did not favor women owning land and was using his position in the official land office to resist the change in the law.

"I insist. Make the deed to Mr. Tucker Barlow and Mrs. Daisy Barlow." Tucker turned the heavy papers back toward Mr. Little. "I believe you have only to write our names on the top lines of both copies before we sign." With one finger he pushed the papers across the desk. Daisy was glad to see the land agent at the mercy of Tucker's insistence.

Mr. Little made a noise not unlike a snort and withdrew his pen from the ink well. "Don't come complaining to me if there's ever someone contesting this deed." He wrote their names as he spoke. "I tried to warn you. That law will never stand up in court. Women don't need to own property. Men are much more capable of handling business." He completed the wording and turned the papers for them to sign.

Tucker signed on the first signature line and turned the first copy to Daisy. She dipped the pen in the ink and blotted the tip. She took her time signing the paper. She took just as long to sign the second copy of the deed. Never had she imagined her name would be recorded in the government office on the deed to her very own land. She put the pen back in the stand, then held up the papers and blew the ink dry. A smile crept across her face as she turned to Tucker. She glowed with this new achievement.

Daisy passed the deeds back to Mr. Little so he could attach the land office seal, making the documents official. He retained one copy to keep on file at the land office, and Daisy carefully rolled her copy and tied it with a string he ungraciously offered. She and Tucker stood.

"Thank you, Mr. Little," Daisy offered, smiling.

"Mrs. Barlow," he grunted in reply.

"Mr. Little, I'm sure I'll be seeing you again. I trust the business relationship we have established today will stand us in good stead for any future dealings we may have." Tucker extended his hand and waited until Mr. Little shook it before turning to open the door. The twins exited first, followed by a very happy Daisy.

Tucker turned and said, "Good day, sir," before closing the door firmly behind him.

"Good day indeed." Daisy could hear Mr. Little grumbling, "Land owned by women! Humph!"

The business at the bank was expedited much more easily. Tucker was pleased to note how Daisy's mood was emboldened by the deed she held in her hand. Mr. Little's refusal to accept her as the legal owner of her farm re-affirmed Tucker's commitment to her. She needed him, even if she wasn't ready to accept him.

He raised one eyebrow slightly when he saw the amount of money Murdock had left for Daisy and the boys. Tucker could see Daisy's pride in being able to prove to him that she and Murdock had planned well. He also knew how quickly it could be gone without continued hard work and expansion of the crops.

If only Tucker's father hadn't been so sick before his death, he might have been able to make that kind of provision for Tucker and his mother. Maybe his mother would still be alive. Even if they hadn't been able to keep their land, maybe she wouldn't have died working in the hotel. There were a lot of things Tucker couldn't change, his past chief among them. But he was determined to pick up where Murdock left off and ensure Daisy and her boys had a hopeful future.

The twins were beginning to accept him. He hadn't sought to buy their approval with the purchase of the horses, but he was pleased to see them opening up to his efforts to teach them about responsibility.

Now, if only he could convince Daisy to trust him.

Would she be willing to work as well with him as she had with Murdock? He wanted her to come to the place where she could embrace his plans for their future. The joy of seeing her revel in the business achievements of the day was countered by the memory of her words when she confessed uncertainty about him to Peggy Dismuke. Daisy was a picture of contradictions. If he were honest, he'd see his contradictions, too. He was determined to avoid adding pain to her grief, but part of him grieved, too. Being so close to her and knowing she was out of his reach emotionally was wearing on him. He wanted them to build a family on their friendship. Would he have to let his guard down to do it?

Chapter Nine

Daisy eyed Tucker and the twins as they came in after working all afternoon on the addition. The new horses were safe in their stalls. She swatted at eager hands that reached for warm molasses cookies before supper.

"Those are for dessert. Go wash up, and we'll eat the soup. Then, and only then, you can have cookies." She smiled at Tucker who feigned a wounded look as he cradled his hand against his shirt.

"Watch out, boys! She wields a mean spatula!" he teased.

James and John hung their hats beneath his, and watched in disbelief as their mother refused Tucker even one cookie.

"The soup smells delicious!" John was first to the table.

"I like the smell of the bread best." James joined his brother.

Tucker took his seat and reached for John's hand. "It all smells wonderful, but I think we may have to fight for it." He chuckled and winked at Daisy before he bowed his head.

She didn't try to mask the mirth in her voice as she blessed the food and her family.

Passing the bread, Daisy spoke. "I see quite a bit of progress on the addition. You're all working very hard. I'm impressed."

James lifted his spoon and blew on the contents to cool it. "I think I might want to be a carpenter when I grow up." He put the soup in his mouth too soon and had to draw in a quick breath to cool his tongue.

"Slow down. Eat some bread while the soup cools." Daisy put a hand on his arm, causing him to lower his spoon. "You could save yourself a lot of pain if you'd learn to be patient."

Daisy realized as she spoke the words that she could benefit from their truth. If only she'd been patient with Tucker when the wagons of lumber had arrived at the cabin or when he was ordering the furniture. She could have saved herself the sadness of knowing she'd hurt him by resisting the things he offered her in kindness.

Tucker interrupted her thoughts. "We accomplished a lot today, but there's still more to be done." He looked to the tired boys. "Those horses of yours are going to need names. Any ideas?" He smiled at their reactions.

"We get to pick the names?" James was ecstatic. "Really? They don't have to keep the names they had at the livery?"

"How will they know to answer to their new name?" This came from John who was always thinking.

"They'll get used to it. You just have to remind them often. People do it all the time," Tucker explained.

"People don't change names," James insisted. "My name will always be James. James Rudolf Mosley." He stuck out his chest with pride at the sound of his full name. "I got the 'Rudolf' from Papa's papa. It's a family tradition."

"That's a fine tradition. I'm sure your papa was proud to have a son to name after his father." Tucker affirmed James. "But people do change names." He grinned as he challenged the twins. "Can you boys think of any time a person would change their name?" He put a spoon of soup in his mouth and savored it while they thought.

Daisy listened from her seat at the foot of the table, not sure she was comfortable with where this conversation could lead.

"What about when a man becomes a doctor?" Tucker offered. "People start calling him Dr. Smith, or Doc, instead of Mr. Smith. See what I mean? Now you try."

"Reverend Dismuke told us once at church that before he was a preacher he was a carpenter. I guess he had to get used to being called 'Reverend.'" John caught on to Tucker's line of thinking.

"That's good, John. What about you, James? Can you think of one?" Daisy asked.

James thought hard. "I know! When we got big enough to talk, we started calling you 'Momma.' No one called you that before. You were Daisy to everyone else." He smiled in triumph at contributing to Tucker's game.

"Good one, James," Tucker agreed. "I know another. I was a ranch hand before I came to live here with your momma and you boys. Now I'm a cotton farmer."

"Can you call yourself a cotton farmer before you farm any cotton?" James wanted to know.

Daisy laughed. "He's got a point. You are a cotton farmer in training."

"We'll see." Tucker laughed with her. "Just give me a chance to prove myself."

Quietly and without looking up, John said, "I heard Mr. Little call Momma 'Mrs. Barlow' today. Her name was Mosley like us before." Everyone was silent for a moment. Then Daisy spoke.

"Before that my name was Miss Daisy Marie Warren. That's the name my momma and papa gave me when I was born. That's what everyone called me until I married your papa. Then I became Mrs. Mosley."

"And now you're Mrs. Barlow, like the people in town were saying today." John's voice was soft and serious.

"That's true, John, but I'm the same person I was when they called me Miss Warren, or Mrs. Mosley, or Mrs. Barlow. I'm still me." Daisy tried her best to reassure John.

"But it's not the same, Momma. You were Mrs. Mosley when you were Papa's wife. Now Papa's gone, and your name's the same as Mr. Tucker's." His chin started to quiver. James began to breathe in deep slow breaths.

"I'll always be Momma to both of you." Daisy's voice was comforting.

"Boys, your momma is right. I've known her since she was a young girl. She's the same person she's always been. She's lived a lot of life since then. She had a good husband in your papa. She's got this farm. She has you boys. But she's still the same inside. Only her heart is bigger." Tucker explained in a way the boys would understand.

"How can you know that, Mr. Tucker?" John asked sincerely.

"John, I've known your momma a long time. I can tell she's the same person when I look in her eyes. I can see right into that soul of hers and see all the love and kindness inside. She's still generous and good. That's how I know." Tucker looked straight into Daisy's eyes. She really felt he was seeing into the depths of her soul, searching for the young girl he'd known all those years ago. The slight tug at the corner of his mouth said he'd succeeded. She wondered what she'd see in his eyes if she searched deeply. The thought made her blush and look away. She wasn't ready to know the answer to that question—yet.

"Now, about those horses..." Tucker pulled his gaze from Daisy and focused on the twins.

"I wanna call mine Trojan. I hear that's a good name for a big horse." James immediately made up his mind.

John thought a moment longer and said, "I'll call mine Beauregard. It sounds important."

"Good names—both of them." Tucker dropped his spoon in his empty bowl. "Now if we can get some of those cookies from your momma without too much of a fight, we'll go out to the barn and make sure Trojan and Beauregard are settled for the night."

"I'll give you cookies, but we need to clarify one thing about names." Daisy brought the platter of cookies to the table.

"What's that, Momma?" James asked.

"Remember that a woman can be a doctor, too. I want my sons to grow up knowing women are important and should be respected."

"Your momma's right. There's another thing that happened today." Tucker snagged several cookies and took a big bite before finishing his thought. "Your momma is now a landowner. That's something that couldn't have happened before."

Daisy's face softened, and she looked at Tucker. "Thank you for your part in that, Tucker. I don't know what I'd have done if you hadn't been there today. Mr. Little made me so angry."

"That's what your papa was afraid would happen. Often new laws are resisted by the people who are supposed to implement them. I'm glad Mr. Little didn't have his way." He smiled at her and rose from the table.

"I mean it, Tucker. I appreciate the stand you took for me today. I won't forget it." Daisy blushed and reached for the empty soup bowls. "Now if you boys are going to see those horses again tonight, you better move. Mr. Tucker and I have some cotton farming lessons to do after you're in bed."

Chair legs scraped across the wooden floor, and small feet ran for the door. James had a cookie in his teeth, and John was trying to put one in his pocket.

"No cookies for the horses," Tucker called as he followed the boys onto the porch. He paused and turned to Daisy.

"You're welcome, Daisy. I only insisted you get what Murdock worked so hard for you to have. It wouldn't be right any other way." He tipped his hat at her and closed the door. She smiled, thinking about the deed safely locked in the box she kept hidden in the chest at the foot of her bed. She would forever be grateful to Tucker for helping to secure her ownership of the farm.

After Daisy washed the dishes, she pulled out the farm journal in preparation for Tucker's lessons on the cotton farm. It was difficult to look at the records and not think of the nights she'd spent recording the figures as Murdock taught her how to balance the many columns on the large yellow pages. She ran a hand across the heavy leather cover and remembered how happy Murdock had been when the crops started to pay off and their nest egg grew enough for them to put a bedroom on the house for the twins.

Daisy pictured him sitting by the fire, urging her to hurry and finish these same books so they could spend time together. She often sat at his feet in front of the fire, and he'd stroke her hair while they talked.

The love she felt for Murdock was so deep and long lasting that his absence created a void in her soul. They'd never talked about what they'd do if one of them passed away. They were so young they never considered the possibility. She should have known better because her own mother had died when she was a child. "Oh, Murdock, I miss you so." Daisy's voice was a soft moan. "If only we'd talked about this kind of thing, I'd know you'd be okay with the choices I'm making." Tears stung her eyes. She wiped them away with the back of her hand. She straightened her back and opened the journal to the numbers for the harvest they'd sold just weeks ago. "Know I'll do my best for our sons, Murdock. I promise."

With the boys in bed and a fresh pot of coffee on the stove, Tucker and Daisy settled at the table to go over the books.

"This is the journal for all our expenses and income." Daisy pointed to the page. "These are the figures for the harvest this year. We sold our cotton just before Murdock was killed." Her voice choked just a bit, and Tucker glanced up at her. He had chosen to sit on the bench the boys usually occupied so he'd be close enough to her to see the records as she explained everything. He reached and put a hand on hers.

"We don't have to do this tonight if you're not up to it," he offered.

"No. I'm fine." She slid her hand from beneath his and shifted a little farther from him in her chair. "It just brought back a lot of memories to bring this out."

"I understand, Daisy. You don't have to do this for me."

She shrugged one shoulder. "Really, I'm fine. This is important information you need to know. The sooner you start to learn the ins and outs of the farm, the better off we'll be come planting season. You've got to have all the facts about the finances. The profits, the time-tables and the costs."

Tucker pulled his hand off the page and reached for his coffee mug. "Teach away," he said, and the lesson began. Daisy showed him the detailed entries recorded in the pages of the journal since Murdock had bought the land. Tucker could see the wisdom they'd gained from their experience as each year progressed. Murdock had been a very diligent man when it came to his work.

An hour and a half later Daisy closed the journal and sat back from the table. "What do you think?" she asked. She seemed tired but not as emotionally spent as he'd first thought she would be. The mundane details in the journal must have helped her to detach from the sadness that threatened her composure earlier.

"Your records are excellent. I can see how you and Murdock managed to get the farm to this point." He stood and grabbed his coffee mug. "If you don't mind, I'd like to sit close to the fire while we talk. I've been folded up on that bench for about as long as a man my size can stand."

Daisy laughed. "It's a wonder you can walk at all."

She put the journal away and joined him by the fire. He added another log and stirred the embers.

They sat in silence for a time.

"It's a lot to absorb in one sitting, but I think I have a good understanding." Tucker rocked slowly. "I did notice something, though."

"What?" Daisy sipped her coffee and stared into the flames.

"You didn't seem eager for me to clear that ten acres at the edge of the northern field."

"I just know how hard it was when we first got here. This next season will be a learning experience for both of us. I don't want us to take on extra work." Daisy finished her coffee and rocked gently.

"According to the journal, Murdock planned to clear that land this fall and have it ready for the next planting."

"That was before. I don't know if we can pick up where we left off last season. I'm not sure it's fair to you."

"So even though I instinctively picked the same ten acres Murdock chose, you don't think I'm up for the task?" Tucker stopped rocking and leaned toward her over the arm of his chair.

"That's not what I meant at all. Tucker, you keep misinterpreting my words." Daisy stilled her chair and leaned forward to meet his gaze. She shook her head as she spoke. "It's hard work. I didn't want to overload you as soon as you got here. Cotton farming is a lot different than ranching."

"I realize that, Daisy. I didn't just get off a train from a city back East. I've worked in Texas all of my adult life. Sure, I've spent most of my time on the ranch with your papa. But I've made a lot of friends over the years.

Some of the closest ones own cotton farms. Your papa's ranch is almost surrounded by cotton these days. I've picked up a fair knowledge of the process. That's just one of the reasons your papa thought I'd be able to help you." Tucker turned to look into the fire. He couldn't tell her the main reason her father had given his approval of their marriage.

Tucker had been surprised all those years ago when Mr. Warren had approached him after Daisy had agreed to marry Murdock. *I know true love when I see it, Tucker. You might hide it from Daisy because she's so young, but I know how you feel about my daughter. Are you going to be able to let her marry Murdock without saying anything? I respect your feelings for Daisy. I'm guessing you didn't act on them because you're a little older than her, and the fact that you work for me—but most of all, because of her obvious love for Murdock. I don't want her to be hurt or confused right now.*

Tucker had thought no one knew his true feelings for Daisy. He'd done his best to conceal them. He had assured Mr. Warren he'd hold his peace and watched the woman of his heart pledge herself to the man of her destiny. He'd forced himself to bury his feelings for her all those years ago. And he succeeded. He was beginning to wonder if he'd buried them deep enough.

Daisy reached out and placed her hand on his sleeve, drawing him back from his thoughts. "Tucker, I'm so sorry. I had no idea. And here I was going on and on about the tiniest details. You should have stopped me."

"Don't apologize, Daisy. It's not your fault." He leaned back in the chair and closed his eyes, rocking again. "I'm not one to talk a lot about what I'm thinking. You should remember that, especially after all the times you and your sisters tried to quiz me about one thing or another." His slight grin gave a playful note to the words he spoke. He enjoyed teasing this woman who had a need to know the details of every situation.

She sputtered a small laugh. "Really? You mean you don't like to talk about your plans? Or what you're thinking? I would never have guessed you'd still be like that, Tucker. I'm so glad you reminded me." She laughed in earnest then.

When Daisy was a teenager, she and her older sister, Jasmine, had often asked him what he was doing or where he was going. She and Lily, the baby of the family, had been relentless in trying to learn his opinions on different people or situations. He never shared the slightest information, saying only that girls tended to want to know too much. They would tease him about being so quiet. She'd even told him once he'd wind up a lonely old man if he wasn't willing to talk to girls. His reply that girls would always be intrigued, as long as they thought he had a secret, had made them both laugh.

"Stop it, Daisy. Or I won't tell you another thing."

Her laughter deepened. Tucker enjoyed the ease of their banter. Many times over the years he'd reminisced about how she looked when she laughed, or how quickly she could become flustered. Even in her youth she'd been able to keep pace with anyone when it came to sharp conversation or a witty exchange. "I mean it. You'll be wondering what I'm thinking for a long time." Tucker teased her knowing it would be a good excuse for all the things he wasn't ready to say to her. "That's it." He rose from his chair. "I'm going to bed now. You'll just have to guess what time I'll be ready for church in the morning—" he grabbed his hat from the peg "—and don't even think about making me wait."

She was still laughing as he closed the door. He suddenly opened it again.

"Come bolt this door, Mrs. Barlow, so I can go to the barn." The door closed immediately. The firelight reflecting the laughter in Daisy's eyes had been more than Tucker could stand. He knew he shouldn't flirt with her the same night she'd been choked to the point of tears over her recent loss. Nor could he sit by the fire watching her laugh and not want to reach out and touch her soft face.

He stood on the porch, waiting to hear her light footsteps approach the closed door. When she slid the bolt into place, he backed down the steps with his hat spinning in his hands. He thought he'd seen a smile pull up at the corner of her lips when he called her Mrs. Barlow. Usually a humble man, a shiver of pride threatened to dance across his barricaded heart.

He turned and headed away from the cabin. Years before he had imagined proposing to her when she came of age. Instead, he'd watched her fall in love with Murdock. She was just as beautiful now as she'd been then. Her golden hair and tiny frame made her look fragile, but he knew her well enough not to be fooled. Daisy was a strong lady with her own mind. Her father may have asked him to come here, but if Daisy hadn't agreed, she would have sent him back to East River within an hour of his arrival. More than anything he had come here to take care of Daisy. His heart was frozen against the pain of rejection, but he couldn't sit idly by, working for her father, all the while knowing she was suffering as his mother had. The protective shell around his heart was in place to prevent others from hurting him. He was surprised that protecting Daisy and her sons was causing him to feel the tingling of new life inside. An unexpected thawing threatened his peace.

Tucker had loved Daisy long ago and never had the chance to show her. He had accepted her marriage to Murdock, squelched his feelings and contented himself to be alone. Now he had the chance to love her, but life had hardened him, and she was too hurt to receive his love. Even if he was able to resurrect it.

Chapter Ten

Freshly brushed hats on clean heads rode in the back of the wagon. Daisy sat next to Tucker as they left a full twenty minutes earlier than necessary. True to his word, Tucker had not told her what time he'd be leaving. She in turn had not told him what time the church service began. It was silly, but they both got a small pleasure from keeping the other guessing.

"Why did we have to leave so early?" James called from the back.

Daisy smiled and looked at Tucker. His eyebrows drew together, and he gave her a mock frown in admission of defeat.

"It's always good to be prepared." He answered James and then winked at Daisy, who knew he was covering for having teased her. "We're trying out these new horses today. I like to make sure I've got plenty of time when dealing with a new animal."

"Maybe you could open yourself up to the idea of sharing information now that you're married," Daisy chided in a lighthearted manner. "It could save you time and trouble in the future." She continued to smile, keeping her eyes on the road ahead of them. Tucker could play at holding back information from her if he wanted. He'd often won the mental games they'd played as friends before Murdock had come into her life. Winning was a refreshing change for her.

"Don't count on any great changes in the personality I've always had, Daisy." There was a sporting challenge in Tucker's tone. "You've known for years I'm not one for telling things just for the sake of telling. I like a good secret now and again."

Chatter from the back of the wagon interrupted them. "Mr. Tucker, I'm glad you let me and John help hitch the wagon. It's important for men like us to know all about our equipment." James was really getting into his role as a young man. Daisy wondered if perhaps Tucker was pushing them to grow up too quickly.

Tucker assured James, "You both did a great job."

John stood and put his hand on Daisy's shoulder. "Momma, did you know Mr. Tucker is gonna teach us how to shoot this afternoon?" His voice showed excitement about the adventure, but it also held a tremor of fear.

"Oh, Tucker, do you think they're ready for that?" Daisy turned in the seat to look at him, her lightheartedness gone in an instant. He held the reins loosely in his hands as he leaned forward with his elbows resting on his knees.

"These boys are ready to be young men, Momma. That means they've got a lot of learnin' to do. They'll need to know all about how to care for their horses and how to handle all the 'equipment' young James was talking about." He nodded in the affirmative. "And, yes, they'll be needin' to learn to shoot. It's important for a lot of reasons."

John sat down next to James, and the boys began their own conversation about all they would learn in the near future.

Daisy touched his arm. "Really, Tucker. I'm concerned about this. Guns are dangerous. Their father…" She remembered how horrified they had all been when she and the twins had come home from town and found Murdock dead in the corral, shot in the chest, blood everywhere. She squeezed her eyes shut in an effort to blot out the images in her mind.

Tucker covered her hand on his arm. "That's one of the reasons, Daisy." He spoke low so only she could hear. "They need to be able to protect themselves, and you, if necessary. They'd be scarred for life if something happened and they didn't know what to do."

He made sense, but the thought of her little boys handling guns troubled her. "What if they accidentally get hurt, or hurt one another?" Daisy's fear was unrelenting.

"I'll teach them about gun safety before I let them touch a gun. That's always first. Then they'll learn how to clean it. Then we'll move to the shooting phase. I promise to be careful and to teach them to be careful. But the last thing we need is for them to be caught unprepared in a dangerous situation." Tucker released her hand and focused on the road ahead. "Besides, they can help put more on the table than fish when they learn to shoot. I'm thinking about turkeys and other fresh meat."

Daisy still wasn't convinced. Her heart longed for the security of the life she'd known before Murdock's death.

Tucker reasoned, "It'll make them feel important.

They're old enough to learn. I'm sure Murdock would have taught them soon."

Her new fear of loss and vulnerability rose to the surface. "I know it makes logical sense, but I just couldn't bear it if something else bad happened to our family."

Tucker's heart squeezed tight when she called them a family. "That's where prayer and faith come into the picture. We'll both pray for their safety, and we'll do our part to prepare them for all they need to know in life. Then we'll trust God to protect them. It'll be fine." A family. He finally had a family to protect. All it lacked was the love he knew would never be his. He'd content himself with friendship. That's all Daisy had promised. It was all he could expect.

Daisy's smile was strained. "You're right. I'll just need to pray—now more than ever."

In an effort to lighten her spirits Tucker said, "I remember when you learned to shoot." His eyes were straight ahead, but there was humor in his voice. He knew she'd been successfully distracted from her worries when she cried out in her own defense.

"That's not fair! You know I wasn't trying to shoot you that day!" She blushed at the memory.

"I'm just saying the lesson I learned that day was to be careful when teaching young people to shoot." Tucker was trying not to laugh. "I still have a tiny scar where you got me with that buckshot." He could no longer contain his amusement. "I've never been so glad to be quick on my feet in my life!" Laughter burst from deep in his chest.

"Tucker, you know you walked right between me and the target!" Daisy again denied all responsibility for what she'd told him then was an unfortunate accident. "If you'd been paying attention, you never would have been hit. Besides all that, it was just a grazing sting. I didn't really shoot you!"

"If that's how you want to remember it, you go ahead. I was there. I know exactly what happened."

Daisy joined in his laughter now.

Tucker knew she was right. He had been distracted that afternoon. She didn't know *she* was the distraction. Tucker had tried to avoid her presence by retreating to the barn, not realizing her father intended to teach her to shoot. He'd come out of the barn thinking Mr. Warren and Daisy had gone back to the house, only to walk right in front of her target as she pulled the trigger for the first time. She'd rushed to check on him, after his dive in the dirt to avoid the full brunt of the blast. Daisy had been convinced she'd really hurt him, but only one pellet had grazed his left side. Horrified when she saw blood oozing through his shirt, she'd assumed he was seriously injured. He'd moaned and rolled in the dirt to torment her, until she found he was faking. Then the real trouble began as she pounced on him for scaring her nearly to death. Mr. Warren had to pull her off. Every hand on the ranch had teased both of them from that day on—him for walking around in a daze and her for bagging big game with her first shot. It was weeks before she forgave him. Smiling at the memory of the concern in her eyes that day lifted his spirits.

The smile faded. Daisy *had* been concerned for him that day. But she saw him as a friend then. And now. The precious love she had in her heart for a man—a partner for life—was for Murdock. Tucker knew the futility of loving someone who'd already given their love away.

Tucker's thoughts settled as they arrived at church, and he found a nice shady spot to leave the wagon. The boys jumped from the wagon and ran to wait for Mrs. Winters. Daisy had explained the woman would teach a Bible class for children fifteen minutes before the service began.

"Mind your manners," Daisy called as they disappeared around the corner of the church.

Tucker set the brake and jumped to the ground. He turned to offer Daisy his hand. She smiled down at him and said, "You know service doesn't start for another thirty minutes?"

"I gathered we might be a little early." He smiled at her before glancing around at the empty churchyard. "Are you going to stay up there until service starts, or are you going to come down here with me and remind me how important it is for me to talk to you about what I'm thinking?" he joked.

"Oh, I think I may just let you help me down and call a Sunday truce to the teasing." She giggled and moved the edge of the wagon seat. "I'm already tired. I was up an hour early not sure when you were going to try to leave."

"So what we have here, ma'am, is a tie."

Tucker lifted Daisy by the waist and set her on the ground. A lightness in her middle caught her breath. She tried to convince herself it was from the motion of being lifted and set to the ground, not from his nearness.

"Yes, I'd say we're about evenly matched," she agreed in a voice barely above a whisper. Looking into his face she was taken again with how masculine he was. Tall and strong, smelling fresh and clean. Her hands still rested on his broad shoulders where she'd balanced herself as he'd helped her from the wagon.

"Oh, you'd say that, would you?" His green eyes danced with merriment. "You think we're a good match?"

She meant as competitors; now he was being almost forward. She dropped her hands. Her eyes darted from side to side. Convinced by the warmth of her face, Daisy knew her cheeks flamed with color. Relief washed over her when Tucker spoke and eased her embarrassment.

"Definitely a day for a cease-fire," he agreed.

He offered his arm, and they walked toward the church. "Should we go inside and wait, or would you like to walk for a bit?"

"If you don't mind—" she turned to look at him "—I'd like to go in and spend a few minutes in prayer."

"That's fine with me." He opened the door. "Do you want me to join you, or would you like to be alone?" He waited for her answer.

Daisy looked in the doorway to the altar area. Her heart still raced a bit from having been so close to him. Had it really only been six days ago they'd come here and been married? So much had happened to her in the past month. She really needed a few minutes of solace with God.

"Would it be okay if I go in alone? I'd love to pray with you, but I feel like there are things I need to bring to the Lord alone today. Do you mind?"

Tucker lifted her hand from the crook of his arm and released her. "Not at all, Daisy." He looked into her face and smiled ever so slightly. "I do understand. I'll join you for service." With a tip of his hat, he left her in the doorway.

Daisy knelt at the altar, hoping to find the comfort and strength she needed. She was flustered beyond distraction at how she'd reacted to Tucker just now. Could she grow to love him as her husband? She knew eventually they would have a more normal marital relationship, but would she really love him? The way she'd loved Murdock? He certainly was handsome, and kind, and committed. The list could go on.

He'd brought the kind of security the twins needed. But she wasn't sure she'd ever feel secure again. Not after losing Murdock and almost losing her farm. She hated feeling vulnerable. The men who'd killed her husband and stolen her horses had made her that way.

Would surrendering her heart to Tucker make her vulnerable to the same kind of loss again? For all his good points, she still couldn't handle the way he did things without even discussing them with her. Was she wrong to resist his decisive ways? A lot of women would see that as strength, but Daisy couldn't help feeling left out when she didn't know what was going on. He spent money— lots of money—without even asking what she thought. Her only hope was now that she'd shown him the bank balances and farm journal he'd understand more about their financial limits.

Daisy found it difficult to pray when she folded her hands under her chin as she knelt. The scent of him lingered on her gloves and drew her concentration away from her dilemmas. It weakened the sense of propriety she felt would require her to resist him for a reasonable time. What was a reasonable mourning period? Reverend Dismuke had said it was not too soon for her to marry. Many people in town hadn't been surprised by their sudden marriage. Peggy, on the other hand, had expressed disbelief that Daisy would even consider marrying again so soon. Maybe Daisy was trying to hold on to a past that was gone. Would that prevent her from considering all the possibilities a future with Tucker could bring?

I'm just not ready, Lord. Help me.

When the steeple bells began to ring announcing service would begin soon, Daisy took her place in the pew and waited for the twins and Tucker to take their seats with her. She sat staring at the cross behind the lectern, meditating on how good God had been to her. She'd seen some very hard things during the past few weeks, but God had provided for her at every step of the way. She missed Murdock terribly, but knew, according to the Bible she put her faith in, he was with God.

She thought about the verse in *Isaiah* that Tucker said he relied on to keep him from giving up. Over the past month she had definitely been walking with the Lord. Sometimes it felt as if she was so weak she could only crawl. Hopefully she would be able to run with God again—even mount up with wings as eagles and soar. She just had to wait on the Lord.

Tucker spent the time before service walking near the edge of the trees beyond the churchyard. He prayed, asking God to continue to give him patience and wisdom. Raising two sons would be hard for any man, but raising another man's sons in a way their momma could be proud of was difficult. His original concern for James and John was beginning to grow into a fatherly love. He could see their pain over their papa from time to time. At the oddest moments they would drift off in thought, and he knew they were thinking of Murdock. Daisy did the same thing. It was challenging to feel as though someone else was in the cabin with them sometimes. Murdock's memory was a powerful force.

Tucker had seen signs of God's healing love working in the hearts of Daisy and her boys. He thanked God for the moments when joy and laughter filled their home. As a lonely child, he'd craved the love of a true family. He had longed to receive the depth of love Daisy and the twins had for Murdock.

He asked God once again to help him walk when he couldn't run, and to build his strength and endurance. He no longer asked to fly like an eagle. He reminded the Lord of how long he'd been faithful knowing it had been God's will for Daisy to marry Murdock. He'd resigned himself to never having her in his life and had chosen to live alone, knowing there was no one else he would ever love. He needed to stay focused on his friendship with her and on building a relationship with the boys.

God had given him this chance to be with Daisy, and he was grateful. But he would keep his heart in check. He couldn't stand to be here day in and day out if he offered to love her and she refused. The only sure way for him to fulfill his commitment to protect her and the twins was to never open the door to the vulnerability of love. The risk of rejection was too great.

Alice Fields had taught him that lesson well. He'd tried to take the place of her former beau, only to be disappointed. Hope that he had found someone to spend his life with had turned to ashes when she returned to the young man who had earlier refused to commit to her. It was a feeling he never wanted to experience again. More than once he'd learned the power that the love of a lifetime held over someone's heart.

Chapter Eleven

Reverend Dismuke preached of God's faithfulness, giving the example of God sending manna and water in the wilderness to the children of Israel. He stressed that God's provision didn't always come in ways we expected, but the Lord always provided for His children. The message comforted Daisy. She knew God would take care of her and the twins. He'd chosen Murdock to take care of her for the past ten years. She believed God had chosen Tucker to be her provider now. If only her heart would catch up to her new circumstances.

Daisy's shoulder brushed Tucker's sleeve as they stood together when the sermon ended. He smiled at her and offered to share his hymn book. He was so close, and so kind, yet so unsettling. He represented the comfort of familiarity and the apprehension of the unknown. Daisy was glad the hymn was familiar, so she didn't have to think as she sang the words. Her heart was stirring with the prayers she'd prayed earlier and the words the preacher had spoken. Healing was painful at best. Was the ache in her heart a little lighter today? Had the divide in her soul begun to mend? How long would the process take?

The final amen was spoken and immediately Daisy and Tucker were surrounded by her friends and curious acquaintances. One by one, Daisy introduced Tucker to almost everyone in the small church.

Judy Thornton and her husband, Randall, were the last people to approach them. Daisy made the introductions, and Judy pulled her aside for all the details of her marriage. The friends hadn't spoken since Tucker had come to town. While Daisy was deep in conversation with Judy, she noticed Randall and Tucker walk outside. She hoped he'd make friends of his own now that he was living in Pine Haven.

Daisy smiled at the thought of her father's caution that it would be much easier to be married to Tucker than to have people make judgments if he were just staying at her farm. She could only imagine how differently this morning would have gone. As her husband, the people of Pine Haven were accepting of Tucker.

She turned her complete attention back to Judy and tried to catch her up on the happenings of the week. There was too much to tell in just a moment. The ladies agreed to have tea in the near future.

Daisy met Tucker at the wagon a few minutes later. The boys climbed into the back and complained of hunger.

Daisy accepted Tucker's hand. "There's a lunch of fried chicken and potatoes ready at the cabin. We'll be there before you know it. There are more cookies, too." She settled into her seat while he came around the wagon and climbed up to join her. "Since there's no need for more cotton farming lessons, we can make a picnic of it if you'd like. It's perfect weather today."

"Sounds good to me." Tucker released the brake and steered the wagon toward the street. Several people called greetings to them as they left the churchyard. "I like your friends, Daisy. They seem like nice folk."

"I'm glad. I know it's not easy to move to a new place and start over without knowing anyone." She folded her hands in her lap and held her back straight to keep from bumping into his shoulder as the wagon climbed onto the road.

Tucker cut his eyes to her. "I know you." He grinned. "And the boys."

"You know what I mean," Daisy countered playfully. "You left an entire life behind to come here. It's got to be difficult." Again she was surprised at the yearning she felt inside when they talked or spent time together. "Don't misunderstand me. I'm glad you're here, but I marvel that you were willing to come."

Tucker watched the road. "I had a lot of reasons." He paused, and she wondered if he was going to explain. "Life doesn't always turn out like we think, Daisy." She sat silent, and he continued. "Those boys needed a father. I know how that feels."

"But you'd never met the twins." What motivated a man to such a selfless act?

"Like I said, I know you." A slight smile pulled at one side of his mouth. She almost didn't see it in his profile. "I know you would want the best for them. If anyone could ever give it to them without help, it would be you."

Daisy looked at her hands as they twisted together in her lap. "Thank you, Tucker. That's very kind of you to say."

"I mean it. You're a strong woman. But boys need a man." They approached the crossroads in the middle of town. He pulled at the reins and steered the horses onto the road that would take them to the farm. "And you needed a friend."

"It was still a big sacrifice for you," she insisted.

"I needed a friend, too." Tucker made a clicking noise inside his cheek to encourage Trojan and Beauregard to pick up the pace. "It was worth it."

Daisy pondered his words and matched his silence for the rest of the journey home.

Ants invaded the picnic, but it didn't keep the boys from enjoying their lunch by the pond. Daisy called them away from the edge of the water more times than she could count. Tucker stretched out on the grass, covered his face with his hat and dozed after eating his fill. She had laughed when he kept reaching into the basket of cookies saying, "Just one more." He'd pronounced her an excellent cook and promptly fallen asleep.

James and John played tag in the distance. Daisy was left to sit on the picnic quilt with her thoughts. She watched the twins frolic and missed their father. He had loved to come here on Sundays and play with them. She was glad the boys had those memories and hoped in time they would play with Tucker in much the same way. They were adjusting to working with him and had been pleased when he taught them about the horses. They respected him, but she wondered how long it would be before they accepted him as their parent.

Tucker moaned and she turned to study him, watching the even rise and fall of his chest as he slept. Tall and broad and strong was the impression he first made on her when she was a young girl. She'd watched him rope and brand cattle on her father's ranch. Daisy was always amazed at how gentle he would be with a colt and how strong he was in the saddle. More than once he'd held his temper when a lesser man would have lost his. She remembered his constant teasing, his sense of humor and most of all his friendship. Memories of their easy banter and the way he listened to her came to mind and made her smile. He really was a dear friend to her then. Never imagining he'd be her husband, she'd laughed with him and told him all her woes. She remembered the day she'd married Murdock, how Tucker had hugged her close and whispered against her hair to wish her happiness. He truly had been there for her in her youth. She understood why her father had sent him to her now. Papa knew their friendship was a good foundation for a successful marriage.

Daisy studied the ring he'd given her on their wedding day. It was uniquely beautiful.

"Do you like it?" Tucker's voice startled Daisy from her reverie.

She flattened her right hand across her chest to calm herself and caught her breath. "Yes, very much. It's beautiful. I never expected a ring." Daisy angled her hand for a better view of the intricate vines and leaves. "Tell me the story behind it."

Tucker propped up on one elbow and pulled a stalk of grass from the ground to twist in his fingers. He focused on the thin blade. "It was my mother's." He looked up at her then.

Her face softened. "Oh, Tucker, what a precious gift. I'm honored to wear it." She fingered the tiny band with her other hand.

"Momma was small like you." He continued to twist the grass and look into her eyes. "She was determined like you, too. And spunky. She didn't like surprises too much, and she always wanted to know what was going on. A planner who didn't want to be caught unawares." He smiled at her. "Kinda like someone else I know," he said with a lift of his brow.

Daisy smiled at him and spoke softly. "I think I would have really liked her."

"I know she would have liked you. She was a survivor, too. I never felt like she'd give up on anything. She taught me to hang on to my dreams no matter what and never settle. Momma always said it would be better to do without than to settle for less than your heart's desire." His eyes grew distant, as if lost in the memory of her as he spoke.

"What was her name?"

"Grace." He spoke the name reverently. "She said her momma and papa must have known she'd need the grace of God to get through the hard life she had to face, so they spoke it over her every day when they called her name." He tossed the grass stalk away and sat up, resting his forearms on his knees as he watched James and John in the distance. "My momma was a good woman. She'd be proud for you to wear her ring."

"Thank you, Tucker." Daisy was humbled by his comparison of her to the mother he so obviously adored. "It's a truly wonderful gift."

A few minutes later they packed up and rode home. The boys were full of talk about who would be the best shooter. Tucker and Daisy went inside, while the twins headed to the barn to wait for Tucker to teach them about gun safety and maintenance. They balked in the beginning, thinking they should shoot first and then clean the guns, but Tucker held fast to his plan.

Tucker set the picnic basket on the table. "I'll be back to let you know before they actually start shooting," Tucker teased Daisy. "I wouldn't want anyone to get hurt accidentally." He smiled and closed the door as her dishrag sailed through the air. It splattered against the door and water ran down the wood in the exact spot his face had been. She could hear him laughing as he went down the porch steps.

Shooting lessons went off without a hitch. James was a good shot, but John was a natural shooter. Daisy had been allowed to watch as long as she promised not to interfere. The boys insisted shooting was a man's business, and they should learn from a man. They thrived under Tucker's watchful eye. She smiled at the bonds she witnessed forming in their relationship. James and John didn't even realize how much they were looking to Tucker for instruction. Once again, she offered a silent prayer of thanks for Tucker's presence in their lives.

After a supper of pancakes and sausage, the boys went to bed early. Daisy and Tucker sat in front of the fire, eating cookies.

"Do you still play dominoes?" Daisy asked.

"Do you still cheat?" Tucker laughed in response.

She planted both hands on her hips and lifted her head. "I don't have to anymore. I know how to win fair and square." The determination of her voice came across as the challenge she intended. She retrieved the box of dominoes from a shelf over the bed and moved to the table to set them out.

"Sounds to me like you're ready to prove something, Daisy." Tucker came to join her, bringing the plate of cookies, and set his glass of milk on the table. He reached for the dotted tiles. "I think we'll just have to see how much you know. Strategy was never your strong suit. You weren't patient enough to plot your opponent's defeat." He turned the tiles facedown. Daisy shuffled them around while Tucker adjusted the lamp so they could see the game.

"Oh, we'll see all right." Daisy perched on the bench and sat at his elbow so she could reach the game. "I'll even let you take the first move."

"No, ma'am, you won't. We'll do this fair and square as you say. Ladies first."

"Not and have you say you gave me an advantage. We'll draw tiles. High tile goes first." They both reached for the same tile, their hands touching for an instant. Daisy jumped back and then laughed to cover her reaction to his touch.

"You can have that one, I was using it as a decoy," she joked and reached across for a different tile. "Show yours first," she taunted.

"No. We'll show them together. On three. One, two, three." They turned the tiles over.

"I cannot believe it!" Daisy was indignant. "How did you get the double six tile?"

"You gave it to me." He smirked and stirred the tiles to mix them up again. "Thank you."

"Well, that's the only thing I'll give you in this game," Daisy insisted.

"We'll see."

Tucker started the domino train, but Daisy quickly proved her skill. After several minutes with Daisy leading the game, Tucker finally caught up to her score and passed her with one brilliant play. On his next turn, as he reached to play another tile, she grabbed his hand and contested.

"Oh, no, you don't! You can't play that there."

He laughed saying, "And just why not?" Tucker tried to tug his hand free, but she wouldn't release him.

"You must have moved something while I was getting more milk."

"Now that is just what I would expect you to do." He used his other hand to try to place the tile. Daisy promptly captured that hand, too.

"Stop trying to play that tile. We're in the middle of a contested move here." She laughed and held both his hands securely, her elbows on the table to leverage her hold on him.

"I moved nothing when you were getting your milk." He grinned and leaned close to her face to make his point. "Now about what I did or didn't do when you weren't paying attention—" he was laughing now, too "—I'll never tell."

"I knew it." Daisy narrowed her eyes and leaned closer still. "You were accusing me of cheating all those years ago, but it was you all along," she goaded him.

"I've seen you swap tiles when you thought no one was looking." He narrowed his eyes and matched her accusatory tone, their faces inches apart. "Don't try to deny it. You can't stand to lose."

Daisy shook her head playfully, "To that I must confess. I do love to win." A lock of hair fell across her forehead and in front of one eye. Tucker pulled a hand free and slowly pushed the stray tress behind her ear. Lamplight danced in his pupils as his gaze followed the motion. Her brown eyes widened. She drew in a small breath as she realized the intimacy of their posture.

Backing away hesitantly and dropping her gaze, she released his other hand and pinned her hair back into place.

"I'll let it slide this time, but I've got my eye on you now." She picked up her glass and paused before taking a drink. "Don't let it happen again." Daisy sipped the fresh milk and set the glass on the table.

A cry from the bedroom brought Daisy to her feet. She was opening the door before Tucker was out of his chair.

John sat straight up in his bed screaming, "I'm sorry, Papa! I didn't mean it! I'm sorry!"

James awakened as Daisy pulled John into her arms and cradled the back of his head with her hand. "It's okay, baby. Momma's here. It's okay." She rocked him and made shushing sounds in his ear.

Tucker stood in the doorway.

"It was just a bad dream, baby," Daisy soothed.

"No, Momma! I shot Papa! In my dream I shot Papa! It's my fault Papa's dead. I should have been here to keep him safe the day the bad men came. It's my fault! I'm practicing to be a good shooter now, but I didn't even try to save Papa! I didn't protect him!" The small boy wailed and refused to be consoled.

"I miss Papa." James joined the crying of his brother, and Daisy reached with one hand to draw him into a circle of comfort with his brother.

Tucker came into the room. "What can I do?" he asked Daisy. She shook her head in response and gently rocked the boys in her arms. The sorrow in her soul slipped over her lashes to wet her cheeks.

"We all miss Papa. It's okay. We miss him because he loved us so much, and we loved him." Daisy tried to soothe them, but even a month after Murdock's death she didn't know how to explain this tragedy to her young sons. She didn't understand it herself. How could she make sense of it to them? The three of them sat on the bed, huddled together, rocking and crying.

Tucker quietly walked away, closing the bedroom door behind him. He put away the dominoes and stoked the fire. Taking his hat from the peg he had come to think of as his own, Tucker looked around the room. Signs of Murdock were everywhere. The peg, the rocking chair by the fire, the chair at the head of the table—all these things had belonged to Murdock. Even the scent of the sausage from supper came from a hog Murdock had provided for this family.

Tucker heard the muffled crying from the bedroom and walked outside. He closed the door and sat on the porch Murdock had built, in the rocker Murdock had made for Daisy, and waited over an hour until he heard her bolt the door with a bolt Murdock had installed.

Walking across to sleep in the barn Murdock had built, the vision of Daisy holding her sons and crying with them filled his mind. Their pain was thick and fresh.

How long would it take for them to heal? What would life be like when they did? What would his relationship with her be when the boys were grown? Would she grow weary of him and only tolerate him? He knew he'd never be who she truly wanted. He had endured his mother's sadness when his own father had died. It had stayed with her until her death. Daisy's father still held firm to a reverential love for her mother's memory. Such love stayed with a soul forever.

Tucker had tried and failed to be that kind of love. Suffering the bitterness of rejection from Alice as a young man had been painful. When the fresh-faced beauty he'd given his heart to in his youth pushed him aside and went back to her first love, his heart had fractured. Her love for another so strong, she hadn't even tried to keep from hurting him.

A man learned from that kind of experience that a woman's heart would always belong to the first man she gave it to. No matter how hard another man tried, he'd never capture the spirit of true love from her. Once spent, it was gone. Like fragrant perfume poured out, a lingering scent only on the one anointed. All others merely caught a hint of the essence of what once had been.

But the pain of losing Alice didn't match the anguish of seeing Daisy fall in love with Murdock and losing the chance to share his love with her. That's when he learned to withhold his heart. It was the only way he knew to protect himself from certain rejection. It would also protect Daisy by not making her feel she must love him. Because he knew she never could.

Again he prayed for the patience to walk when he wanted to run. Then he prayed what he was sure was a selfish prayer.

God, please heal this family of the pain they still suffer. Let us become a family.

Chapter Twelve

Morning dawned colder than the previous days. The sound of Tucker hammering could be heard before the twins finished their morning chores or Daisy had breakfast prepared. With only two days before the men came to build the roof, he had a lot to do.

"Breakfast!" Daisy called from the front door. James was carrying the morning milk when he followed John from the barn. Neither boy moved with their customary liveliness. Tucker watched them go up the steps and through the door before he approached the front of the house. He wondered what mood would meet him inside the cabin. Last night was probably not the first time Daisy had dealt with nightmares since Murdock had died. Were the episodes further apart now? Had he sparked some new pain by teaching the twins to shoot? Never one to avoid the inevitable, Tucker entered the cabin.

Silence greeted him. He hung his hat and poured his coffee. John watched with sad eyes as Tucker pulled the chair back to take his seat. Tucker felt like an interloper but knew it was best for the boys to accept his presence.

He'd earned the right to be here by taking on the responsibility for this family.

"Good morning."

"Good morning, Tucker. I trust you slept well." Daisy set a basket of hot biscuits on the table and took her seat.

"Yes, thank you." He hesitated to ask after her night given the events of the previous evening. He reached for John's hand. Slowly John reached out without looking up. Tucker bowed his head and prayed.

"Lord, we thank You for this fine breakfast. May You bless it and the hands that prepared it. Guide us as we work today. Help us to look to You for comfort and healing. Amen."

"Amen" came from Daisy. Not a sound came from the boys.

"Eggs?" Daisy passed the bowl to James. "You're after it mighty early today, Tucker."

"The men I hired to help with the roof will be here on Wednesday. We've got to make sure we're ready before they arrive." He spooned a generous portion of eggs onto his plate. "Are you boys done with your chores? We could get started right after breakfast."

James pushed his eggs around on the plate with his fork. "I'm not feeling very well today. I think I need to stay inside." He never looked up from his food.

"Me, either. My stomach hurts." John didn't even pretend interest in his food.

Daisy reached out to touch James on the forehead. "No fever." She stood and did the same to John. "You're not warm, either." She sat back down. "What is it, boys? Why are you trying to convince me you don't feel well?" Daisy waited patiently. The twins looked at each other as if silently communicating what to tell their mother. It appeared James was to be the spokesperson.

"We don't want to help with the addition." He didn't look at Tucker but stared straight at Daisy.

"And why is that?" she asked with restraint.

John hung his head lower.

"We don't want anything to be different. Everything's changed too much. We want it back like it was—like Papa built it."

Tucker set his fork down and waited while Daisy processed this declaration.

"I see," she said. "Is this how you feel, too, John?" The voice was low, but tight with the effort to control her emotions.

"I don't know." John was not as certain as his brother.

"Tell me what you mean, John." Daisy pressed him.

"James and me talked after you fell asleep last night." John still didn't look up. "He thinks Papa wouldn't want us to change things—that Papa had it like it was supposed to be."

"Is that true, James?" Tucker admired Daisy's patience, but could wait no longer to get to the bottom of the situation. He knew the pain the boys were in and wanted to help, but he needed to hear from them what they were thinking.

James looked at him defiantly. "It is. Our papa built this house. And you just came here and started changing things. We don't want it different." A small chin jutted forward.

Daisy inhaled slowly. "James, apologize to Mr. Tucker."

"I won't do it. It'd be a lie. I don't like him changing things. I won't say I do."

"James!" Daisy began.

"James—" Tucker held up his hand to signal Daisy that he wanted to speak "—there are some things you need to understand."

"I don't want to understand," James interrupted.

"I want you to listen to me for a minute, son. I'll speak respectfully to you, and I'll expect the same from you," Tucker admonished.

"You're not my papa! You can't talk to me like you are!" James stormed from the table and ran out of the house, slamming the door behind him. Daisy's call for him to stop was ignored. She rose to follow, but Tucker stopped her.

"Let him go, Daisy."

He turned to John and calmly asked, "Is that how you feel, John?"

"Not really, sir." John looked up for the first time. He put a hand on the table and worried his fork between his fingers. "At first, I didn't know what to think about you being here." He looked at Tucker's face and held his gaze steady. "I miss Papa something terrible. I didn't want anyone to take his place. It was like if we left everything the same, maybe one day we'd wake up and Papa would be here—like it was all a bad dream."

Tucker patted John's hand on the table. "What about now?" he encouraged him to continue.

"Now I know you better. I know you liked my papa. And you're Momma's friend. I didn't want to like you at first, but now, I think it's kinda like you're trying to help us." The young head fell again. "And I know Papa's not coming back. It wasn't just a dream."

Daisy sat quietly. A lone tear slid down her cheek. Tucker imagined the intense clenching of her heart. One of her sons was tormented by the thought of letting go of his papa. The other was dealing with the emotions of actually doing it.

Tucker put a hand under John's chin and lifted his face. "Thank you, John, for being so honest. I think we'll be able to help your brother because of the way you've described all you've been feeling." Tucker pushed his chair away from the table. "Let's go find him and talk to him, man to man." He extended a hand to John.

John sniffed loudly and put his small hand in Tucker's much larger one. "Okay. But you may have to make him be quiet so we can tell him. James talks more than he listens." John spoke with the honesty of a child.

Tucker smiled. "We'll both talk to him. I'm sure he'll listen then."

He laid a hand on Daisy's shoulder as they walked by her on the way to the door. "Do you think you could put our breakfast back on the stove so it'll be warm when we finish our conversation? We're going to need a good breakfast because we've got a hard day's work ahead of us." She dabbed at her eyes with her apron and gave him a watery smile, nodding her head.

Tucker and John found James by the creek. He was skipping rocks but didn't turn around when Tucker was certain he'd heard their approach. Tucker picked up a few pebbles and encouraged John to do the same. They all stood on the bank for several minutes, skipping rocks in silence. Tucker threw his last rock and sat on a fallen tree trunk close to the water's edge.

"Seems like we've got some things we need to talk about, James." Tucker was the first to speak.

John came to sit by Tucker, but James continued to skip his stones.

"There's something you don't know about me, James."

Still no response. "My papa died when I was five years old." James dropped his hands to his sides. The pebbles he held fell and rolled into the creek.

John looked up at Tucker in disbelief. "Really?"

"Yes."

"Then you know how we feel," John decided.

"I do," Tucker said.

"Did your momma marry some stranger then?" James asked but didn't turn around.

"No, she didn't. As a matter of fact, my momma never married again."

"Then you don't know how we feel, do you?" James was still defiant.

"I know how it feels for no one to care except my momma." Tucker kept his tone calm.

Silence permeated the air for several minutes. Tucker gave them time to absorb this new information.

"After my papa got sick and died, my momma took care of me all by herself. She had to work in a hotel, cooking, and washing dishes, and cleaning rooms. They paid her by giving us a room and food but almost no money. Sometimes, if a customer liked the food a lot, or wanted some extra work done, like washing their clothes, they'd give Momma extra money. That's how she bought our clothes and shoes."

"How'd you both live in just one room?" John was curious.

"At first I was little, and we'd sleep at the same time. Momma would make me a pallet on the floor next to her bed. She'd even give me her pillows so the pallet was extra soft. Then later Momma would sleep in the afternoon after her work was done, and I'd sleep at night while she prepared the meals for the next day. When I got older, I'd go to school in the morning. I think she took naps between cleaning the rooms and cooking the next meal."

"I never knowed anybody whose momma had to work a real job. Except Reilly Ledford. His momma sews dresses for ladies. But he don't have a papa." John relayed his only known comparison to Tucker's situation.

"What about your house before your papa died?" James finally asked.

"The laws were different then. The only way Momma could have kept our land was to marry again. Because Papa had been sick so long, he had to borrow money from the bank to pay the doctor. When he died the bank owned the land, and me and Momma had to move."

"That's not right!" James said. "Your papa probably wanted your momma to have that house."

"I'm sure he did," Tucker agreed, "but it wasn't possible without a husband to work and pay for the land. So we moved to town, and Momma got the only job she could find. I got a job helping at the hotel when I was twelve. I'd help clean tables in the restaurant or carry people's luggage to their rooms. It took all my money to help buy the things we needed. The last year we were there, I was able to get a small room for me so we'd both have a bed. Then we didn't have to take turns sleeping anymore."

"And she worked there for always and didn't want to get married to another man?" John wondered.

"Momma worked there for ten years. One day she got real sick. The doctor said she was so tired from all the work she just couldn't get well again." Tucker felt complete honesty was the only way James and John would see why sometimes adults made decisions that were difficult for children to understand. "And then she died. I got a job on a ranch outside of town and worked there for a couple of years. Then I met your Papa Warren at a cattle auction, and he hired me to work for him. I've been there ever since, until the day I came here and married your momma."

The twins thought about all he'd said for a few moments. "Is that why you married Momma? So she wouldn't have to go work at the hotel and make us sleep in a hotel room by ourselves at night? And so she wouldn't get tired and sick and…die?" John spoke again, his face full of worry.

"That's why I know what your momma was facing trying to raise the two of you without your papa. And how hard it would be for her to keep the farm your papa wanted you to have."

Tucker stood and went to put a hand on James's shoulder. "Easy or not, like it or not, life needs to be dealt with as it happens. That's how boys become men."

John walked to the creek bank and stood on Tucker's other side. All three stared over the rippling water.

"I won't try to take your papa's place. But I must take my place of responsibility. I came here to take care of your momma and both of you. That's what I'm going to do." Tucker asked, "Can you understand that?"

"Yes, sir," both boys replied. James's voice was quieter than John's, but just as sincere.

"Do you boys understand that your momma married me so you would be taken care of?" The twins nodded. "This is a difficult time for her, too. How about the three of us work together to help her through it?"

"I will," John agreed instantly.

Tucker had a hand on the shoulder of each boy now.

He jostled them playfully. "What about you, James? Are you willing to give your best effort for us to become a family?" Tucker wanted to make sure James was on the same page with his brother.

"Okay. I will," he spoke softly, "but it still hurts."

"I know it does. I promise it will heal in time, but we've got to pull together and help one another now." Tucker turned and went down on one knee so he was eye level with the boys. He looked directly at James.

"One more thing. You can't disrespect your momma— or me. Do you understand?"

"Yes, sir," James answered. "I'm sorry."

Tucker wrapped the boy in a hug. "I forgive you. I know you were acting out of pain. I want you to know it's okay to feel the pain and work through it, but it's not okay to hurt others in the process. You'll need to apologize to your momma." He opened an arm to include John in the hug.

"I promise you both I'll do my best to take care of you and your momma." He released them and stood. "Now let's go eat a man's breakfast, so we can do a man's work. You ready?" They all walked up the hill together. Tucker hoped he'd been able to help the twins. And in turn help Daisy. He prayed as he walked toward the cabin.

Lord, please let these boys understand. Death is hard to deal with at any age. Please show mercy to these children. And I'm going to need more wisdom, too.

Daisy watched the boys work with Tucker that afternoon. They hauled scraps of lumber to the woodpile, held boards for him to saw and carried the nail bucket to wherever he was nailing. Tucker taught them a new tune to whistle while they worked. Daisy was sure she'd be hearing that song deep in the night in her sleep.

She took lemonade and cookies to them for an afternoon snack. They all laid aside their tools. The twins sat on the edge of the floor, feet dangling where the new back steps would be one day soon.

Tucker walked to the side of the house, and Daisy followed him. He drained his lemonade glass and wiped his mouth with his sleeve. She chuckled. "Try licking that off your face next time, so I don't have to wash it out of your shirt. Sugar is messy."

"Anything to oblige, ma'am." Tucker made a big show of trying to lick his lips clean of any lemonade residue.

"You are a silly one." Daisy laughed.

"How about you and I take a walk after supper tonight?" Tucker looked over the fields as he asked. "We haven't had much opportunity to talk without the boys nearby. I think it's time we did."

"Okay." She spoke tentatively. "Anything in particular you want to discuss?"

"No one particular thing." He turned and smiled at her, his green eyes alight with something she hadn't seen there before. "I'd just like the chance for us to spend some time alone." He handed her his glass. "Thank you very much. That was very refreshing." He touched the side of her face with the back of his hand and headed back to work.

She stared after him and said, "After supper, then." Her free hand moved to cover the side of her face, and a small smile tugged at her lips.

What could Tucker possibly want to talk about? Her impatient streak had wanted him to tell her immediately, but she knew his stubborn streak would hold out until after supper. Or could it be when he'd said there was no particular thing he meant it? Did he want to spend time with her—without the boys—like they would have if they'd had time for courting before they'd married? That would be an entirely different matter. One she couldn't get out of her mind for the rest of the afternoon.

Chapter Thirteen

The boys sat on the floor in front of the fire, reading after supper. It was almost November. Daisy didn't want them behind in their work before they had to transition back to the town's school after Christmas. They asked her earlier in the afternoon what it would be like this year. She hoped that all of Tucker's spending wasn't giving them the idea they'd celebrate the birth of Christ by exchanging costly gifts. The homemade treasures in the chest at the foot of her bed were more valuable to her than anything from the general store.

Telling the boys they'd be in earshot if needed, Tucker and Daisy went out the front door for the promised walk.

The stars were amazing against the deep, bluish-black sky. Daisy threw her head back and spun in a circle, taking in the beauty of the night. Frogs croaked near the creek, and crickets chirped their night song.

"It's such a beautiful night. I don't remember the last time I was able to enjoy this time of night." She stopped spinning and stood looking overhead with her arms wrapped around her middle. "I've been so busy trying to be a momma and papa that I haven't taken time to relax."

"Shall we?" Tucker extended his arm, and she looped her hand in its protective circle. She appreciated the warmth of his nearness in the evening chill, but she was careful not to get too close. Her mind and heart sent each other mixed signals when she was in close contact with Tucker. They walked to the end of the lane in companionable silence.

"How are you, Daisy?" Tucker ventured as they strolled back toward the cabin.

She shrugged one shoulder. "Getting better I suppose."

"I'm glad to hear it." He pulled his elbow into his side and squeezed her hand against his torso, placing his other hand over hers. The warmth of his hand gave her a slight chill. He pulled her closer. Part of her wanted to pull away. Part of her didn't.

They walked on a little way before he spoke again. "You know, I'm a pretty good listener. It seems you and I have quite a history of you telling me your woes. I remember many talks about school, and your frustrations with your sweet sisters, and even boys." He stopped walking and stared down into her face. The full moon lit her golden hair like a beacon in the darkness. "I'm here if you need me. I didn't just come to work the land and help raise the boys. I'm here for you, too."

"Thank you, Tucker. That means more than you know." She started walking again. She would be more comfortable talking if she wasn't looking into his face. "I heard what you said to the twins this morning down by the creek."

"You did?" He paused for a moment. "I guess I'm

going to have to be watchful so you don't sneak up on me in the night," he chuckled.

She joined his laughter. "I promise to warn you first." Sobering, she added, "What you said to them was precious. I think it will help them to heal." It was her turn to stop and look at him. "I had no idea your childhood was so challenging. Your mother was a strong lady." Daisy lowered her gaze to the ring on her hand. "I hope I'm able to be as strong for my sons as she was for you." She ambled forward again, effectively pulling him along with her.

"You already are. She'd have loved the way you nearly shot me when I rode up on the property! No one could call you weak." They laughed again.

"You have no idea how scared I was. I could have shot you. Again." She smirked in the darkness. "I don't know what I'd have done if it hadn't been you, or if I'd missed, or if there had been more than one person."

"Thanks for not shooting me—again," he joked. "And thank you for letting me stay," he added, his voice tender.

"I know it was the good Lord looking after us the day you rode up the lane." She applied a reassuring pressure to his arm. "I needed a friend."

Tucker cleared his throat. "Tell me how you're doing. We saw last night and this morning how the boys have been struggling. How are you healing? Do you want to tell me what happened?" Tucker's voice was comforting in the darkness as they walked.

"It was terrible." Daisy's voice wavered, but she kept talking, hoping the telling would help her. "More terrible than anything I've ever seen or imagined. Murdock had taken the boys and me to town so I could visit with Peggy Dismuke and Milly Ledford. You remember the dressmaker?" His hand still covered hers, and she was grateful for the comfort it brought.

"I remember."

"We were going to spend the day, and Murdock was going to come pick us up before supper. The boys were playing with Milly's son, while she and Peggy and I visited." Tears spilled over her lashes and trailed down her cheeks at the painful memories. "We had just sold the cotton, and Murdock thought we needed a day away from the farm. If only we hadn't gone."

"You can't torture yourself like that, Daisy. Murdock was giving you the gift of a day of leisure. He had no way of knowing what would happen."

"I know, but I can't help wishing." Daisy wiped her eyes. "When Murdock didn't come by suppertime, Reverend Dismuke and Peggy offered to bring us home." She gasped and sobbed at the same time. "It was almost dark when we pulled onto the property. Reverend Dismuke saw Murdock first. He tried to keep me away, but I had to see him, to hold him in my arms."

"What about the boys?"

"Reverend Dismuke and Peggy were able to get them into the cabin, but they knew their papa was gone. Then we realized the horses were missing. I don't know what I would have done without the Dismukes that day."

"I'm glad they were here for you and James and John." Tucker stroked her hand with his fingers.

"The next day Sheriff Collins came and tried to determine how it all happened. The thieves must have come up while Murdock was working in the barn. The sheriff thinks he surprised them when he stepped into the corral to get the horses so he could hitch up the wagon to come back to town. He didn't stand a chance against two of them. Not without a gun."

Tucker stopped walking and pulled her into his arms. Daisy buried her face in his shoulder and cried like she hadn't since the first week it happened. She had been determined to be strong for the boys. She didn't want them to hear her sobbing at night, so she'd held it all inside. Now she released the pent-up sadness and anger that threatened to drown her soul.

It was several minutes before she quieted. Finally Tucker spoke softly against the silkiness of her hair. "I'm so sorry for all you've suffered, Daisy. You and the boys." He still held her in the circle of his arms. Part of him never wanted to let her go.

Daisy pulled herself away from his chest and dabbed at the wetness of his shirt with her shawl. "Oh, I've gone and made a mess of you," she muttered.

Tucker caught her hands in his. "Don't worry about it. I'm just glad I was able to be here for you." He already missed the scent of her nestled beneath his chin.

"Thank you, Tucker." Daisy looked into his face and smiled a watery smile. "You really are a good friend. I haven't been able to talk to anyone about this since the funeral. I was trying to protect the boys. It all got bottled up inside."

"I'm here for you now. For anything you need." He released her hands, and they started to walk back toward the cabin.

Daisy spoke again. "I'm getting stronger every day. I won't lie and tell you it's easy. I've never known such pain, not since my momma passed. But this is a different pain. This was like losing my future. Murdock and I had so many plans." She walked slower with each passing word. "It's all gone now," she ended on a whisper.

"Not all of it, Daisy." He wanted to take away her pain. Tucker captured her hand again and gave it a reassuring squeeze. "Murdock lives on in his sons. You've been able to save the dreams he had for the boys. We can continue to cultivate the land. By the time the twins are grown we can have most of it growing cotton. There's plenty of room for each of them to build a house and raise a family. And there'll be enough harvest money to provide for three families and more." Tucker wanted to spark a vision in her for a future together.

"Are you sure, Tucker? Can we really do it?" Her voice was woeful and hopeful at the same time.

His thumb crossed her knuckles as he answered. "I'm sure, Daisy. Together we can make your dreams come true. I hope in time they can be our dreams."

They were back at the front steps now. He could hear James and John laughing inside.

"I enjoyed our walk—" Daisy turned to him "—and our talk." She stretched up on her tiptoes and touched her lips to his cheek, like she had as a young girl when he'd consoled her over the crisis of the moment. "Thank you."

Caught off guard by her kiss, Tucker released her hand. "I did, too." Tucker took a step backward and watched her in the moonlight. "Good night, Daisy."

"Don't you want to come in for coffee?"

"Not tonight." He wanted to go inside, but he wouldn't. He wanted to be there for her. His heart ached with the sorrow she'd shared. He'd done everything he knew to comfort her, but he needed to keep a safe distance tonight. Her tears had soaked through his shirt as if to trace the cold fissures of his heart. The release of her grief threatened to seep into his brokenness with healing strength and awaken long dead hope. No good could come from that. Only more pain for both of them.

"I stoked the fire and brought in more wood while you washed the dishes. You should be fine until morning." He stepped back from the steps, and she stood on the porch. "Bolt the door, and I'll be on my way." He lifted a hand slightly. "Good night."

"Good night." Daisy opened the door and slipped inside before turning back to him. "Sleep well."

Tucker heard the bolt slide into place and headed for the barn. Daisy shared her deepest pain with him tonight. Would there come a time when she could share her deepest joy? Was he willing to let her close enough to learn his deepest pain?

Mack whinnied at him in annoyance when he lit the lamp so he could read his Bible. His lamp burned late into the night.

Wednesday night after supper Daisy led the boys in their usual Bible study. Tucker joined them and even helped to answer some of the twins' questions about the verses they read.

That night she and Tucker sat on the porch and talked while drinking coffee. They slipped back into the comfortable friendship they'd shared for years. She would laugh and tell him her frustrations. He would listen and offer sound advice. If she caught him glancing at her hair or the curve of her neck, she pretended not to notice, though part of her was beginning to enjoy his attention. He was always a gentleman, and she grew more at ease in his presence with each passing day.

The men Tucker hired headed back to town just before

dark on Thursday. The roof was on and covered with new shingles. She was surprised by the grand size of the room, but she still couldn't imagine how the new furniture would look in the space. She wouldn't allow herself to think about living in the room alone—or with Tucker.

After the boys went to bed that evening, Daisy and Tucker sat in front of the fire talking. Daisy asked, "Will you pray with me tonight?"

"Is something wrong?" Tucker was attentive at once.

"Oh, no. You had asked once before if I wanted you to pray with me. I needed to be alone that day, but I think it would be a good idea if we make it our practice to pray together," she explained.

"Okay. Is there a particular thing you want to pray about?"

"Our family." Daisy lowered her gaze to her lap. "I want us to pray together for God to help us be the family He wants us to be." She hesitated. "I realize you've never been married before." She paused again. "And I'm very grateful for all you're doing for us." This time she stopped entirely.

"Daisy, you don't have to say anything." He put a hand on the arm of her chair. "I'm in no rush. I'm enjoying our friendship." He lowered his head to peer into her eyes. "I hope you are, too?" The last part was a question.

She smiled a little and looked up at him. "I am." She picked her hands up and dropped them back into her lap dramatically. "I'm just so confused. I don't want to be, but I am," she lamented.

"Don't be, Daisy. I'd never want you to be upset on my account."

"That's just it, Tucker. One minute I'm missing Murdock, and I'm sad for the boys that he's gone. The next minute I'm so grateful you're here I could almost kiss you." Her face reddened as she admitted her conflicting thoughts.

Tucker reached into her lap and took her hand, the one with his ring on it, and looked deeply into her eyes. "I understand. You'll always love Murdock. I would expect nothing less from you. Your loyalty is admirable. I know you were his destiny. I saw it when you were courting." Tucker touched her face with his other hand. "The twins will miss him, too. That's part of the grieving process. It has to happen naturally. Daisy, I know what you're going through."

"How can you know? I don't even know how I feel right now."

"I've seen it more than once." His eyes were earnest, as if he willed her to believe him. "Your father loves his housekeeper. He has for years. But he's never advanced the relationship because he couldn't bring himself to replace your mother."

"Do you think that's why?" Daisy had seen the strength of her father's friendship with Beverly Norton, but she never even thought of him with any woman other than her mother.

"I do. And my mother loved the owner of the hotel where she worked, but would never let him court her. Her commitment to my father went beyond his death. She was unwilling to consider another husband."

"Maybe she didn't court him because he wasn't the right man to be a father for you. Maybe he was good for her, but she was protecting you."

"It wasn't about me. She could never love anyone like that again. The same is true for your father. The same is true for you." Tucker's voice faded a little as he finished speaking.

"Oh, Tucker. Right now I'm still grieving for Murdock. I just need time."

"Time doesn't really heal all wounds, Daisy. You'll heal from the pain, but the love you shared with Murdock will forever overshadow any other relationship."

"Tucker…" She tried to interrupt, but he didn't stop.

"It's okay, Daisy. I knew that when I came."

"How can you be sure?"

"It's happened to me before."

"What?"

"When my mother passed, I went to work on a ranch. There was a girl there. Her name was Alice Fields."

Daisy searched her memory, but she couldn't recall him ever mentioning anyone named Alice. Tucker's voice was devoid of emotion as she listened to him now.

"She was the cook's daughter. Alice had her cap set for the foreman's right-hand man. They even got engaged. Then he got scared of the responsibility and called it off. She turned to me for comfort."

"What happened?" Daisy wasn't sure she wanted to know this story. She had a strange foreboding it would have a profound effect on her relationship with him.

"I was still hurting over the loss of my mother. It was nice to have someone who I thought understood my pain. We started courting. Her pa advised me to be cautious. She was young. Only sixteen. And vulnerable. Or so I thought." He stared into the fire now. Daisy sensed he was back on that ranch, seeing the events play out again in his mind's eye.

"You don't have to share this with me." Wouldn't it be better not to know? Did she want Tucker to give her some reason he could never love her? After she already married him?

He kept talking as if she hadn't spoken. "I fell hard. As hard as a young man of seventeen can. A few months later I proposed." Tucker leaned back in his chair. He didn't look at her. "She did everything but laugh in my face. Said she was courting me till the other man noticed. Said she could never love me. Her heart would always belong to her first love."

"She was young, Tucker. She didn't know any better." Daisy tried to soften the blows he endured so long ago.

"She knew what she was doing. She was young, but she knew her heart. And she was willing to do anything to satisfy it." He turned to look at her now. "That was right before the cattle auction where I met your father. He offered me a job, and I took it. I heard Alice got married the next month." He rubbed his hands down his thighs as though to relieve the tension of his soul.

"So you see, Daisy, I know you'll always love Murdock more. I came here for your friendship. If our friendship grows into a deeper marriage over time, that's well and good." He reached for her hands again as she wrung them in her lap. "If not, we'll be fine as friends."

Daisy pressed his hands with hers. He'd been such a help to her. She yearned to help him, but didn't know how.

"I came here with my eyes wide-open. I understand your conflicting emotions." He brushed his thumb across the ring on her finger. "As for wanting to kiss me—" he paused and tilted his head to one side "—you can do that anytime you want to." He smiled slightly. "But not until you're ready. Okay?"

She nodded. Her head swam with his revelation. She

never suspected his painful past all those years before. Perhaps youth had cast a hue of peace and love over her world. At the time, she assumed everyone was as happy as she was.

Tucker's voice cut into her thoughts. "I'd be honored to pray with you about our family."

Daisy was startled by his abrupt return to the reason for their conversation. She bowed her head after him and listened to him pray.

"Lord, You know the heavy hearts of this home. We're asking for Your healing touch on these broken spirits. We trust You to guide us as we grow together into the family You ordained for us to be. Help us follow Your leading at the pace You set. Don't let us get ahead of You or lag behind. We ask it all in the name of Jesus. Amen." Tucker squeezed her hands and released them.

He stood and moved to the door. Restraint tightened his voice. "Good night, Daisy."

She followed to latch the bolt. "Good night, Tucker. Thank you."

Daisy leaned against the bolted door with her face in her hands. It had truly been difficult to admit to Tucker that she was beginning to have feelings for him. Had she opened a door she couldn't close? If she'd known about Alice, she might never have told him. Grieving Murdock's death was emotional and difficult, but understandable because of the love they'd shared. Tucker had been in mourning for years for something he'd never had. How could he recover from the loss of hope?

The coming of November brought cooler nights and days that could be warm or cool. Tucker came into the house for breakfast wearing a jacket Daisy hadn't seen before. He warmed his hands by the fire before hanging it on the peg under his hat.

"A jacket? Either it's cold out this morning, or you don't plan on working up a sweat today," Daisy teased him as she set the table for breakfast.

"You're a funny girl," he jibed. "It's starting to get chillier at night. I'm feeling it a little deeper in my bones today." Tucker grabbed a mug and poured coffee.

"I didn't think about how chilly it was last night. I'm sorry." Daisy fretted at herself for not considering his comfort more. "You need to sleep in here tonight. I can make a pallet in the boys' room."

James and John came in from their chores and joined them at the table. "You're gonna sleep in our room, Momma?" James asked while climbing onto the bench beside his brother.

"No, James, your momma is going to sleep in her bed tonight—" Tucker looked pointedly at Daisy before continuing "—and every night until I have her room ready." He turned to the boys. "John, will you pray this morning?"

They joined hands, and John prayed before bowls filled with biscuits, ham and fried potatoes were passed around the table.

"This looks delicious," Tucker said as he heaped potatoes onto his plate.

"I hope it tastes as good as it looks." Daisy speared a piece of pan-fried ham and dropped it onto her plate. "So what's the plan for today, gentlemen?"

"Mr. Tucker says we're gonna finish your room real soon. He said even though it's Saturday, we're not going to town. We're gonna work on the room. He says we gotta finish so we can start clearing more land for next year." James rattled off the information without stopping.

Daisy chuckled. "Is that so? Then you boys better eat up and get busy."

"I'm hoping to get the windows and back door in today after I finish the siding. You should be in by the middle of next week." Tucker reached for a second biscuit and pierced the side of it with his fork so he could pour it full of honey.

"That soon? I better get to work on some curtains then," Daisy said. "Do you mind if I go over to Judy's while you work today? I promised her I'd come visit soon."

"Can you wait until next week? I really can't leave today, but I'd like to go with you. I think an outing would be good for the boys, and when I met Randall on Sunday he was giving me some good information. I'd like to talk to him again." Tucker took another bite of his biscuit. "Maybe you and Judy could set up a time when we see them at church tomorrow. Something for Friday evening or next Saturday."

Daisy was surprised at how quickly he'd taken to Randall, but agreed to make the arrangements the next morning.

The boys finished eating before Tucker and went to the barn to gather their tools. Tucker stood and headed for the door.

"Thanks for breakfast, Daisy. It was definitely as good as it looked." He lifted his hat from the peg.

"Tucker, about last night…" She paused, as if unsure what to say, but wanting to say something.

"We both said a lot of things last night, Daisy." He turned his hat in his fingers.

"I appreciate everything you told me," she said. "You've always been the one who listened to me. I'm glad I could be a friend to you. Thank you for sharing your heart."

"Sorry to have burdened you so. It's been years since I thought about Alice. I wanted you to know I understand the way your pain anchors you to your past." He put his hat on. "You won't be pressured by me. For anything." He opened the door and looked out across the porch. "I do appreciate your friendship." The door closed, and he was gone.

Daisy stepped to the window and watched him walk to the barn. Before their conversation last night, she'd begun to think they could eventually build a true marriage. Now she knew he really meant it when he said he came to be her friend. She was grateful for his friendship, but what about James and John? How would they learn to love their future wives? Would time rob them of the memory of how Murdock had loved her?

The dishes were washed and the sounds of hammering and sawing filled the air when Daisy made her way to the barn to collect Tucker's dirty clothes. She hadn't been in the barn since he'd come to Pine Haven. He'd immediately taken charge of the animals and the boys' chores. Sunshine lit a shaft of dust across the middle of the building as she opened one heavy door. The smell of freshly spread hay assaulted her senses as she walked by the clean, empty stalls. Tucker let the horses roam free in the corral during the day.

She smiled at the order he'd restored to the stalls and tack room. It had been reduced to complete disarray during the weeks she'd tried to handle the farm on her own.

Now feed sacks were piled neatly, and even the tools her sons used were stored in a perfect row. Glancing upward she noticed the loft had not escaped his attention, either.

Tucker's blanket was rolled and placed in a corner of the tack room where he slept. The few personal belongings he'd brought with him were stored neatly in the small space. Only his shaving brush and cup sat out where he'd left them to dry. Next to that, a towel hung on a nail under the small mirror he'd leaned against a post. A mental picture of him grooming intruded on her thoughts. His Bible was on a shelf near the only lamp in the room. The smell of his soap permeated the area. Daisy shook her head and stepped deeper into the room in search of his dirty clothes.

"Can I help you find something?" Daisy jumped in surprise as Tucker spoke just inches behind her.

She spun around, and he laughed at her guilt-ridden expression.

"You scared me!" Daisy stamped one foot.

"Did I now?" He still laughed. "I didn't expect to find you here. Is there something in particular you're looking for?" He stopped laughing and raised an eyebrow as if to taunt her. "Or did you just come out to see if I'm neat enough to move into the house next week?"

Daisy's heart was still racing as she took a backward step toward the corner of the small tack room. A room that seemed to shrink as he closed the space between them.

"Are you ready to tell me what you're looking for, Mrs. Barlow?" He was so close their breath mingled in the cool air.

She giggled. "Your dirty clothes, Mr. Barlow." Were

her nerves betraying her excitement at his nearness? "If you'd like them washed today."

Without touching her, and without taking his eyes from hers, he reached around her and snagged a dark bag made of heavy fabric from the corner. He stood up straight, and she felt drawn to him, as if by a magnetic pull.

"Here you go, ma'am. Sorry I forgot to bring them to you this morning." He lifted the bag up beside them because there was no room between them.

"Oh, my." Daisy wrinkled her small freckled nose. "These smell strong. Must be the scent you get from being cantankerous." She grabbed the bag and dashed around him, fleeing to the safety of the open spaces outside the barn.

Daisy spilled the contents of the bag onto her workbench and set about scrubbing Tucker's clothes. She doused the first shirt into the hot water and pulled it up to rake across the washboard. By the time she got to the third shirt she knew she was in trouble. The rhythm of her heart kept pace with her hands as she repeatedly dragged the wet fabric across the board.

She reached to brush her hair back from her forehead as Tucker crossed the yard to return to his work on the cabin. Never looking her way, she wondered if he were avoiding her.

If the confinement of the tack room for such a short time with him set her heart racing, how would she manage to control her growing feelings for him once he moved into the cabin? The only place she would be able to retreat would be the room he was building her. Could her mind escape him in a space he created for her? Would she want to escape him?

Thoughts of Alice, and Tucker's belief that Daisy could never love him, warned her that she might not need to keep her distance. He might avoid her.

Chapter Fourteen

A bright sun warmed the blustery day as they rode home from church on Sunday. Tucker was careful to keep some space between Daisy and himself on the wagon seat. He was finding it more and more difficult to concentrate on anything else when she was near.

During the service he'd been mesmerized by her closeness and the scent of her. He turned to admire her beauty as she folded a blanket across her lap and tucked it under her legs. The years had not been unkind to her. Her hair still shone with health, and she was as vibrant as ever. She'd maintained her tiny shape even after having twins. Many women didn't fare so well after ten years working the land.

Thinking back, he hoped he hadn't hurt Daisy by telling her about Alice. She needed to know he didn't expect to be loved. Not like she'd loved Murdock.

Yet something tugged at his cold heart. A tug of hope that maybe she wasn't like everyone else. Maybe she could love again. Was she still thinking about kissing him? What would he do if she did? Could he open up to her and put their friendship at risk?

Daisy shivered and rubbed her gloved hands together. "I saw you speaking to the sheriff after the service."

Tucker shifted his gaze to the road. "There's no new information on the thieves."

"Thank you for talking to him. I hope they've left the area."

"There's no way to know for certain. We'll keep alert and pray." Changing the subject, Tucker asked, "Did you speak to Judy Thornton?"

"Yes. We can go to their place Friday for a supper of venison stew."

John leaned over the wagon seat and tapped Tucker on the shoulder.

"Yes, John?"

"Mr. Tucker, you know what Reverend Dismuke preached today about showing your scars and helping other folks get better?"

"I did hear him say that. I think I have a pretty good understanding of what he meant. What did you think about that?" Tucker gave John time to form his answer.

"I think," John began and then hesitated. "Well, I think that's kinda what you did when you told me and James about you being a kid and your papa dying and all." John looked serious. "I think you showed us your pain, so our pain could heal. Is that what the preacher meant?"

Tucker nodded his head, but kept his eyes on the road. "That's one way to look at it, John. I sure hoped telling you and James my story would help you feel better." He flicked his wrists to urge Trojan and Beauregard to pick up the pace. "I don't want you boys to suffer like I did. That's why I came to live here and married your momma. I wanted to be a comfort to you all."

"That's what I thought." John clapped his small hand on the top of Tucker's broad shoulder. "I'm glad you did." Just as quickly as he'd interrupted, John sat down.

Tucker's heart compressed. John's words were evidence this family—his family—was growing in love. Deeply moved by John's words, he felt Daisy's gaze on him. But he couldn't look at her.

She spoke quietly so only he would hear. "Wow. Kids sure have a way of getting to your heart, don't they?"

"Yes. They do." His voice was lower than Daisy's, and those were his only words for the rest of the trip home.

Monday morning Tucker finished installing the windows. By lunch he was ready to start on the back steps.

"I'm glad the wind died down through the night. I plan to finish the steps and put in the windowsills this afternoon," Tucker told Daisy at the table.

"Really? You're working hard and fast. Don't hurt yourself." Daisy put a steaming bowl of soup in front of each of the boys.

"If it works like I hope, I'll be able to cut the door to the inside of the cabin in the morning. We can move your bed in there tomorrow evening. The new furniture won't be here, but you can have privacy." Tucker dipped his bread in the soup before taking a big bite. "This is delicious."

"Thank you." Daisy reached for the basket in the center of the table and took a slice of the still-warm bread. "I better get busy and finish the curtains today. I had no idea you'd be through so quickly." Daisy was making the curtains from fabric she'd bought on a whim. The soft green fabric had seemed to speak to her on the day she'd married Tucker. Mr. Croft had wrapped it in brown paper and tied it with string. She didn't even open it that night when they'd returned home, but had slipped it into the chest at the foot of her bed. The day Tucker told her he was building an addition she knew she'd use it for curtains.

"Can we go outside and play?" John asked. He dropped his spoon into his empty bowl.

"Yes, you may." Daisy excused both boys from the table.

"You've been working so hard, Tucker. I'm very grateful for your thoughtfulness in building this addition."

"Glad to do it. It's best for a lady to have space away from the main part of the house whenever possible. Those boys are going to be young men before we know it." He wiped the inside of his bowl with the last of his bread and popped it into his mouth.

"It will be good for you to come in out of the barn, too. It's getting awfully chilly at night now." Daisy stood and began clearing the dishes from the table. She was still uncomfortable with the thought of Tucker staying in the house—with her—but she knew it wouldn't be right for him to keep sleeping in the barn. "I've felt mighty guilty being so warm in here while you were out in the cold. It doesn't seem fair, as hard as you work every day." She had her back to him and was watching out the window as the boys chased each other.

Tucker rose and brought his bowl to the dishpan. He reached around her and placed it in the warm water. "No need," he said, resting a hand on her shoulder. "I've been fine. It's only one more night." He tapped the window to motion for the twins to join him for the afternoon's work. "Thanks for lunch." She missed the light pressure of his hand on her as soon as it was gone.

Daisy stood at the window, watching Tucker and the boys as they headed to the side of the house. Her heart had ached so much when Murdock had died and the boys lost their joy or will to play. It was refreshing to see them run and frolic again. Tucker plucked John's hat off his head and ruffled his hair before racing ahead of him. John soon caught up and retrieved his hat, laughing the whole time. James jumped to try to take Tucker's hat, only to be surprised as his hat was taken and launched high into the air with a flick of Tucker's wrist. Daisy smiled and prayed a prayer of thanks for the happiness she was seeing as the twins built a relationship with Tucker.

Lord, Tucker is so good with my sons. Help me to build the relationship I need with him. He deserves to be loved and appreciated. He's such a dear friend. I hope I can make him happy one day. She closed her eyes for a minute and dared to add, *Soon.*

Tuesday was busy. Tucker pushed Daisy's bed and chest away from the corner of the room and cut a hole in the wall. The door to her new room was mounted into place before lunch. Tucker swung it back and forth to ensure it was level before oiling the hinges.

Daisy was able to get the table clean enough for them to eat the ham left from breakfast on slices of bread. She handed out apples and glasses of milk to the hardworking men in her life.

"I may have to bake something special tomorrow as a way to thank you all for this wonderful room," she said as they crunched away on the juicy red fruit. "I'd do it today, but I'm afraid it might be full of sawdust."

"Yummy! Will you make cake or pie, Momma?" James got excited.

"Or more cookies?" John wanted to know.

"Why don't we let Mr. Tucker decide? After all, the room was his idea." Daisy looked to Tucker for his input.

"Do you still make buttermilk pie, Daisy?" He smiled at the memory of her pies.

"Oh, my goodness! I haven't made a buttermilk pie in ages." Daisy reached for a small box on the shelf above the kitchen cabinet. She opened it and started flipping through the small pieces of paper inside. Finally she stopped and pulled one from the rest. It was more worn than the others, discolored from time and previous handling. Holding it up for them to see, she said, "Here's the recipe." She perused it quickly. "I have everything I need to make this." She closed the box. "Buttermilk pie it is."

"What's buttermilk pie?" James sounded uncertain.

"Did we ever have that, Momma?" John asked.

"I don't think so, John. James, you'll just have to wait and see."

"I bet you'll like it, boys. Your momma made the best buttermilk pie in the county when she was a young girl. Even won a ribbon at the county fair when she was fifteen." Tucker smiled at Daisy. He remembered how young and beautiful she was that summer. How he'd had to outbid several young lads to win her pie. Even then, in his mind's eye he could see the lady she would become.

"You are going way back for that memory, Tucker." Recollection dawned in her eyes. "Seems like you were the high bidder that year."

"I bought your momma's pie at the auction. She deserved that ribbon. It was the best pie I ever ate." Tucker made a show of rubbing his stomach in a satisfying motion while licking his lips. "Didn't know I'd ever get the chance to eat it again after she moved away from home."

At the time he'd wished she was older so they could have shared the pie that night at the fair instead of him having to eat it alone.

"I haven't made it in years. Can't promise it will be that good now, but I'll do my best." She looked to James and said, "I'll need your help churning butter tomorrow morning, so I'll have fresh buttermilk for the pies."

"Yes, ma'am."

Tucker pushed his chair away from the table and stood. "Now you boys go take a few minutes to see your horses. I've got a couple of chores to handle. We'll start the cleanup after your momma puts away the food. Don't want to start stirring up the sawdust for a few more minutes. I'll need your help to move the furniture." James and John were out the door and halfway to the corral before Daisy could wrap the remaining bread in a towel.

"I can't believe you remembered that pie." Daisy stacked the plates from their lunch and moved them to the dishpan. "Murdock didn't care for it, so I quit making it."

Tucker drained the last of his milk from the cup and handed it to her. Their fingers brushed, and she almost dropped it.

"I have a lot of fond memories, Daisy." He gave her a smile. "I'll confess I'm looking forward to the ones we'll make together and share." He stepped to the front door.

"As long as you don't try to shoot me again." Laughing, he went out relishing the sight of her—mouth agape, cheeks pink and speechless.

The cleanup went quickly with all of them working together. The twins helped Tucker move the bed and chest into the new space. Daisy was certain he could have managed more efficiently without them, but knew he was teaching them by letting them help.

"Can you help me hang the curtains?" Daisy asked Tucker when the boys went to do their afternoon chores.

"I can. Give me a minute. I'll need to get some things from the barn to hang them with."

Daisy laid the curtains across the quilt that covered her bed. She smiled to see the soft hue of the curtains pick up the green of the vines woven among pink roses. She ran a hand across the intricate stitches in the quilt her mother had made before marrying Daisy's father.

She stood lost in thought when Tucker stepped through the doorway. Late afternoon sunlight streamed through the window on the back wall. He cleared his throat. "Do you want me to come back later?"

"No," she answered. "I was just admiring how well the curtains match Momma's quilt." She straightened the corner of the quilt and picked up one of the curtains. "Papa had Jasmine send it after Murdock died. He thought I needed something of Momma's close to me for comfort."

She sat on the side of the bed, taking care not to wrinkle the freshly ironed curtain she held. "He was right. Those first nights when I would lie down, all I could think about was Murdock. Then the quilt arrived. It reminded me of how much Papa loved Momma. But it also made me remember how he got on with his life after she passed. It was like having known her somehow strengthened him to move forward. His love for her didn't die. It propelled him into the future and helped him take care of us. Now at night when I curl up under this quilt I think about how strong and wonderful love is. I think about how even when you're separated from the ones you love, that love can motivate you to keep living."

She looked up from the quilt and met his kind gaze. "It also makes me think about how I wouldn't even exist if it hadn't been for the love my papa and momma had for each other." She gave him a watery smile. "You know all of us are named after flowers because of Momma?" At his nod she continued. "Jasmine had such exotic beauty, like Momma, with pearly skin and black hair. Her eyes dark and deep like richly brewed coffee. She was long and graceful from the beginning. I'm more like my papa. The blond hair, brown eyes and freckles are like his momma. He told me once that Momma said I was so petite, and looked so fresh and light, that I reminded her of a daisy. My baby sister, Lily, is dainty and fragile, like a delicate flower, with vibrant blue eyes."

"I can see why they chose the names they did for each of you," Tucker said.

"I'm the most ordinary of the bunch, but Papa knew I needed to be reminded of Momma's love. That's why he sent the quilt."

Tucker came to stand near her. He touched her hair and looked into her eyes. "You may be fresh and fair, but you have never been ordinary. Far from it." Daisy saw a swirling of emotion in Tucker's eyes. Could it be longing?

Heat climbed into her face at his compliment. His nearness caused her heart to race.

"Thank you, Tucker." The quiver in her voice could be interpreted as sadness or anticipation. Tucker must have thought it was sorrow because he immediately dropped his hand and reached for the curtain she held.

"Tell me how you want this to look." He moved to

the window and held the curtain up so she could choose the correct placement.

Now she was sad. Sad Tucker had misunderstood her emotions. She didn't want him to think she would move into the room he'd built for her and bring Murdock's memory along as a way to shut him out. As she'd sat on the bed and reminisced about Murdock, the memories hadn't tormented her. The love they'd shared was beginning to serve to move her forward into the happy life she knew Murdock would want for her. She wasn't even surprised to feel it happening. It had been a gradual moving from a place of constant pain, to loss and then toward hope. What she didn't know was how to communicate the changes in her heart to Tucker.

The curtains were hung and Daisy went to look out the window. She realized a couple of things immediately. Tucker had planned the layout so she wouldn't see the path to Murdock's grave from either window in this room. It had been barely visible from the window in the cabin before he'd built the addition. Now she'd have to make a special trip up the hill to see it. She was comforted by the thought of being separated from the constant reminder of her loss.

Then another thought hit her.

"Tucker!" He came back into the room when she called. She met him with an accusing stare. "You moved that outhouse so I wouldn't see it from this room." She put her hands on her hips and waited for him to reply.

"I did." He stood unflinchingly. "It took a little figuring, but I wanted it out of sight as much as possible. Just had to keep it on the side of the house away from the well."

"You worked off your anger that day by doing all kinds of manual labor, and the whole time you were planning this for me." Her toe tapped under the edge of her skirt.

"And you have a problem with that?" He smiled.

She shook her head and blew out a breath before walking across the room to stand in front of him. "Not one bit. I just can't believe how thoughtful it was. You are sweet." She reached up and put a kiss on his cheek. "Even when you're upset." Caught off guard by the day's growth of beard and the scent of his soap, Daisy drew her bottom lip in and bit it and tried to back away.

Tucker captured her waist with his hands and pulled her so close they were almost touching. The emotion she'd seen in his eyes an hour ago was still there, but there was more. "You definitely know how to upset me, Daisy Barlow. I'll give you that." He released her and turned for the door. "I'll be in the barn until supper. I've got to work on some tools."

Daisy stared at the doorway after Tucker went through it. Could he receive her love if she gave it? Or would he think it was pity? An unwelcome notion fluttered through her mind. Pity might be what Tucker felt for her.

Chapter Fifteen

Supper was eaten and tired boys went to bed early.
Tucker sat by the fire with Daisy. "So do you like the
room?" he asked before drinking from his coffee mug.

"It's perfect. I can't believe how big it is. Or how
much more room there is in this main area without the
bed and chest." She turned in her chair and looked behind her at the empty space where she'd slept for most
of the past ten years.

"Well," she asked, "now that you've finished this addition what will you do?" Daisy settled back into her
chair.

Tucker thought for a minute. "That ten acres is going
to need to be cleared. I'm thinking I'll head over in that
direction tomorrow."

"Why don't you take a day to rest? You've worked
nonstop since you got here." She had a distinct feeling
she would miss not having him nearby every day.

"I'll rest on Sunday."

"What about your things for tonight?" she asked "You
didn't bring anything in yet."

"I'm good in the barn for now." Tucker added a log to the fire.

Daisy stilled her chair and turned to him. "Tucker Barlow, you said that room would keep you from having to sleep in a cold barn. The room is ready. There is no reason for you to stay out there anymore." She tapped the toe of her shoe on the wooden floor and frowned up at him.

"I know why I built the room." He turned from the fireplace and pulled his hat from the peg on the wall. "And I know why I'm sleeping in the barn right now." He set the hat onto his head and adjusted it slightly forward. "I'll see you in the morning for breakfast." Tucker winked at her before he opened the door and left.

Daisy sat dumbfounded in her chair at his abrupt exit. She placed the fingertips of one hand over her lips and silently gasped at the possible meaning of his words. She was dragged from her thoughts by his knuckles rapping on the front door.

"The bolt, Daisy," he reminded her.

She vaulted from her chair and opened the door. He ambled backward, surprised. Daisy stepped onto the porch in front of him and looked straight into his face. The moonlight behind him kept his face in the shadows and lit the porch with a soft glow. She reached one hand up and laid it flat against his chest.

"Tucker, did you come here out of pity?"

"No, Daisy. You are not a woman to be pitied." His brows drew together. "Bolstered, perhaps. Protected, even. But never pitied." His tone was genuine. Just as she knew he was.

Daisy stretched up on her tiptoes and pressed her lips softly against his. The warmth and gentleness of his response held no pity. Her hands found their way to his shoulders as she lost herself in the sweetness of the moment.

She backed away from him and lowered her eyes, not willing to risk him seeing the hope in her gaze.

She retreated into the cabin.

"Good night, Tucker." She closed the door slowly and threw the bolt.

Without taking a breath, Daisy prayed. *Lord, I've done it now. I just took a big step down a slippery slope. I hope I'm ready.*

She opened her eyes and drew in a gulp of much-needed air.

Daisy checked the twins before picking up the lamp on the table and heading into her new room. She set the lamp on the floor beside the chest, knelt beside it and reached inside for her nightclothes. She was lowering the lid when she caught sight of the bag containing her wedding ring from Murdock.

Carefully raising the lid, she retrieved the small velvet pouch. She untied the drawstring and turned the bag upside down, allowing the gold band to slide into her palm. She closed her hand tightly around the ring and treasured the past it represented. Opening her hand again, she slid the ring back into the bag. This time she tied the drawstring into a bow and then knotted it. She tucked it deep in the corner of the chest where she kept her mementos. Tonight she knew she was truly tying up the past. Murdock had been good to her. He'd been a wonderful husband and father, but he was gone.

Daisy had no choice but to move on. She'd pledged herself to Tucker for the sake of her sons and her land. But she knew that pledge meant she must also honor

Tucker and become his true wife. Was she finally ready to move beyond her fear of loss?

She stood and stared around her at the room Tucker had built for her. And for him. Tucker had proven he was here so she and the boys could have a good future. Daisy realized that he, too, deserved the future he was working so hard to give her.

The chatter of twins covered the awkwardness Daisy felt the next morning when Tucker came in for breakfast. He brushed his arm against hers as he reached for the coffeepot. When her face flushed warm, he smiled and moved to sit at the table.

"Are you boys ready for schoolwork today?" Tucker wanted to know.

"Oh, do we have to?" they sang in unison.

Daisy and Tucker laughed. "Yes, you do," she answered while putting a platter of pancakes on the table.

James reached to spear one with his fork, but Daisy sent him a look that warned him to wait. She took her seat, and they prayed. "Now you may put food on your plate, James."

"What will you do today, Mr. Tucker?" John was pouring syrup liberally onto his plate.

"I'm going to start clearing the ten acres I told you about—at the edge of the northern field."

"Can't we help you?" James asked with his mouth full of pancakes. Daisy signaled for him to mind his manners.

"You can work with me in the afternoons if all your schoolwork and chores are done. And remember, James, you've got to help your mother make butter today so we can have buttermilk pie tonight." Tucker smiled at Daisy.

"I've done my morning chores," John asserted. "Can I go get the schoolbooks, Momma?" He was rising from his seat as he spoke.

"Sit down, son." Daisy motioned him back to his bench. "You've got to eat well if you're going to work hard. And the table will have to be cleared before the books can be brought in here." She pointed at his plate. "Finish your sausage and drink your milk."

To Tucker she added, "I wish they were this eager to do their lessons. I think they like your teaching better than mine."

"He teaches us fun stuff, Momma," James said. "Things men need to know about life and work—not book stuff. The lessons we do here and at school are boring." He crossed his arms and huffed.

"James, apologize to your mother." Tucker immediately squelched James's attitude.

James hung his head. "I'm sorry, Momma," he muttered under his breath.

"James," Tucker warned.

"I'm sorry, Momma," James repeated more sincerely. "I just want to learn how to be a man. I don't need all that other stuff."

Tucker leaned his elbows on the table. "A man has to be educated to take care of the business of life. You'll need to know how to read and understand contracts, like a deed when you buy land. And how to calculate sums to make a deal for a major purchase like seed for your crops. Farming and ranching require more than just hands-on training for working the land or the animals. You've got to be able to take care of the business side, as well."

"I hadn't thought of that," James admitted.

"Have you ever seen your momma working on the journal for the cotton?" Tucker asked.

"I remember Papa and Momma working together on the journal at night. Papa taught Momma how to do the figures and all." John's voice was restrained.

"She needs both of you to study so one day you can learn how to handle the journals. You'll need to be able to decipher the figures and keep the ledgers. There's more to life than a hard day's work. A man has to know business, too." Tucker rose and came to stand behind the boys. He put a hand on each head and leaned them backward until they were looking in his face while holding on to the bench to keep from toppling over.

"So are you boys going to work hard at your schoolwork today?" he asked.

"Yes, sir!" James was the loudest.

"I am," John agreed.

Tucker released them and said, "Good, because I'm sure I'll be needing some help after lunch." He turned to Daisy. "Thank you for breakfast. It was good."

Daisy followed Tucker onto the porch. "Here's a little something in case you get hungry before lunch." She offered him an apple and a chunk of bread wrapped in a towel.

He took the towel from her. "I want you to be careful while I'm away from the cabin. I won't rest easy until I know those thieves have been captured."

"We'll be fine. I think they must be long gone from this area. It's been over a month now." Daisy's tone wasn't as convincing as her words.

"Just be careful. For me." He touched the side of her face for a brief moment before stepping from the porch. He climbed on Mack and rode off to work.

* * *

That night, supper was eaten and so was most of an entire buttermilk pie. Tucker was glad to see Daisy had baked two.

After the boys were in bed, he asked Daisy if she'd go for a stroll with him so he could walk off some of the pie he'd eaten. They took the familiar trek to the road and back, walking slowly with Daisy's hand hooked over his arm, his other hand caressing her fingers. More than once he rubbed his thumb across the ring he'd given her at their wedding.

"Did you sleep well?" Tucker asked.

Daisy chuckled a little. "I did," she answered. "I did think about you in the barn, though." Her voice was very low. He had to lean in to hear her.

"You did?" He was almost teasing her, but not quite. He tilted his head to see her better in the moonlight.

"I did," she repeated the same words awkwardly.

Tucker laughed. "What else did you did?"

"Oh, stop." Daisy joined his laughter for a moment, but her voice was serious when she spoke again. "I've been doing a lot of thinking these last few weeks." Daisy looked down as she walked, casting her face in shadow even under the bright moonlight. He waited when she paused. "Last night when I went to get ready for bed I found the wedding ring Murdock gave me." Tucker tensed.

"Are you okay?" Once again a first love rose up to recapture a heart he thought might be warming toward him. He should have known better.

"Yes. I'm actually better than I thought I could be by now." She stopped and turned to face him. The light now covered her face, and he could see her clearly. "I know you came here for the boys to have a chance at a future on this land." She looked down and slid her small hands into his strong ones before looking back into his face. "I also know you came here to give me that chance." Tucker gave her hands a gentle squeeze. "I'm just beginning to realize how good that future can be." She smiled at him.

There was an invitation in that smile that had him leaning toward her and pulling her just a step closer.

Daisy continued, "I want you to know I put the ring away. I'm trying to move forward with my life now. I can't forget the past, but I know I can't live there, either."

"Oh, Daisy, I don't want you to forget it." Tucker brushed his hands slowly up and down her arms. "I only want to give you a good life, so you can be happy and fulfilled."

"Thank you, Tucker. I really want that, too." She took a deliberate breath. "I know we're married, but what I'm asking is that we go slowly."

"Oh." He backed away a step and paused for her to continue.

She stumbled over her next words. "We've been friends for a very long time. And I really enjoy your company." She rubbed her arms as if his touch had left her cold.

"Good. I like you, too." He was matter-of-fact. Her mixed signals were confusing him.

"I'm just asking that we go slowly to a deeper relationship as husband and wife," she finished, looking up at his face.

Tucker recognized fear when he saw it. Daisy was afraid to move forward even though she was beginning to want to. He knew her mind must be a jumble of emotions. The only way to help her through it was to be patient. In all likelihood she would never be able to love him. No matter how much she tried.

Tucker pulled her into his embrace. With great effort he offered her comfort that demanded nothing from her. He whispered into her hair, "You set the pace that is comfortable for you. Our future is worth the investment of the time it takes to get it right." He kissed the top of her head before turning toward the house and offering her his hand. "Shall we?"

Daisy slid her hand in his. He walked her back to the cabin and told her good-night.

The cool of the barn kept him awake. He stretched out on the bedroll he had cushioned with hay. His mind swirled with thoughts of Daisy. One minute he knew she was thinking of Murdock. The next minute he found himself hoping she was thinking of him.

God, I'm still walking in faith here. It's been a long time since I ran or flew like an eagle. I'm just not sure where I'm going at the moment.

Chapter Sixteen

The days passed and were spent in much the same manner. Chores and school were completed in record time by two boys wanting to clear land and work their new horses. Tucker taught them how to dig up stumps and move heavy boulders. Every night they tumbled into bed exhausted, and every morning they eagerly began again.

Some evenings Daisy and Tucker walked outside. Sometimes they sat by the fire drinking coffee or milk and talking. Their friendship was deepening.

Daisy enjoyed the casual way Tucker reached for her over the past couple of days. He might rest his hand on the small of her back while putting his mug in the dishpan, or place a hand on her shoulder when she sat at the breakfast table before he left for the fields. She drew comfort from his nearness, but wasn't threatened by it. They were growing closer. The pain of her grief still flared at odd moments, but she was adjusting to Murdock's death and accepting Tucker's presence. She no longer saw them as two people solving a problem. Now she hoped they were two people who were growing into one.

On Friday they loaded into the wagon shortly after lunch for the trip to the Thorntons' ranch. Daisy brought two loaves of fresh bread and two buttermilk pies.

Randall and Judy Thornton's three children were a little older than James and John, but as close neighbors, they all played well together.

"How late will we get to stay, Momma?" James was always happy to see his friends.

"We probably won't stay long after an early supper. We'll need to get back before it's too dark." Daisy answered.

Tucker contradicted Daisy. "Randall and I talked about riding over the ranch. There are some things I'd like to see, and he agreed to show me. We may have supper a little later than usual. You'll have plenty of time to enjoy your visit." He smiled at Daisy. "We haven't had much free time. I think it'll be okay to spend some extra time relaxing and visiting tonight."

"Oh, boy!" James was excited.

"Are you sure, Tucker? It's getting cooler earlier in the evenings now. We can come again another day, too." Daisy was unsure. To think of being out after dark left her ill at ease. Hadn't he cautioned her just this week about the need to be careful?

"I'm sure," Tucker said as he reached for her hand. "We'll be fine. It's a clear day and promises to be a clear night. I stowed a couple of blankets in the back of the wagon. The boys can wrap up in one, and you can have the other to protect you from the night air. You can even ride in the back with them if you want." He gave her a sympathetic smile and squeezed her hand. "Remember the Thorntons are moving away as soon as he sells the ranch." Tucker released her and took the reins in both hands again.

Some of the joy of anticipation Daisy was feeling ebbed away at the reminder. Judy had been a dear friend for years. Daisy would miss her.

The Thornton children raced up the lane to meet them as soon as they topped the last hill. James and John leaped over the side of the wagon and tore off across the fields, carefully avoiding anywhere the cattle had been. Daisy was amused when James tumbled and rolled as he hit the ground.

She laughed and said, "I declare that James goes so fast after everything in life, it's a wonder he doesn't get hurt. He's constantly on the go."

"John does seem to be more cautious," Tucker acknowledged.

"He is," Daisy agreed, "but James is determined not to be left out of anything. He'd rather be hurt in the attempt than bypass a possibility."

"You used to be that way when you were younger."

Daisy thought about his remark for a moment. "Sometimes the hurts of the past teach you caution."

"That can be true. I think John is wary of the consequences of moving full steam ahead." Tucker watched the boys run as he pulled the reins to lead the horses off the main road and drove toward the front gate. "I understand John because in some ways he's like me. He likes to think and plan before moving. Sadly, even at his young age, he knows there are times when things can't be like you planned. James wants to enjoy the process and is sometimes in the game before he knows all the rules."

Tucker set the brake and hopped to the ground before

turning to Daisy. He reached for her waist and lifted her to the ground. She rested her hands on his shoulders to keep her balance. He set her on her feet, and one side of his mouth lifted as he released her. His eyes invited her to respond to him.

She wasn't ready to put their growing relationship on display for their friends. "Thank you, Tucker." Daisy shyly turned away as the front door of the house opened, and Judy came onto the porch.

The Thornton house was much larger than their cabin. White siding seemingly rose to the sky and large dormers lined up across the face of the second floor. There were stables behind the house, and a bunkhouse that slept as many as twenty men. A large barn stood beside the bunkhouse. Several men were moving around the numerous outbuildings, working the busy ranch. Every time Daisy came here it reminded her of home and Papa.

"Daisy!" Judy descended the steps and drew her friend into a hug. Backing away to look at her, Judy spoke quietly. "You look good, Daisy. I can see your heart is mending." She turned and greeted Tucker. "Welcome to our home, Mr. Barlow. At least it's ours for the time being."

"Thank you, Mrs. Thornton. From what I've seen so far, it's a real nice place. You and your husband must be very proud." Tucker returned her greeting and put a hand up to acknowledge Randall Thornton as he approached from the stables.

"Good to see you again." Randall extended his hand to Tucker.

"You, too, Randall," Tucker said as they shook hands.

"Are you ready to ride?" Randall wanted to know.

"Already?" Judy spoke with mock rebuke. "Well, you

men go have your ride. Daisy and I are going to sit in the shade of the porch and catch up on lady talk."

Tucker retrieved the basket filled with pies and bread and left it on the porch with the ladies. His hand rested on Daisy's shoulder for the briefest moment as she sat in the rocker opposite her friend. "We'll be back in time for supper," he told her.

"Enjoy yourself," Daisy encouraged him. "It'll be nice for you to ride some open range after all the weeks you've been confined on the farm."

Daisy and Judy talked while the children played in the yard. Daisy saw Tucker and Randall ride off a few minutes later. Tucker's mount was a large black thoroughbred, but she preferred the way he looked on his pinto, Mack. Something about the uniqueness of his horse matched his spirit. He didn't fit into a mold, but rather, his value came from his individuality. Tucker was strong and dependable. He was more than one usually expected in a man who worked the land. His sacrificial heart and deep sense of caring, even his humor, set him apart from other men of equal strength. If only he didn't harbor such deep pain.

"So tell me about him." Judy's voice brought Daisy back from her thoughts. "I was so glad to hear you married. My relief in finding that Tucker has been a friend for so long was great. How horrible it would have been for you to lose your land and for those boys to never own what Murdock worked so hard to give them. But it would have been worse for you to marry someone you couldn't abide just to keep Murdock's dream alive." Judy watched the men disappear over a hill. "It certainly doesn't hurt that he's such a fine-looking man."

"Judy!" Daisy's cheeks turned pink at Judy's last statement.

"Now, don't you try to pretend with me, Daisy Mosley—I mean Barlow." Judy grinned widely and narrowed her eyes. "We've been friends too long for you to think I can't see how you feel about this man."

"You're embarrassing me, Judy!" Daisy started to fan her face with both hands.

Judy reached to lay a hand on Daisy's arm. "I'm sorry," she said soberly. "I'm just so happy for you."

Uncomfortable talking about Tucker, Daisy redirected the conversation. "I've been praying for your parents. I'm trusting they'll be better just by having you there to care for them,"

"Thank you. That means so much. I hope having the kids around will inspire them, too. The Bible says a merry heart doeth good like a medicine. Maybe the joy of having us home will help them heal." She lifted a hand and gestured toward the cattle grazing in the distance. "I'm going to miss this place.

"I will truly miss you, too, Daisy." Judy smiled at her friend. "I'm glad to know your future is safe. God has been good to both of us. Even if our blessings have come on the heels of great sorrow."

"You're right. I will miss you, too." Daisy's tone was reflective.

The rest of the afternoon and evening seemed to hurry by. The large dining room table hosted lively conversation as the two families shared news of their lives and future plans. The children had been saddened to learn they would soon part, but were determined to enjoy every minute of the time they had left. A roaring game of tag ensued immediately following the heavy meal. The adults watched from chairs on the front porch.

"Your place is nice," Tucker directed his opinions to Randall. "Larger than it seems on first sight. Very impressive."

"Thank you. It's been a long labor of love, but we made it." Randall smiled at Judy. "It'll be difficult to part with, because it's become such a part of who we are."

"It will be nice to be with my family again," Judy added. "We haven't been able to spend time with them since we moved here. You know how demanding a ranch can be, don't you, Tucker?"

"I do. That experience also makes me appreciate the value of what's been accomplished here," Tucker responded.

"I love this place." Daisy sighed. "It reminds me of home."

"It really is like your father's ranch," Tucker agreed. "Of course, the house is newer, as are all the buildings, but the size of the ranch and staff are comparable."

The enthusiasm in his words reminded Daisy of the sacrifice he'd made to come to Pine Haven for her and her sons. "You're a farmer now, but you still sound like a rancher."

"I will admit this place speaks to the rancher in me." Tucker looked across the fields, and she wondered if he could ever be as happy on their farm as he had been as a rancher.

The evening wore on, and, too quickly, they said their goodbyes. The children promised to see each other on Sunday, and the adults agreed to at least one more meal together before the Thornton's moved away for good.

"Very nice family," Tucker observed as he and Daisy rode home under the moonlight.

"Yes, they are," she agreed. "I'll really miss them."

James and John slept soundly under the blanket he'd had provided. An afternoon of running and playing had caught up to the small bodies. Daisy was wrapped snuggly in the other blanket. As the wind started to pick up, he turned his collar up around his ears and set his hat lower on his head.

"Do you want to share the blanket with me?" Daisy offered.

Tucker smiled his thanks, but said, "No, I'm fine."

"Well, at least sit closer, so you'll be warmer." Daisy tried unsuccessfully to scoot closer to him on the wooden seat. She was hindered by the trappings of the heavy blanket.

"Be careful, or you'll roll off the wagon like a sack of potatoes," Tucker laughed. "I'll come to you." He slid nearer to her and, holding the reins in one hand, put an arm around her shoulders, pulling her head toward his shoulder. "I'm sorry about the wind. You were right. We should have left earlier."

Daisy burrowed into the warmth of his coat collar and shook her head. "The extra time with the Thorntons was worth it."

"I'm going as quickly as we can safely make it in the dark. We'll be home in about a half hour. Just stay close, and you'll be okay."

Daisy pulled the blanket around her head and shoulders and was unaware of the kiss he dropped on the top of her head as they rode in silence. She must have gotten warm enough to relax because, when they arrived at the cabin, Tucker had to gently shake her shoulders to wake her.

"We're home," he whispered near her ear.

Daisy sat up and yawned heavily, while stretching her neck and shoulders.

"Oh, Tucker, I'm sorry. I didn't mean to fall asleep."

"No apology necessary. You've had a busy few weeks and needed to rest." He set the brake and climbed down from the wagon. "I just hope you didn't get a crick in your neck."

She chuckled and slid to the edge of the seat before standing and reaching for him. "I'm good. Just a little stiff."

Tucker reached for her waist and hoisted her to the ground. He smiled at her disheveled appearance. With both hands, he pushed loose strands of hair behind her ears before cupping her face and leaning down to brush a soft kiss across her forehead. "You need to get these boys in bed so you can rest. I'll take care of the wagon." He put a hand on each shoulder and spun her around to face the front steps. "Go ahead. I'll bring the boys in. You turn down the blankets."

When he entered the room a moment later, Daisy had lit the lamp on the table and prepared the boys' bed. Effortlessly he laid James on the far side of the bed and returned to the wagon. She removed James's coat and shoes before Tucker came back with John. He took John's shoes off while Daisy pulled his limp body from his coat. She piled an extra quilt on top of the sleeping boys and followed Tucker into the main room.

"Let me make some coffee," Daisy said, lighting the stove.

"That's sounds like a good idea." Tucker lit the fire

he'd laid before they left that afternoon. "I'll take care of the horses and be back in a few minutes."

When Tucker reentered the cabin, he found the coffee warm on the stove and Daisy sleeping in her chair by the fire. He quietly poured a mug of the rich brew and went to stand by the fire to warm himself. He stood with his back to the fireplace and wrapped his cold hands around the warm mug.

Sipping the dark liquid, he watched her sleep. Thick blond lashes cast shadows across her pale cheeks. The dotting of freckles across her nose had faded due to the cooler weather. He knew from years of loving observation that those freckles would resurface with new color at the beginning of spring and deepen in beauty through the hot summer months.

Ten years was a long time to be separated from her. In the beginning Tucker had often wondered why God put such a dire love for her in his soul and then refused to let him have her. Over time he'd realized sometimes in life people don't get what they want. It was a difficult lesson, but he'd learned it. He had accepted God's ways were best even when he couldn't understand the reasons.

Standing in the dimly lit cabin tonight, Tucker prayed a prayer of thankfulness that Daisy was his wife. Hope had faded to disappointment ten years ago. Now it threatened to spring to new life with each passing day. Every comforting touch she permitted, each smile of agreement, any time she laughed, the hope grew.

Daisy stirred in her chair, and a quiet moan escaped her. Tucker drank in the sight of her for one moment more. Then he put his mug in the dishpan, pulled the coffee off the burner and turned off the stove.

He squatted in front of her chair with a hand on each chair arm and spoke gently. "Daisy, it's time for bed." She muttered softly. "Daisy, it's time to go to bed," he said again.

"Murdock?" Daisy whimpered. "Murdock?" She sat straight up then, completely disoriented. He doubted she knew she'd spoken aloud.

"It's Tucker, Daisy." He gently shook her shoulders. "Daisy, wake up."

"Oh, Tucker." She put a hand to her forehead and rubbed her brow with her fingers. "I'm sorry. Did I fall asleep again?" She smiled at him through tired eyes.

Tucker pulled his closed lips inside his mouth to form a thin line before he spoke again. He gave her a small smile that didn't reach his eyes. "Yes, you did. It's time for you to go to bed." He took her hands and tugged her out of the chair. "Do you think you can bolt the door and make it to bed without falling asleep again?" he teased.

"I can try." She grinned sleepily.

He put on his hat and coat and stepped into the cold night. "Good night, Daisy," he whispered as he closed the door behind him. He waited to hear the bolt move and then turned toward the steps.

One minute she was reaching for him, and the next she was withdrawing to a place where she wasn't ready to let him be.

How could he move into the cabin with her, sit in the lamp-lit room every night, listen to her voice, and not lose his heart completely to her?

Even now Murdock was the man of her dreams.

Why had Tucker allowed himself to hope for more from Daisy than it was possible for her to give?

With each porch step he descended a little further away from the hope he'd been relishing moments before.

Chapter Seventeen

Saturday morning Daisy stood on the parsonage steps and waited for her friend to answer the door. Her mind struggled with Tucker's mood today. He'd been quiet on the way to town. After they left the boys to play with their friend Reilly, Tucker told her he had business to tend to and would be back in an hour.

Recent days had seen a new closeness in their friendship. What could be troubling him now? From the sidewalk in front of the general store, she'd watched him drive away. His blank expression offered no clues.

Peggy opened the door and welcomed Daisy. "Join me in the kitchen. I'm baking today." The rich aroma of cinnamon filled the air.

"It smells delicious," Daisy said as she hung her coat by the door and followed Peggy into the kitchen.

Peggy put a plate over the cake pan and, holding the pan and plate together, flipped it upside down. She pulled the pan free to reveal the golden cake.

"How about a nice cup of tea and a piece of warm cake?" Peggy went to the stove and picked up the kettle.

Daisy sat at the worn table in the middle of the room. "That sounds good."

"How are you, Daisy?" Peggy set a cup of tea in front of Daisy.

"I'm doing well." She stirred the tea with a spoon, watching the swirls as the milk she added mellowed the brew. "Better than I expected."

Peggy turned to look at Daisy, whose face glowed with a faint blush. "Are you falling in love?" The blush deepened. "You are! Oh, Daisy, how wonderful!"

"It is," Daisy agreed. "But it's not easy. I'm afraid of hurting Tucker. He's been so good to the twins and me."

"How could you hurt him, Daisy? Most men are content with a woman to cook and clean. A lot of men don't concern themselves with love. It's a bonus to Tucker for you to love him." Peggy passed a piece of cake to Daisy. A trail of cinnamon and brown sugar ran through the middle of the thick slice.

"Do you really think so? You weren't so keen for me to marry Tucker in the beginning," Daisy pointed out, lifting her fork.

"That was before David talked to me about how good Tucker would be for you."

"There is one problem," Daisy said softly.

"What?" Peggy asked. "I'm sure it's not anything that can't be fixed."

"I still dream about Murdock." Tears poured down Daisy's face. She hadn't been able to speak to anyone of her dreams. "Not so much now as before, but I don't know how I can move ahead until the dreams stop."

Peggy patted Daisy's hand where it lay on the table. "Tell me about your dreams."

Daisy sniffed and stared at the table, the cake forgotten. "They usually begin with me washing dishes and looking out the front window, or on the porch looking across the fields in front of the house. I see Murdock walking away in a haze of light. I call out to him, and he turns and looks at me, smiles and waves, and then turns back and disappears into the haze."

"What do you think about the dreams?"

"I think he's going away, and I'm trying to hold on to him." Daisy's tears stopped, but her composure was still vulnerable.

"Maybe in your heart you're trying to hold on to him," Peggy offered.

"I dreamed it again last night, but it was different." Daisy's voice quivered.

"Do you want to tell me about it?"

"It started the same. I was on the porch. Murdock was walking away. I called to him, like in every other dream. Only this time—" she sniffed again "—he didn't turn around. So I called again. He still didn't turn around. He just kept walking." Daisy was crying again now.

"How did the dream end?" Peggy asked.

"That's just it. This is why I'm concerned about hurting Tucker."

"I don't understand." A frown creased Peggy's brow.

"The dream didn't end. I had fallen asleep in the chair by the fire. After I called out to Murdock in the dream, Tucker woke me up. I was startled, but I didn't know what to say. I don't know if I cried aloud or only in my sleep."

"Have you told Tucker about the dreams?"

"No. Not even then." Daisy dried her eyes and took a deep breath. "He's been so kind. For the last several days we've been becoming more friendly, if you know what I mean."

Peggy smiled. "I think I may have an idea."

"Nothing serious, but we've been making a real effort to strengthen our friendship and build a good relationship. I don't want to endanger that now. It's too fragile." Daisy put her face in her hands and rested her elbows on the table.

"I have a feeling everything is going to be just fine." Peggy declared.

"Why do you think so?" Daisy lifted her head.

"Because you, my friend, are in love." Peggy smiled. "I think your last dream may have been the last one you'll have. In your heart you're letting go of the past. It's been a hard road, but I think you're ready to pursue your future."

"I did think that might be the case, but I feel guilty for letting go of Murdock," Daisy bemoaned.

"You won't ever let go of the essence of Murdock. Those boys will keep him in your life. But it's time to release him as your husband," Peggy assured her.

"Thank you, Peggy. You're right. I think I'm ready to release Murdock." She smiled. "And embrace Tucker."

She silently prayed. *Lord, help him to be willing, too.*

As Tucker and Daisy met back at the wagon later that afternoon, Mr. Croft came out of the general store.

"Mr. Barlow, Mrs. Barlow. How are you fine folks today?" Donald Croft walked to the edge of the wooden sidewalk and greeted them.

"Just fine, Mr. Croft. How are you?" Tucker helped Daisy into the wagon and answered for both of them.

"I'm fine myself, thanks for asking." To Daisy he

said, "I'm sorry I didn't get to speak to you earlier, Mrs. Barlow. I trust my Liza was able to get you everything you needed today."

"Yes, thank you. The twins loaded everything in the wagon earlier."

"That's good, that's good." He addressed Tucker again. "I wanted to let you know I ordered your furniture."

"Will you let me know as soon as it arrives?" Tucker climbed up to sit next to Daisy. James and John vaulted into the back of the wagon, carefully avoiding the day's purchases.

"Well, that's what I come out here to tell you." Mr. Croft nodded his head in the affirmative. "I heard back from the company. It seems they had that particular set on hand. They were set to ship it out last week. Should get here by Tuesday." He held up a hand. "Now I know that's a might earlier than we thought, so if you need me to hold it for a week or two, until you get the money, I can."

"That won't be necessary, Mr. Croft." Tucker released the brake. "I'll be able to pay you as soon as it comes. I'm not one to order something before I can pay."

"Oh, no, sir, that's not what I meant, Mr. Barlow. I was just trying to be helpful. I didn't mean to offend. I'm not the least worried about the money. Just wasn't expectin' it to come so soon."

"No offense taken." Tucker held the reins in hand.

"Oh, well. That's good." Mr. Croft stumbled over his words. "And don't you worry about a thing. As soon as it comes, I'll send a boy out there to let you know. I can even deliver it, if you want."

"Just send word. I'll pick it up." He lifted his hat in dismissal and set it back on his head.

"Thank you for your business, Mr. Barlow. Good day to you and the missus."

As they rode home, Daisy tried to think of a way to draw Tucker out of his silence. He had kept to himself all day, barely speaking a dozen or so words to her. He had even grabbed a biscuit and a slice of ham that morning and eaten it while he hitched the wagon instead of coming into the house.

She finally asked, "Did you get everything done in town that you wanted to?"

"I did." He kept his focus on the road ahead.

Daisy looked to make certain the boys wouldn't hear her next question. "Did you speak to the sheriff?" Daisy didn't want to ask, but she couldn't stand not knowing.

"Still haven't caught them," Tucker replied. "He did say he got word some more horses were stolen. Looks like they've made a big circle and have headed back this way."

"How can we know it's the same people?" Daisy was troubled at this turn of events.

"Can't. We'll have to be extra cautious and pray somebody catches them soon." He did look at her then. "I'm sorry, Daisy. I know you want this to be over." Turning back to the road he added, "No more than I do, I promise you that." He made no further attempt at conversation.

Tucker's continued withdrawal convinced her she must have cried out in her dream last night. Without wanting to, and really without being able to avoid or control the circumstances, she'd hurt him. The question in her mind was how to fix it. She turned slightly to study him as he drove the wagon.

His red hair was starting to curl in the back. It was time for a haircut. She'd ask if he wanted her to trim it after she cut the boys' hair tonight. Maybe he'd relax and talk to her then.

"Boys," Daisy called over her shoulder. "I want you to finish up your chores quickly when we get home. I need to cut your hair before supper. I don't want to be on the porch too late in the day. You might take a chill."

"Yes, ma'am." The boys were riding near the back of the wagon, away from the supplies she'd bought at the general store and the crates that contained Tucker's purchases.

"Would you like me to cut your hair, too, Tucker?"

He rubbed a hand across the back of his neck. "That'd probably be a good idea. Haven't had a cut since the day I left to come here."

Daisy's heart was warmed at the thought of him preparing so carefully before he came to offer to save her family. "Really?" She couldn't help but tease him. "And what else did you do the day you left to come here?" Daisy leaned in close to ask.

Tucker exhaled a short breath from his nostrils and smirked. "I told both my girlfriends goodbye and sold my interest in the saloon."

"Tucker!" Daisy jerked up straight in surprise. "That's terrible! What if the boys heard you say that." She was incredulous. First he wasn't talking at all, and now, in an instant, he was teasing her mercilessly.

He chuckled and smiled. "Then you'd have to explain to them why you're always asking me questions. Sometimes a man just doesn't want to talk." He gave her a smug look. "We sure don't want to tell our secrets when we're not sure how they'll be received." His voice had been so low she'd had to lean in to hear the last sentence.

"We can share secrets," Daisy offered, looking directly at him as she spoke. "If you want."

Tucker observed her open gaze and decided to test her intentions. "Okay. You go first."

"Okay," Daisy agreed, inhaling deeply. "What secret do you want me to share?" She was still turned toward him and leaning in close.

Tucker knew the boys couldn't hear so he asked, "You were calling for Murdock in your sleep last night." He kept his eyes forward. "Will you tell me how you're feeling? Are you still grieving terribly?" He cleared his throat in an attempt to cover how vulnerable he felt having to ask her this question.

"Is that what's been bothering you today?" Tucker slid her a sideways glance before turning back to the road. He'd known she would notice his cool manner but hadn't been able to relax and be himself. He couldn't erase the memory of hearing her call Murdock's name.

"I wondered if I spoke out loud." Daisy shifted away from him slightly, but remained close enough to keep the conversation private. "I had a dream about Murdock."

"Are you okay?" Tucker wanted to know how she was feeling about her late husband. It was only natural that a part of her would always love Murdock, but a part of him was beginning to hope he could help her heal and move on with her life. If she was still dreaming about her first husband, she might not be ready. He didn't want to confuse her heart by falling in love with her again. Not if she wasn't ready to receive his love. He'd lost her before. He wouldn't rush ahead now and risk having her mistake his love for pity.

"This may seem crazy to you, but that dream helped me realize something." She appeared to be having a difficult time choosing her words. Tucker held the reins tighter, as if by doing so he could hold his thoughts in check. "Peggy told me I should consider telling you about this."

"So you've discussed this with Peggy?" Tucker longed for Daisy to confide in him. He'd come all this way to be here for her, and she still wasn't comfortable enough with him to share her most sensitive thoughts.

"I saw her today. She was very helpful." Daisy turned back toward Tucker. "Peggy helped me see that my dreaming about Murdock was a way my heart was trying to hold on to him."

Tucker wrestled his heart back into the bonds of patience he'd only recently begun to loosen. "I see." Echoes of rejection hammered in his ears before she spoke another word.

"No, Tucker. It's not what you're thinking." Daisy became more animated, but quickly lowered her voice. Leaning in again, she said, "I've had the same dream many times since Murdock was killed. Each time I called him back, and he turned to me." Tucker sat in silence, watching a sad smile crease her face. "Last night in the dream he kept walking. He didn't look back." She looked at him with pleading eyes. "Can't you see? I'm finally able to let him go. He's not coming back. I know that in my head, but now my heart has realized it. I'm letting go of him."

Tucker sent her a puzzled look full of uncertainty.

Daisy elaborated. "When I called him back, and he

didn't respond, it was my heart knowing I've released him."

He wasn't sure he understood her. Why would she still be calling for Murdock, if she'd really let him go?

"All day long today, I've noticed how distant you've been," Daisy said pointedly. "Today I didn't miss Murdock." Tucker looked down at her and waited. A glimmer of hope started to flicker in his soul. The fire of hope had been extinguished the night before when Daisy spoke Murdock's name. Was it possible for her to speak the same name again and reignite the flame?

Daisy looped her arm into his as he held the reins and lifted her eyes to meet his. "Today I missed you." She grinned mischievously. "I've grown accustomed to your easy friendship and fun manner. When you didn't want to tease with me today, I felt part of me slipping downward into the sadness I'd just begun to escape."

Tucker smiled at her now. "Is that so?" He pulled his elbow into his side, pressing her hand against him. Did he dare consider that Daisy could actually let go of her past? She was stronger than any woman he'd ever known. Stronger, even, than his mother. Maybe there was a chance for them. "Well, we can't have that, can we?"

Looking ahead so he could lead the horses onto the lane to their cabin, Tucker asked, "So you want to cut my hair, do you?"

Daisy reached up timidly and threaded her fingers through the red curls at the base of his neck. "I think it would be a good idea. If you can trust me with the scissors."

He reached up and captured her hand in his. "You must promise there'll be no bloodshed." He tugged on the hand he held. She laughed and he tugged again. "Promise or it's no deal."

"I promise to make every effort to prevent bloodshed." She giggled.

"Is that the best you've got?" He put her hand on his thigh and, and without releasing it, pressed his hand on top of hers.

"You can't guarantee something like that. Accidents happen." She still laughed. "I promise to do my best."

Tucker gave her hand a squeeze and released her. He was pleased when she let her hand continue to rest on his leg as they pulled up to the cabin. His pleasure came mostly from the hope that once again they were forging toward a deeper relationship. He prayed again for God to help him.

God, thank You for continuing to heal her pain. She's releasing her past. Will there be room in her heart for me?

Chapter Eighteen

Daisy arranged everything she needed to cut hair on the table between the porch rockers. She moved a straight back chair so she'd have good light to work.

"John, are you finished with your chores?" Daisy saw her youngest twin come out of the barn.

"Yes, ma'am." He started walking to the porch.

"Let's get your hair cut first, then." John hopped onto the chair, and Daisy draped a towel around his shoulders. He sat extremely still. She carefully worked around his face and ears, after she'd cut the top and back. She was shaking the hair from the towel, and he was going to get his brother within minutes.

James wasn't as eager. "You need a haircut. Hop up on the chair, and let's get it over with," Daisy admonished.

He obeyed, but not without complaint. "Why does my hair need to be short, if Mr. Tucker can have long hair?"

Tucker came out of the barn in time to hear Daisy tell James to get in the chair. By the time James started to try to convince her he didn't need a haircut, Tucker was on the porch steps. "James, don't argue with your momma. She said you're getting a haircut. That's the end of it."

Daisy was adjusting to Tucker's active role in the boys' discipline. She knew he had every right to correct them, and the boys had accepted this new authority quicker than she had. Their initial resentment had faded when he gave them, not just correction, but also his attention.

"Yes, sir." James pushed his bottom lip out and hung his head. Daisy took full advantage of his posture to trim the back of his hair.

James was too boisterous to be silent for long. While Daisy cut his hair, he told her all about his day in town playing with Reilly. He was still jabbering away when Daisy finished and removed the towel from his neck.

"You and your brother have a few more minutes before I'll need to wash your hair. Don't go far. I'm heating the water now. Baths for both of you tonight." James opened his mouth to protest, but she silenced him by holding up one hand.

"Don't even try, James. It's Saturday. You know the routine." Little feet dragged across the dirt as he headed to the barn to relay his mother's message to John.

Daisy turned to Tucker who leaned against the porch rail and gestured for him to take his seat.

"Remember your promise." Tucker lowered himself into the chair, but kept his eyes on her face.

"I remember. But don't make me nervous." She moved to stand behind him and laid the towel across his chest, overlapping the ends at the base of his neck. "That always makes me snip an ear."

Tucker instantly put a hand over each ear. "I do hope you're kidding." He pulled his shoulders up close to his ears for added protection.

"Stop that. You're making the towel fall." Daisy

pulled his hands away from his ears. "You'll have loose hair down your collar and everywhere. Now be still."

Tucker straightened, and she repositioned the towel under his chin.

"How much do you want me to take off, sir?" Daisy asked in her best barber voice and made a show of wiping the comb on the towel across his shoulder. "You want a good cut, or do you prefer to keep a slightly scruffy look?"

Tucker smiled at her tone. "I'd like to keep my ears, please, sir. Just clean it up around the neck and sides for me. And cut this out of my eyes, too." He flicked the hair away from his forehead with one hand.

Daisy laughed. "Okay. I'll leave your ears this time, but there are no guarantees about future cuttings. I've been known to be distracted from time to time."

She reached up and ran her hands through his hair to get a feel for how long it was and where she'd need to trim. She wasn't prepared for her reaction to the simple act of touching his hair. Suddenly what was supposed to be an act of kindness for a friend became a very intimate moment. Until she caught her fingers in a knot above his ear, and he cried out in mock pain.

"Ouch!" He leaned his head to one side to lessen her hold on him and chuckled. "Are you going to cut it, or pull it out by the roots?"

Daisy jerked her hands away, glad he couldn't see her face. "You just be still. You're worse than the boys. I'd never have thought you'd be so tender-headed." She could feel the heat of his body. It warmed her, but also sent a tingle up her spine.

"I didn't know you were so strong," he countered, rubbing the spot her fingers had snagged.

Forcibly gathering her wits, she cut the red curls away from his neck, and they fell to the porch. She was able to cut the back and sides without being directly in his line of vision. Neither of them spoke. Daisy wondered if the nearness affected him as much as it did her. She stepped around the chair. His eyes closed as she combed his hair down in the front so she could cut it straight across. The sight of him with red hair almost covering his eyes as it curled on the ends made her laugh.

Tucker opened his eyes and sent her a teasing glare. "What is so funny, Mrs. Barlow?"

"Why, you are, Mr. Barlow, with your red curls hanging in your face."

In a swift motion, he reached out and encircled her waist with both arms and pulled her against his chest. With a quick breath, he blew his hair away from his face. He sat staring up at her with clear green eyes. She put her hands on his shoulders, the scissors open in one hand, bracing herself away from his face, and realized again how tall he was—the top of his head even with her shoulders.

"So you think I look funny, do you?" His brows rolled up and back down again inquiringly as he looked into her face.

"No, sir, Mr. Barlow, not at all." She giggled.

"Are you ticklish, Daisy?" he teased, and a dark gleam entered his eyes.

"Mr. Barlow, if you value your ear, you will release me at once," she warned with a grin. "I cannot be held responsible for these scissors if you try to discover the answer to that question." Tucker released her so quickly she stumbled backward, and he had to catch her.

"Easy there, ma'am." He set her upright and put his

hands up in surrender. "We don't want anyone to be hurt here today." He winked at her then, and she laughed.

Daisy took a deep steadying breath and approached him again. "You be still, or we won't ever finish." She straightened the towel and combed his hair back in front of his eyes, causing him to close them.

"I'm in no hurry," he said with a grin.

"Well, I've got water on the stove to bathe those boys. I'm sure it's boiling by now," Daisy said as she finished cutting his hair. She was surprised by how relaxed and playful Tucker had become. Her prayers for God to open his long-shuttered heart must be working.

"You really are an easily distracted barber," Tucker said as she removed the towel and shook the loose hairs into the dirt in front of the porch. "I'll definitely be back to see you again." He stood and put the chair back in line with the others on the porch. Daisy began to gather her tools.

Tucker came up behind her, leaned close to her ear, and asked quietly, "Do you think I could get a shave next time? Or would that be too dangerous for me?"

She turned and snapped the towel in his direction as he bounded from the porch laughing.

"You come back in half an hour. I'll have the water ready for you then," she called at his quickly retreating back. "I don't want to be out on the porch all night while you boys take your baths."

"Yes, ma'am. I'll be there."

Sunday morning dawned unseasonably warm. Daisy's heart was lighter than it had been in months as she sat in church with Tucker and the twins. She spent the time before service in prayer thanking God for the healing balm that Tucker was to her.

She reflected on how God had impressed that into her spirit on the way into town the day she married Tucker in this very room, and a smile crossed her face. Tucker turned in time to see it, and he reached for her hand, holding it in his for the duration of the service.

Reverend Dismuke approached the lectern. "This week I studied *2 Corinthians* 5. Verse seventeen says, 'Therefore if any man be in Christ, he is a new creature: old things are passed away; behold, all things are become new.' It's exciting to me that we can experience new beginnings all through our lives."

"Many times we come to a hard place, or the end of something familiar, and we feel at a loss. This verse gives us hope, because even when the old is gone, God has something new for us."

Daisy didn't hear much of the rest of the sermon. She prayed for Judy and Randall Thornton and the new beginning they were about to encounter. Her sons had a new beginning when Tucker came and protected their future. He also filled the much needed place of a strong man in their lives to lead them into manhood. She sat, holding Tucker's hand and thanking God for new beginnings. She chanced a glance at him and caught him looking at her. Daisy squeezed his hand in silent thanks for who he was becoming to her.

Sunday night, after a supper of beans and cornbread, the twins spent time with their horses. Tucker and Daisy sat on the front porch enjoying the mild weather.

"Randall Thornton told me today the railroad is coming through this county," Tucker informed her.

"Really? We were told last year it was going to run to the south of us."

"That was the original plan, but the water supply south of here has dried up, so the land scouts chose Pine Haven as the best alternative." Tucker used one boot to rock his chair as he looked out over the fields. "It'll sure make getting the cotton to market easier for all the local farmers. The profit margin will go up considerably. Ranching is a lot easier when there's a railroad nearby, too."

"How long did Randall think it would be before they get here?" Daisy asked.

"Next year some time, probably in the fall," Tucker responded. "He said the scouts are already purchasing property in the area. He sold them the south edge of his property so they can lay track. Said they'll probably want to run across the south of our property, too. The scouts were on their way back to meet with the owners of the railroad when he saw them last week. They won't be back in Pine Haven until January, but if they approach us, I want to consider selling them an easement. They'd be able to run the track across the land, but we'd still own it and be able to plant on either side of the tracks. I think we'd both benefit from an arrangement like that. What do you think?"

"That sounds wise," Daisy agreed. "I'll be glad to see the railroad come here."

"It has the potential to completely change the lives of this community," Tucker observed.

"Do you think so? I hoped it would come so I could take the boys to see Papa. I miss him terribly."

"It will be easier to do that, but I remember how it changed East River. Your father's ranch is able to sell cattle and transport herds much easier, but people are constantly moving in and out of town. Something about transportation unsettles folks. They start hankering to move away in search of something they don't really know. The town isn't like it was when you left, Daisy."

She looked at Tucker so intently that he stopped the motion of his chair. "Tucker, I'm glad you were willing to make the move into the unknown." She didn't blink. "I don't know what the boys and I would have done without you."

"I didn't move to the unknown, Daisy. I came to you." Tucker pushed his boot against the boarded porch and smiled before looking back at the setting sun.

After a dessert of pumpkin pie, Daisy sent the boys to bed and went to hear their prayers. Tucker stepped outside to bring in more firewood. When he unloaded the logs onto the hearth he heard their voices from the other room.

He went to door and leaned against the jamb. His arrival went unnoticed by the boys. He watched Daisy's back as she talked with them.

"If we love Mr. Tucker, does it hurt Papa?" John asked as he climbed into bed.

"No, son." Daisy squeezed his small frame into a hug. "It means your papa taught you so much about love that you have room in your heart to love more than one person." Daisy cupped John's face in her hands and looked deep into his eyes. "Your papa would be so proud of your heart. I am, too." Daisy kissed his forehead and brushed his cheek with the back of her hand. "Now you lie down and go to sleep." She pulled the quilt up close under his chin.

"Momma?" his voice was just above a whisper.

"Yes, John."

"Do you have enough room in your heart to love Papa *and* Mr. Tucker?" Tucker held his breath. He hadn't meant to overhear, but now he needed to know her answer.

"Oh, John, I already do. I love your papa. He was an amazing man, and he gave me wonderful things. Like this farm. But most of all he gave me you and your brother." She took his chin between her thumb and forefinger and gave him a playful squeeze, then smiled at James who was listening closely from the other side of the bed. "And I love Mr. Tucker. He's been my friend for many years."

"But, Momma?" John persisted. "Do you love Mr. Tucker like you loved Papa? You know, like a papa and a momma kind of love, with all the kissing and stuff? I saw you smiling at Mr. Tucker today like you used to smile at Papa. Is that what it's like?" Tucker was amazed at John's young mind. He was trying to understand things Tucker was still struggling with in his heart. Could Daisy love him?

"Yes, John, my heart can do that. It just has to heal from the pain of losing your papa. Like your heart is healing." She patted the side of his face and stood. "Now you boys need to get to sleep."

Daisy headed for the bedroom door. "Momma?" This time it was James.

"Yes, James?"

"Isn't God love? That's what Mrs. Winters said in our class at church today. She said God is love, and that He heals us, too."

"That's true, James," Daisy answered. After hearing

John's insight, great curiosity filled Tucker. What would James, who was so like his mother, say?

The boy asked in a serious tone. "Then won't it help your heart to heal if you go ahead now and love Mr. Tucker? Is that how God makes it work?"

Daisy stood and Tucker quietly backed away from the touching scene. He heard a slight tremor in her voice when she responded. "Yes, James, I think you've got that exactly right. God uses love to heal our hearts.

"I'm so glad we had this talk tonight, boys. Sleep well." She closed the door quietly and leaned her forehead against it.

"Are you okay?" Tucker asked from his chair. He'd only just taken a seat; Daisy's Bible was in his lap. He didn't realize that in his haste to move away from the boys' bedroom door, he'd opened the Bible and now held it upside down.

Hope that she would completely embrace him as her husband was growing with each passing day. Overhearing the bedtime conversation let him know the twins expected the relationship between him and Daisy to move to a deeper level.

"I'm more than okay, thank you." Daisy wiped her eyes with the bottom of her apron and went to pour coffee for them. "It just touches my heart to learn the lessons of God from my sons. That's all." She sniffed and brought a mug to Tucker.

His fingers wrapped around the mug and captured hers. He looked into her eyes and smiled. "We can both learn a lot from those two."

At breakfast on Monday, Tucker told the boys he'd need their help in the fields for the morning. Their elation at foregoing schoolbooks for a day was enormous. A jovial meal was followed by the twins heading off to prepare their horses for the day of labor. Tucker lingered in the cabin with Daisy.

"Will you make us a few sandwiches? We may not make it back before supper. There are a couple of large stumps I need to get moved today."

"Sure. Do you have any requests?" Daisy asked.

"Some more of that pumpkin pie?" His eyes lit up.

"Okay. Only if you promise me you boys won't eat and then fall asleep up there instead of working. I don't want to hinder your progress in clearing that acreage."

Tucker went to help James and John. Daisy prepared their lunch and left the basket on the table. She went to make her bed, humming her way through the morning chores. With her back to the door, she fluffed the pillows.

The sound of Tucker clearing his throat drew her attention to him standing at the threshold of the room.

"I didn't hear you come in." She joined him at the doorway. "Be careful. I don't want either of you to be hurt trying to move those stumps. We can get a couple of men to help if you want."

Tucker looked into her face and cupped the side of her delicate throat with one hand. "We'll be fine." He rubbed the pad of his thumb across her cheek. "You have a good day. And you be careful, too. We still need to be cautious." He dropped his hand and stepped toward the front door. The warmth of his touch left a coolness behind. Daisy wondered if that's what had happened to her heart. Had she wanted the touch of healing love, only to resist it and leave her heart cold?

She followed him and put a hand on his arm as he

reached for the latch. "I'll be careful." She rose up on her toes and pressed her lips to his for a brief moment.

He raised his eyebrows and looked at her with a slight smile.

"You said I could do that whenever I wanted to," she reminded him. She clasped her hands behind her back and lowered her head.

Tucker put a hand beneath her chin and lifted her face. Her brown eyes met his green ones. "I'm pleased for you to take me up on that offer." He smiled and stepped outside, then whistled to get Mack's attention. Daisy stood on the porch, watching the three of them ride around the side of the cabin toward the fields. She put a hand to her throat and caressed the place Tucker had held in his hand. With a smile she turned and went back to her chores. The tune she hummed was a happy one.

Chapter Nineteen

By midafternoon Daisy had the wash on the line and was going inside to put bread in the oven. She stepped onto the porch and heard the sound of horses galloping over the top of the hill on the lane that led to the road. She knew Tucker and the twins were working in the opposite direction. Dropping her basket, she ran into the house and bolted the door. She snatched the shotgun from the rack over the fireplace and went to bolt the back door. She was at the front window within seconds with the gun ready to fire.

Two riders came steadily up the lane. She pushed the barrel of the shotgun through the front window. Her elbows rested on the cabinet by the dishpan. Her aim was hindered by the speed of the riders. She narrowed her sights on the man in front. He was of average height and wore a striped poncho. A felt sombrero rested on his head. The second rider was in her periphery. A fleeting glance told her he was probably a Texan.

Afraid there would be no time for Tucker to come to her aid, Daisy fired a shot high in the air. Dust flew into a cloud at the hooves of both horses as the riders pulled hard on the reins and jumped to the ground on the opposite side of their mounts. Each drew a gun and aimed for her window.

"Don't shoot!" the first rider called loudly.

"Drop your guns," Daisy ordered the strangers, "and step out where I can see you."

"How do we know you will not shoot at us again?" Concern laced the heavy Mexican accent of the lead rider. Neither man moved a muscle.

"Who are you? What's your business here?" Daisy was no-nonsense in her questioning.

"My name is Paco Morales," the first rider spoke again.

"This is my amigo Lawrence Walker. We are here to see Señor Tucker Barlow." He adjusted his sombrero in an attempt to see her better. "We are at the right cabin, no?"

"What's your business?" Daisy hoped that was Tucker's horse she heard riding in the distance.

"We are here to join with him in the business of ranching," Paco answered. "Are you Señora Barlow? The daughter of Señor Warren? We come from his ranch in East River."

Daisy heard Tucker's voice from the side of the house. "Paco! Lawrence! What's going on here?" He came into Daisy's line of sight. "Daisy!" he admonished. "Did you try to shoot my friends?"

"It's so good to see you Señor Tucker. Your wife is a strong woman. If you did not come we would be in danger still, no?" Paco shook hands with Tucker and clapped him on the back.

Daisy lowered her gun, and lowered herself, trembling, onto a chair by the table. She could hear the men talking and knew she was not in danger. But she'd been frightened too many times lately to take chances.

Through the open window she heard Tucker welcome his other friend. "Lawrence, it's good to see you. Let me see if I can talk Daisy out of shooting anyone and maybe get us something to eat."

She caught sight of Tucker as he turned and whistled twice—long and even. Then he cupped his hands around his mouth and shouted, "Boys, take care of all these horses for me, and come inside for supper." He must have had the twins hang back at a safe distance when he'd come to investigate the gunfire.

Tucker opened the front door and spoke to Paco and Lawrence over his shoulder. "Give me a minute, please." He entered the cabin and closed the door. Daisy dropped her face into her hands and wept like a frightened child.

She crumpled into Tucker's arms when he went down on one knee beside her chair. She nestled into his shoulder, and he cradled her head with one hand. "It's okay, Daisy. You're safe."

She spoke against his shirt, scolding him in garbled words she knew he wouldn't understand. He pushed her away from his chest. She tried in vain to resist his effort to pull her hands away from her face. She hated being afraid. It went against her nature. Yet she couldn't mask the shadows of terror in her gaze.

"Oh, Daisy, I'm so sorry." He pulled her back into his arms. "You must have been frightened to see more strangers ride up here, but you're safe now."

She jerked away from him. "Why didn't you tell me someone was coming to see you?" She flung the words at him. "I could have killed them!"

"They weren't supposed to be here until next week.

I don't know why they're early." He rubbed his hands up and down her arms in an attempt to calm her. "That was a great idea to fire off a shot so I'd come back to the cabin. No one can accuse you of cowardice." He leaned in to smile at her still-angry face. "If anything, we might need to post a sign at the road warning people about what a good protector you are."

Daisy made a kind of snorting sound, somewhere between crying and laughing. Tucker laughed with her. She stood and wiped her cheeks dry with both hands. "Maybe if men didn't just show up and startle women they wouldn't be in such danger." She knew the argument was feeble, but felt compelled to defend her actions.

"Wait a minute." Daisy's face clouded with the beginnings of a fierce rage.

"What is it?" Tucker's tone was clipped, reflecting his surprise at the sudden change in her expression.

"What business of ranching are these two men here to join in with you?" She leveled an accusing stare at him and crossed her arms.

The front door burst open, and James and John exploded into the room. "Are you okay, Momma?" The twins wrapped themselves around Daisy's middle.

"I'm fine." She put a hand on each boy's back to comfort them. "I fired the shot so Mr. Tucker would come quickly."

"He ran when he heard that shot, Momma!" James was full of drama. "He jumped on Mack and was riding away before we could move! He told us to follow him, but not come over the last hill unless he gave the signal." James took a deep breath for air. "Then he told us to go to Mr. Thornton's if we didn't hear the signal five minutes after he rode over the hill. It was exciting, Momma!"

"I'm glad you're okay." John didn't let go of her waist. He'd wrapped both arms around her and clung to her still.

"I'm fine now. The men who rode up are friends of Mr. Tucker."

James had gained a second wind. "We know. We saw 'em outside. They're holding our horses for us while we check on you. That's what men do. They help each other with their horses."

"You young men better go outside and help those men with their horses, then." Tucker stood by the door that had swung wide when they entered. "I'm proud of both of you for following my instructions so well. If there had been a true emergency, everything you did would have been a great help. Those will be our signals from now on. Gunshots when we need help and two long whistles when everything is safe. And don't forget to ride to the Thornton ranch if we ever need more help."

"Yes, sir." The twins marched outside like real men. They flourished under Tucker's instructions.

"Is it safe to come in?" Paco peered into the front door as the boys went down the steps. Lawrence came onto the porch after handing the boys the reins to all the horses.

Tucker looked over his shoulder. Daisy sent him a glare. She was not anywhere near being satisfied with their conversation. He gave a wink before mouthing, "Later," to her. Swinging the door open again, Tucker welcomed his friends to the cabin.

"Come in. I'd like you to meet my wife."

Paco and Lawrence removed their hats as they came through the door.

"I'm so sorry we frightened you, *Señora*. We did not

know you did not know we were coming today." Paco took the lead in the conversation again. He dipped his head in her direction.

"I'm Lawrence Walker. It's nice to meet you, Mrs. Barlow." The younger man nodded a greeting. "Please forgive us for catching you off guard."

Daisy listened to all of this and did her best to steady her breathing. "If you'll excuse me for a moment, gentlemen?" She turned on her heel and went into her room, quietly closing the door behind her.

Paco looked at Lawrence and then at Tucker. "You are in trouble, amigo." Paco chuckled. "I think this sister is more like Jasmine than Lily. This one is like a fireball. You better be careful with her." He laughed.

"I'll say," Lawrence added with a chuckle, "or she'll shoot you one day."

"She already has," Tucker admitted, and they all erupted in laughter.

Daisy opened the door to her room and came out. "Is something funny?" She moved to the table and uncovered the dough she had left to rise earlier. "I'd hate to miss a good laugh." She narrowed her eyes on Tucker. "Unless, of course, it's at my expense."

"Now, Daisy." Tucker came to stand beside her and put an arm around her shoulders. "You've got to admit there's some humor in the fact that you tend to want to shoot any man who comes in your vicinity."

She slipped from Tucker's embrace and retrieved a baking pan. Returning to the table she began to grease and flour the pan. Daisy stopped in midmotion and looked up at the men standing around the table in the small cabin. Lifting a floury finger she pointed at each one of them in turn.

"Consider yourselves warned." She jerked a thumb in Tucker's direction. "You can ask him if I know how to hit a target." They all laughed, and she joined them.

"Now if you'll all go make yourselves busy somewhere else, I've got to add some more vegetables to the soup if we're all going to eat supper tonight." She picked up the bread and dropped it into the pan.

The three men headed out the door. Tucker was the last to leave and turned to her. "I'll explain everything as soon as we get a moment alone."

"Yes, you will." Daisy pointed at the door. "Now go so I can get my thoughts together, or I'll grab that gun again."

"Amen." All the men echoed Daisy as she finished giving thanks for their supper. She passed the bread around the table and asked Paco, "You said you came from my father's ranch?"

Paco took a slice of the warm bread and passed the basket to Lawrence. Reaching for the butter, he answered her question with one of his own. "Did Señor Tucker not tell you I work for your papa?" Paco shook his head in Tucker's direction. "It is not good to keep secrets from your *señora*." To Daisy he said, "I work for your papa for many years now. Seven years. I meet him on a cattle drive before the railroad come to East River. He is a good man, your papa." He smiled at Daisy.

"I didn't know. I'm sorry. What did you do for Papa?" she asked. Paco's friendly manner made it impossible to be upset with him. Daisy was happy to meet someone who could bring her news of her family.

"I was a ranch hand for many years." Paco wiped the

corners of his mouth. "This soup is very good, *señora*. It is much like your sister Lily makes."

"How is Lily?" Daisy's face softened as she thought of her family. Lily had been only twelve years old when Daisy moved away.

"She is well. She is a lovely woman." Paco praised her sister.

It was hard for Daisy to imagine Lily as a young woman. She still remembered the braids of blond hair and the dainty features of a schoolgirl. It was bittersweet to hear her described so kindly.

"It's so nice to have you here, Paco. I look forward to hearing news of my family."

Tucker spoke up then. "Lawrence worked for your father, too. He's only been there a couple of years, but Paco saw a lot of potential in him and decided to bring him along."

"I had no idea you both worked for my father. I'm sorry for the reception I gave you this afternoon." Daisy lowered her stare to her bowl and stirred her soup absent-mindedly. "I've had some difficult experiences lately. It's left me a bit jumpy at times.

Lawrence said, "We understand, ma'am. Mr. Tucker explained about you being nervous of strangers. No harm done." The young man couldn't be more than eighteen. His dark hair was too long, but it was clean. His clothes were neat, but his manner was clumsy, like a colt.

The rest of the meal passed quickly. Paco and Lawrence gave Daisy news of her sisters and father. Before leaving to take a walk after supper, Paco gave her letters from her family. He and Lawrence said they'd been in the saddle for several days and wanted to walk for a bit.

Daisy went to take the wash off the line, and the

boys headed to the corral to see Paco's and Lawrence's horses again.

When she came back into the cabin with the basket of wash Tucker was alone in the front room.

Tucker began to explain the arrival of Paco and Lawrence. "I'm sorry I didn't know they were coming today. I would have warned you."

She wasn't interested in that detail. "Why are they here, Tucker? The when has already been established. What I want to know is what they meant when they said they were here to work a ranch with you." She set the basket on the bench and walked to the other side of the room so the table was between them. She put her hands on her hips and tapped the toe of her shoe, willing herself to remain calm.

"I'll get to that part. I just want you to know I intended to tell you all about this before they arrived."

"I wish you'd just tell me what's going on." Daisy's patience was almost completely gone. She never liked being in the dark in a situation. Today she felt completely blindsided by something Paco and Lawrence thought she was aware of. She placed her hands, palms down, on the table and took a slow breath, waiting for his answer.

"They are here to work a ranch," Tucker began again.

"We don't have a ranch. We have a farm," Daisy contradicted him. "And we don't need full-time help. We hire migrant workers during the planting and harvest. We do the rest of the work ourselves."

"I'm well aware this is not a ranch." Tucker began to show his impatience to her. "If you'll let me finish I can explain."

"I'm listening." Daisy's tone was curt.

"Please let me finish."

"Please do." Her toe tapped louder.

"Daisy, stop interrupting me for one minute, and I'll explain." She opened her lips again, but he held up a hand to silence her. "I bought the Thornton ranch. They're here to work it for me."

The blood left Daisy's face. She lost all her breath and opened her mouth only to close it again. She knotted her fists and released them at her sides. Again she made fists until she felt her nails digging into her palms. Just when she started to trust him, he overwhelmed her with a major surprise.

"You did what?" The quiet restraint of her voice was extremely menacing.

"You heard me." The frustration in Tucker's tone was electric. "I didn't want to tell you like this, but you won't listen."

All the progress they'd made in recent days disappeared. He still kept things from her. Important things. It was especially painful after her efforts to be so open with him about her grief and feelings for Murdock—and even about her feelings for him.

"I won't listen?" Daisy turned her back to him, only to immediately spin around again. Her voice rose a notch. "I won't listen? I don't seem to remember you trying to tell me anything lately." She pushed both palms against her forehead and thought.

"Oh, I do remember something." She lowered her hands and leveled her gaze at him, speaking slowly and calmly. "On Saturday you said you wanted us to share secrets." Her eyes grew wider with each sentence. "You wanted me to tell you my secrets. And I did." She stopped and nodded her head as the memory of their ride home from town flitted through her eyes. "But I don't remember you sharing any secrets with me."

"Daisy, be reasonable," Tucker implored. "We've been busy. There's more to this than I can explain in just a couple of minutes."

She launched into speech. "We can't afford a ranch! We make a decent living, but you've spent money like there's no tomorrow ever since you got here. How are we supposed to keep up? We don't have money for a mortgage payment." She listed every reason as soon as she thought of it. "How could you do this without talking to me?"

"There is no mortgage. I bought it." Tucker's tone was clipped and controlled. "The ranch will pay for itself. And I'm not accustomed to having to ask permission before I make a business decision." The intensity of his irritation caught fire. She saw it in his face as he retreated to a place she couldn't go. A solitary haven behind protective walls. She knew she was driving him there, but couldn't stop herself.

"How can you be sure it will pay for itself? A ranch is a huge undertaking." Daisy refused to listen to him. Her anger at not being included in the decision process thwarted all rational thought.

"It may come as a surprise to you, Daisy, but I've actually got some experience in this area." Tucker snatched his hat from the peg by the door. "Now if you'll excuse me, we have guests. I'm going to spend some time with them tonight."

The quiet shutting of the door sent a more powerful message than if he'd slammed it shut.

Chapter Twenty

James and John came in full of tales Paco had told them about life on a ranch. The stories were animated and colorful. It took Daisy almost an hour to get them in bed.

She stepped onto the porch for firewood and was surprised to see Tucker sitting there with Paco and Lawrence. All three men had a cup of coffee and were talking quietly. Tucker stood when she came outside.

"I just need some wood." Daisy spoke quietly and headed toward the woodpile. Tucker stopped her with a hand on her wrist.

"I'll bring it when I come in. You go on to bed. I'll be in after a while." Tucker held the door for her to go inside.

"Well, I'll just say good-night." Daisy included them all in her statement. Then she had no choice but to enter the cabin and prepare for bed. Paco and Lawrence wished her a good evening as the door closed. Did Tucker just announce he'd be sleeping in the house without discussing it with her first? He was definitely trying her patience.

Daisy hadn't cried herself to sleep in weeks. Tonight she wept quietly and prayed until exhaustion took her into a deep sleep.

Tucker was at the stove the next morning when he heard Daisy open the bedroom door.

"Good morning," he ventured.

Daisy just looked at him blankly, but didn't speak.

"Were you able to rest?" he asked.

"Yes." She pulled the cast iron skillet to the front burner and started slicing bread.

Tucker came to stand behind her and put his hands on her shoulders. Daisy tensed and stood completely still. He leaned in close to her ear and whispered, "I'm sorry."

Daisy let out a deep sigh and slumped her shoulders. "Me, too," she admitted. "I was rude and impatient."

He knew they had to get past this argument to heal their relationship, but he wasn't sure how to do that. Her next words surprised him.

"Please forgive me."

Tucker turned her to face him and looked into her eyes. "If you'll forgive me."

Daisy reached up a hand and covered his where it lay on her shoulder. Meeting his gaze, she said, "I do. I don't know where we go from here, but I know we have to be forgiving." She asked, "How did you sleep? Oh, wait. Where did you sleep?"

"In the chair by the fire." He nodded to his usual place in the cabin. "It's the warmest I've been in weeks," he added wryly.

"Oh, Tucker, that couldn't have been comfortable. You should have let me know when you came in. I'd have given you the bed."

"And risk Paco and Lawrence discovering we don't share a room?" He shook his head. "I don't think so. Our personal business will stay personal. I won't give anyone cause to discuss our relationship." He cupped the side of her face with his hand. "I'm sorry I didn't get a chance to ask about sleeping in the house before you came onto the porch last night. I was trying to protect you. I didn't want to risk them hearing you throw the bolt and make judgments about us. I moved my things into the far corner of your room while you were taking the wash off the line yesterday. I hope nothing was in your way."

"I didn't notice anything. I went straight to bed without turning on the lamp. Thank you for considering that Paco and Lawrence might have questions," Daisy said. "I didn't even think about it."

"As for the Thornton ranch, I should have told you about all of this earlier. I really had no idea they'd get here so soon."

Daisy huffed another small sigh. "You don't see the real problem here, do you, Tucker?"

"I didn't tell you about the ranch before Paco and Lawrence got here. That's why you're upset, right?"

"No, Tucker." Daisy shook her head. "I'm not upset because you didn't tell me about Paco and Lawrence coming to work the ranch. I'm upset you *bought* the ranch without discussing it with me first. I thought we agreed we'd discuss all business before we made the transactions."

"Daisy," Tucker began, only to be interrupted as James and John entered the room.

"Good morning, Momma. Morning, Mr. Tucker." James spoke immediately. "Can we get started on our chores early? I wanna go with you and Mr. Paco and Mr. Lawrence when you go to the Thornton ranch today.

Mr. Paco says there's a lot to learn about ranching, and I wanna get started right away." Sometimes he didn't know how the boy talked so fast, while never seeming to stop for air.

"Not today, James. Your momma let you off yesterday. Today you'll be studying before you go working at anything other than your chores."

"Yes, sir." James hung his head and went to the front door.

John was at the door before James and stopped as he reached to unlatch the bolt. He put his hand on the latch and turned to look at his mother. "Momma?"

Daisy turned to face John. "What is it, son?" There was a hint of uncertainty in his voice.

"The bolt is latched."

"I know son. We latch it every night. It's for our protection," Daisy confirmed his observation.

"But Mr. Tucker is inside." John eyes were searching her face.

"And…" Daisy prompted.

"And if Mr. Tucker is inside, and the bolt is latched, then does that mean Mr. Tucker stayed inside?" There was a childish innocence in his voice.

"Yes, Mr. Tucker stayed in the cabin last night." Daisy blushed. "Now go do your chores. Both of you." She turned back to the stove, but John didn't move.

"Momma?"

"Yes, John." Daisy kept slicing bread.

"Does that mean Mr. Tucker will stay inside every night now?"

Tucker looked at Daisy. He shrugged to indicate he didn't know the best way to answer the child. Her eyes clouded with indecision and then cleared. She turned her gaze back to the stove.

"Yes, John, Mr. Tucker will be staying in the cabin from now on. It's too cold for him to stay in the barn anymore. He built that fancy room on, so yes, Mr. Tucker will be staying inside. Now go do your chores, or you'll be late for breakfast."

The front door opened, and both boys tromped down the steps and ran toward the outhouse before beginning their chores.

Tucker stared at Daisy's back, startled by her announcement.

"I can feel you looking at me, Tucker Barlow."

"I'm trying to figure you out, Daisy Barlow. I don't know from one minute to the next what is going to come out of that pretty little mouth of yours." He couldn't keep the happiness out of his voice.

"It's important to me that we don't send mixed signals to the twins. They've been through enough. It wouldn't be good for them to see you inside one night and outside the next." She dropped the first pieces of bread in the pan to fry, and it sizzled as the smell of the melting butter filled the room.

"So you're saying you only told them I'd be staying inside to keep them from getting mixed signals?" Tucker asked carefully.

"That's part of it." She still refused to look at him.

He came to stand close behind her again. "I think it will be important, Daisy Marie, for you and I to get all our signals straight. And the sooner, the better."

The tingle on Daisy's neck remained long after she heard Tucker close the front door as he, too, went to handle his morning chores.

Lord, this man is so frustrating I don't know what

to do. One minute I want to leap into his arms, and the next he's gone and done something I completely disagree with. What am I going to do?

If Daisy were truly honest with herself, she'd admit that she didn't know if she should disagree with him about buying the Thornton ranch. It wasn't so much about the ranch to her, as it was about him not including her in the decision. And it was about the ranch because she didn't know how they would pay for it. How was it possible there was no mortgage? Then she remembered that he'd said her mouth was pretty. And she smiled. Daisy really needed to talk to Tucker, but not with so many people around.

As if to confirm her frustrations, the front door opened and both boys came in followed by Paco and Lawrence. Tucker came a few minutes later carrying a folder much like the one Mr. Little had used at the land office. She could only guess what it contained.

After breakfast the men rode off to the Thornton ranch. Daisy got James and John started on their reading and went onto the porch to read her letters from home. Her sister Jasmine wrote briefly in a strong, bold hand, talking of the ranch and her love of the land. Lily wrote of cooking and gardening. Graceful strokes of ink curved across the pages of her letter, which ended with an update on their father's health.

Daisy smiled at the differences in the two letters and tucked them into her pocket. Then she opened her papa's letter, carefully breaking the seal on the back of the envelope. She prayed there would be wisdom for her on the pages inside.

Dearest Daisy,

I trust this letter finds you in a better state than my previous note. I received your news that you have followed my advice and married Tucker. I pray for both of you every day. Knowing you as I do, I'm sure there have been many moments of frustration as the two of you adjust to one another. Even dear friends must adapt.

To marry when you are a woman is different than when a girl marries. A girl can survive on dreams, and hopes, and, dare I say, love. A woman knows she must deal with the realities of life. It is somewhat sad to me that this is true. For a woman should not be robbed of her dreams simply because she has grown beyond the age of innocence. I pray you will have new dreams, and that those dreams will come true.

Tucker contacted me by telegraph and letter about his plan to buy the neighboring ranch. He sought my advice and counsel, but not direction. I agree with his assessment of this property. He has my full endorsement in this decision. I have the utmost confidence Tucker's strong business sense will benefit your family for years to come.

If I had to guess, I'd say you have not yet come into agreement with Tucker on this business of ranching. Your sister Jasmine was always the one who had a love for ranching. Your love for farming drove you to the life you now have. Sometimes it's as though life, or God, throws things into our path solely for the sake of causing us to grow and stretch beyond who we currently are.

Please give my love to James and John. I hope

above hope that the coming railroad will afford us
the opportunity to see one another.

Be good to Tucker. I continue to pray for God
to heal your heart and bless your new marriage.
All my love,
Papa

Once again, a letter from Papa brought hope to Daisy's
troubled mind. She sat wondering if it was wrong for her
to want to be included in the business decisions Tucker
made for their family. She knew many women had no
idea of their husband's financial holdings, but Murdock
had always included her. She'd worked alongside him
for everything they had. He'd taught her how to handle money and run the farm. She had no desire to sway
anything in a negative direction, but she did want her
abilities to be put to good use. She hoped Tucker would
come to value the skills she brought into their marriage.

Daisy sat on the porch meditating and praying for
almost an hour. She couldn't say she'd reached a reso-
lution in her soul, but she was comforted and helped by
her father's letter. Praying helped her most of all. Daisy
knew Tucker was a good man. And she knew he had her
family's best interest at heart. She just didn't want there
to be any secrets between them. She had opened up to
Tucker; she needed him to be open with her.

When Daisy stood to go inside and help the boys finish their lessons, a rider came up the lane. Thankfully
she recognized him immediately because of the dis-
tinctiveness of his white mount. She really wasn't up to
shooting anyone today.

Jay Winters, the postmaster's son, rode up to the porch.

"Hello, Jay. What brings you out our way?" Daisy greeted the lad.

"Mr. Croft wanted me to ride out here straightaway and let Mr. Barlow know the furniture he ordered has arrived. It came this morning." Jay pulled the reins to keep his horse from getting too close to Daisy. She reached out from the porch and rubbed the mare between her dark eyes.

"Mr. Barlow is out right now, but I'll let him know as soon as he gets back. Please tell Mr. Croft thank you for the message." Daisy patted the mare a final time.

"Do you think Mr. Barlow wants it delivered? Mr. Croft told me to be sure and ask."

"No, I don't think so. If he does, we'll send word." She took a step back on the porch. "Thanks for coming, Jay."

"You're welcome, Mrs. Barlow. Have a good day." With a tip of his hat, Jay sent his horse up the lane at a fast trot.

Daisy watched Jay leave and turned to enter the cabin. Out of the corner of her eye, she caught just a glimpse of something red in the trees near the end of the lane. She turned to see what it could be, and it was gone. "Hmm. Must have been a bird," she mumbled to herself and went into the cabin.

"Are you boys about ready for your spelling words?" Daisy moved to the table where James and John studied.

"I am." James was eager to finish. She knew he'd rather be with his horse or with Tucker and their visitors over at the Thornton ranch.

"What about you, John? Are you ready?" Daisy picked up the spelling primer.

"Who's that, Momma?" John pointed out the window over the kitchen cabinet.

Daisy moved toward the window saying, "It's probably just Jay Winters coming ba…" Her feet tangled in her skirt, and she fell to the floor with a thud. Pain shot through her right ankle when she stood. James and John jumped up to help her.

"Are you hurt, Momma?" James asked as he reached for a chair to help her sit.

"I'll be fine." She refused the chair. "How silly to stumble over my own feet." She tried to laugh. Daisy shuffled over to lean on the kitchen cabinet so she could see out the window. Panic filled her mind as a flash of red became visible close to the spot she'd noticed before coming inside.

"Boys! Go out the back door as quickly and quietly as you can. Run straight for the tree line behind the smokehouse. Stay as low as you can so you won't be noticed. Then run for all your worth to the Thornton ranch and get Mr. Tucker." Daisy limped to the front door and slid the bolt. Grabbing the shotgun from over the fireplace she stumbled back to the front window and watched two men on horseback weave their way around the front edge of the property toward the barn. They kept just beyond the line of the trees in an effort to move unnoticed.

"We can't leave you, Momma!" John was trying not to cry. "I can stay here and help you shoot. Who are those men?" His bottom lip was quivering now.

"John, you have to be a big man for Momma today. I'm not planning to shoot anyone. I need you and James to go get Mr. Tucker. I can't run, or I'd go with you." The twins had come close to her when they'd heard the panic in her voice. She looked directly at them. "It's important to stay calm and to not be seen. Can you do it?"

"We can." James spoke for both of them. "And Mr.

Tucker will come and protect you, Momma. That's why he came to live here." He hugged her and headed for the back door. "Come on, John. Let's go!"

John hugged Daisy for a brief instant. "Can I take the pistol and fire it so Mr. Tucker will come? That's the signal."

"John, that's a great idea. Get a chair and get it off the mantel." John pulled a chair to the fireplace. "Be careful," she warned.

"I will, Momma. Mr. Tucker showed me how." John seemed older than his eight years as he took the loaded pistol in his hand and climbed off the chair.

"Don't fire it until you top the last hill past the cotton field. You'll be close enough to Mr. Tucker then that he'll be sure to hear the shot. I don't want whoever is out there coming after you." Daisy looked at her boys at the back door. "Go now. And be careful. I love you."

"Come bolt the door, Momma," James insisted. "Mr. Tucker wouldn't want us to leave you without the door being bolted.

"Okay. Be quick." She shooed them out the door and slid the bolt. She hobbled back to her vantage point at the front window, looking for any sign that the intruders noticed her sons. She must have forgotten to breathe because she had to gasp for air when the two men came into full view near the end of the lane. The one leading the way wore a red bandana tucked into the front of his shirt. That was the red she'd mistaken for a bird earlier. They must have waited in the woods for Jay Winters to ride away before making their move toward the barn. The second man wore a dingy brown hat and spit over his shoulder as he surveyed the horizon.

Daisy didn't recognize either man, but she did recognize Murdock's horse. The one with the red bandana rode Murdock's bay, Dutch. The three white socks and star on his face ensured that Daisy would recognize the horse anywhere. His beauty was probably why the murderous thief had kept him.

Daisy watched from the shadows as the men crossed the lane. They showed no signs of interest in the cabin as they neared the barn. She would lose sight of them if they went into the corral. Which is exactly what they did. She moved to the boys' room hoping to keep them in sight through their window. Just as she lowered herself onto the edge of the bed and rested the barrel of the shotgun on the windowsill, she heard a shot in the distance.

The two riders had entered the corral and were trying to lasso Trojan and Beauregard. The sound of the shot caused all the horses to start. The man in the brown hat sat straight in his saddle, looking in the direction Daisy had sent the boys. Then a second shot rang out.

The thieves appeared to argue. Their heated exchange lasted for a couple of minutes, and they went back to work trying to lasso the horses. Trojan and Beauregard must have sensed danger because they refused to cooperate. After several attempts, the man on Murdock's horse snared Trojan around the neck. Beauregard was only able to hold out for a short time before he, too, was captured.

When the men led the horses through the barn, Daisy came back to the front window so she could see them when they came out. She opened the window slightly before they exited the front of the barn, in full view of the cabin. Daisy lowered the shotgun into position. She almost jumped out of her skin when the butt of the gun knocked a tin cup off of the cabinet, causing it to bounce on the wooden floor.

The bouncing cup echoed in the cabin sending the sound into the yard. In an instant the thieves were both focused on the cabin, pistols drawn.

Daisy knew she had no choice. If only she hadn't knocked over the cup, they would have left without knowing she'd seen them. She drew in a deep breath and prayed.

Dear Lord, protect the horses. And me.

As the thief with the red bandana took aim at the window, Daisy closed her eyes and pulled both triggers. She heard the window shatter and a bullet flew by her head. Daisy opened her eyes as cries of pain erupted in the yard. Both men had fallen from their horses. Trojan and Beauregard ran for the field behind the cabin. Dutch was dancing all around the thief in the red bandana as he rolled in the dirt writhing in pain. The man in the brown hat had one foot hung in a stirrup and was clutching his belly. Blood stained his shirt.

Thundering hooves sounded over the hill behind the cabin. Tucker came into view first, followed by Paco and Lawrence. All three had their guns drawn and were ready for battle. As they reined in their mounts Daisy was surprised to hear laughter. Guffaws! It was the last sound she heard as blackness overtook her.

Chapter Twenty-One

❦

"**D**aisy. Honey. It's me, Tucker. Daisy." Strong hands patted her cheeks firmly. "Daisy." Then the cold water came. Splashing her into consciousness. She sputtered and spewed, shaking her head from side to side. When she opened her eyes she was cradled in Tucker's arms. He knelt on the floor beside her, holding her firmly against the broad expanse of his chest. A chest that was covered with a very wet shirt.

"I am so sorry, Señora Barlow. I did not know how else to wake you up." Paco stood above them with an empty pitcher. The smile on his face offered sympathy and humor.

"Were you trying to wake her or drown her?" Tucker shook his head and drops of water rained on Daisy.

"Are you okay, Daisy?" Tucker's voice gentled, and he looked into her eyes.

"The thieves? Are they...?" Daisy muttered.

"Tied up outside under Lawrence's watchful eye. Paco and Randall Thornton will go with Lawrence to take them to the sheriff. And the doctor. They told us they came back here figuring you'd have new horses and maybe no husband around." Tucker's gaze searched hers. "Did they hurt you?" His voice grew very serious. "In any way?"

Daisy smiled a weak smile and patted his chest. "No, dear. I'm fine."

"You're sure?" he asked her.

"I'm sure. They never saw me until just before I pulled the trigger."

"That's my girl." Tucker pulled her closer and pressed his face into her hair. "I couldn't live with myself if they'd harmed you," he whispered low so only she could hear.

"The twins?" Daisy worried aloud.

"They're great." Tucker sat back so she could see his face. "They did exactly what you asked. Thank God, we were on our way back here when John fired the warning shot. Randall was coming with us to get the folder with the paperwork I left on the table. I forgot to take it to him this morning. He picked up the boys and let Paco, Lawrence and I come ahead to protect you." Tucker chuckled.

Paco laughed out loud. "Señora Barlow does not need your help to shoot people, Señor Tucker. She does pretty good all by herself. Those muchachos outside are lucky she is not a better shot. She is shooting two at a time now. And not one injury to a horse."

Color returned to Daisy's face, and she attempted to sit up. "You fellows better stop teasing me and help me up. I can't just lie on the floor all day." Tucker helped her sit up and then stood to pull her to her feet. She flinched when she tried to put weight on her throbbing ankle and fell against him.

"Sorry. I fell earlier." She smiled up at him.

Tucker picked her up to carry her to her room. She

wrapped her arms around his neck. "Thanks for coming to my rescue." As they crossed the threshold into the new room, Daisy slid her fingers into Tucker's hair and pulled his face to hers. He stopped and stood still while she kissed his lips. When she pulled back he looked into her face and a groan escaped him. This time he leaned in and kissed her.

Tucker lifted his head. "Thank God you're not hurt."

Daisy saw the protective look in his eyes. No longer a look that protected him from a relationship with her. Now the look promised to draw her in and keep her safe.

He lowered her onto the quilt. "Boys, come see your momma." The twins were in the room in an instant. "Stay with her while I make sure those thieves are dealt with."

To Daisy he said, "Don't go anywhere. I'll be right back to see about your ankle." He adjusted his hat and took one more look at her before he left the room.

"Momma, are you okay?" John spoke with calm concern.

"Yes, son." The boys stood by the bed. She reached a hand to both of them. They eagerly latched on to her. "You were both very brave."

James launched into speech. "We ran so fast nobody could catch us! Then Mr. Thornton let us both ride on his horse with him."

Tucker entered the room. "You boys did exactly what needed to be done. I'm proud of both of you. Why don't you head out to the well and get some cool water for your momma? I'm gonna see about her ankle."

With a quick, "Yes, sir," they were gone.

Tucker propped her up by pushing another pillow be-

hind her shoulders. Then he sat on the edge of the bed
to inspect her ankle.

Daisy blushed at his touch. He was very gentle.

"How bad is the pain?" Tucker didn't meet her eyes.

"Right now, I'm still so upset about all that happened,
I don't know. It's tender to walk on."

"I'll wrap it tight to keep the swelling down."

He found what he needed in his roll that still sat in
the corner of the room. By the time it was wrapped, the
boys could be heard in the kitchen.

Tucker checked his work. "Better?"

"Yes. Thank you."

He stood. "I want you to rest for a while."

"That's not necessary." Daisy started to sit up in the
bed.

"I insist."

Her nerves had started to settle some while he worked
on her ankle. The pain had begun to ease. She leaned
back against the pillows. "I could use some rest."

He moved to the door and looked back.

"You called me honey." She smiled at him.

"You called me dear," he countered with a grin. He
closed the door as she closed her eyes.

Paco and Lawrence rode up as they set lunch on the
table. Randall Thornton had headed to the ranch after
helping deliver the thieves to Sheriff Collins with the
news that one of their horses had been recovered. James
and John were in the barn with their horses. They were
so happy Dutch was home.

"Señora Barlow? Can we come in?" Paco called.
Tucker opened the door and laughed. "Please don't shoot
me," Paco continued to hail Daisy from the porch.

"Keep it up, Paco. Ask Tucker how patient I am," Daisy chided. "I wouldn't think there was a man in fifty miles of here that isn't scared of me now," she teased him with a laugh.

"I promise to be good, *señora*." Paco laughed, too.

Lawrence came in with Paco. James and John had heard their horses arrive and came to join the men in the cabin.

"Lunch is ready." Tucker motioned for the men to sit at the table. "Daisy's ankle prevented us from having a hot meal. I'm not much of a cook, but we do have pumpkin pie."

"Go wash up," Daisy reminded her sons. She set glasses on the table and reached for the tea pitcher. Tucker took it from her and asked her to sit while he filled the glasses. The boys climbed onto their bench.

Tucker took his place at the head of the table and reached for John's hand. He bowed his head and prayed. "Lord, we thank You for this bountiful meal. Give us wisdom and guide us in all we do. And we especially thank You for protecting our home and family from danger today. Amen."

"Amen," echoed around the table.

Daisy was looking at Tucker when he lifted his head. His green eyes reflected her mood. Her expression was confused, but hopeful.

The food was passed around the table. Then silence reigned while hungry men satisfied themselves with good food.

"*Señora*, this pie is delicious. I wonder if you use molasses to make it so sweet, no?" Paco seemed to know a lot about cooking.

"Actually, yes, I do." Daisy asked, "How do you know so much about food, Paco?"

"I spend a lot of time in the kitchen at your papa's ranch. I help your sister Lily. She is a good cook, too. Remember I told you?"

"I didn't realize you spent time in the kitchen. I thought you said you were a ranch hand," Daisy responded as she sliced pie for James and John.

"*Sí,* I was a ranch hand, but I also help in the kitchen. I need to learn from her so I can cook for the hands in the bunkhouse. The cook sometimes cannot come when we need him." Paco waved his fork in the air as he spoke. "So I spend extra time in the kitchen with Miss Lily. Now I am a good cook, too." Paco toasted them all with the fork and then took a big bite of pie.

"Mr. Paco, can you cook chili?" James wanted to know. "I love chili!"

"I make very good chili. I use lots of peppers—so maybe you need to drink lots of water or tea when you eat my chili." Paco smiled.

Tucker reached for a piece of pie. "Daisy, this is delicious."

"Thank you, Tucker." Daisy rose to refill everyone's tea glass. Tucker offered to do it, but she insisted. The wrapping of her ankle had helped the sprain, which wasn't as bad as she'd first thought.

"Oh, by the way," Daisy said, "Jay Winters came by this morning before all the commotion. Mr. Croft sent him to let you know the furniture arrived this morning." She lifted Tucker's glass and filled it. "He asked if you wanted it delivered, and I told him not unless we sent word for them to bring it."

"That's good. We can go to town this afternoon and

pick it up." He lowered his fork and cut his eyes at Daisy. "Will you be okay here, Daisy? I need to go so I can pay Mr. Croft."

"I'll be fine," Daisy assured him. "Especially now. I won't have to worry about those murderous thieves ever again." The relief was evident on her face. It eclipsed any signs of the stress of having faced down her husband's killers. She was grateful the entire episode had lasted only a few brief minutes. Certainly the shock of it could hit her later, but right now relief overrode all other emotions.

"If you're sure?" Tucker waited until Daisy nodded in the affirmative before addressing Paco and Lawrence. "Can I get you gentlemen to help me today? Paco, I'll feel better if someone is here with Daisy. Will you stay here while Lawrence and I go pick up the furniture?" Tucker cut another bite of pie with his fork.

"I would be glad to stay, Señor Tucker."

So Paco stayed at the farm to keep Daisy from being alone. He spent his time in the barn and the yard, telling her he didn't want to intrude on her privacy. James and John rode to town with Tucker and Lawrence. And Daisy prepared her room for the arrival of the new furniture. She stripped the bed of the sheets and quilt. Then she made a big pot of chili, with extra peppers for Paco, and left it simmering on the stove.

Daisy couldn't resist one more trip into her room. She stood at the foot of the iron bed—the bed she'd shared with Murdock. She caressed the curves of the metal and remembered the day they'd bought it shortly after they'd finished the cabin. When they'd set it up, she'd been so proud. They had slept in the covered wagon for weeks while they'd raised the cabin. It had seemed like ages

since they'd been in a real bed. This was the first, and
only, bed they'd owned as husband and wife.

Daisy smiled as she remembered having her babies in
this bed—and nursing them in the middle of the night.
She remembered the times the twins had climbed in bed
with them because they'd been frightened by a storm or
a bad dream. She laughed when she recalled how Murdock would tickle them until they begged for mercy.
Then she thought about the love they'd shared and how
she'd treasure it forever in her heart. She was able to
say a prayer of thanks for all the good Murdock had
brought into her life.

And now she stood at the foot of this bed and realized
she was ready to move on with her life. The capture of
the men who murdered Murdock brought that chapter
of her life to an end.

The sound of the wagon coming up the lane reached
her ears. She was glad the bed would be in the boys'
room now. It was time.

In what seemed like a flurry of activity, and really
was no time at all, the men had moved the old bed into
the boys' room. There was enough room to keep their
original bed, so now both boys could have their own
space to sleep. Tucker told Daisy he thought they would
appreciate that as they grew. She agreed.

The new furniture was arranged to please Daisy. She
only had the men move the dressing table twice. The
bed and chest were perfect from the time they set them
up in the room.

Tucker had another surprise for Daisy. When the last
of the furniture was taken off the wagon, and the twins
had gone with Paco and Lawrence to the barn, she no-

ticed a large crate in the corner of the bedroom. They must have put it there while she was out of the room.

"What's that?" Daisy asked Tucker.

"Are you sure you want to know?" he answered her with a question.

"Stop doing that."

"What?" He knew exactly what she meant, but he wanted to hear her say it again.

"Stop answering my questions with a question."

"What question?" He tormented her.

"Tucker Barlow, what is in that crate? I have no more patience in me today." Her skirt moved back and forth as she patted one foot on the floor.

"Would you like to do the honors?" Tucker offered her the iron bar he held.

"No, thank you. I just want to see what's inside. You open it."

"Your father was right when he reminded me how impatient you are." He smiled and pried the first corner of the crate loose. She tried to peek, and he shooed her away.

"My father told you I'm impatient?" She couldn't imagine her father talking to Tucker about what she knew Papa considered to be her character flaws.

"Yes, he warned me about that, and how you like to have your way." Tucker pried another corner loose.

"Everyone likes to have their way. Anyone who says they don't isn't being honest." She moved closer to watch him pry another section of the lid loose. "How many nails did they put in that box?"

"See, Daisy, you've got to learn to wait." Tucker methodically worked his way around the top of the crate, loosening one nail at a time. Finally he reached the last one, but he didn't lift the lid.

"Are you sure you want to see?" he asked again.

"Yes." She was tapping her toe.

"You're not going to be upset with me because I didn't talk to you about this first, are you?"

"Oh, Tucker, I can't stand it another minute. You have to let me see." Daisy pushed him aside and knelt down to slide the lid back so she could peer into the corner of the crate. She pulled at the straw that had been used for packing and threw it onto the floor. She gasped and reached into the box and touched the fine copper of the fancy bathtub. She fell backward onto her heels.

With one hand to her chest and her mouth hanging open, Daisy turned to stare at Tucker. "I can't believe it! It's beautiful!" She stood as quickly as her ankle would allow and threw her arms around his neck. "I love it! Thank you! How ever did you know?" She went on and on without stopping to breathe. "Why did you buy this?"

"So you like it?" He smiled.

Daisy laughed out loud. "You're doing it again. Well, I'll answer your question now, because I'm so pleased with you at the moment. I love it! It's the most beautiful bathtub I've ever seen. And judging from the size of this crate, it's huge!"

Tucker laughed at her exuberance. "This was a combination gift. I bought it for you because it's beautiful, and I bought it for me because I'm too tall for that wash tub you've been filling with water for me to bathe in on Saturday nights. I'd do better with a bowl and a cloth."

Daisy grabbed her side and bent double laughing at him as he tried to demonstrate how he had to fold up to get into the small wash tub she used for herself and the twins.

"Stop laughing at me, and go finish supper. I'll get Paco and Lawrence to help me get this out of the crate."

At the table, Tucker informed Daisy that Paco and Lawrence would be moving to the bunkhouse at the Thornton ranch after supper. They'd made the arrangements with Randall that morning.

"It's best for them to get right to work. Randall has agreed to show them the entire operation before their family leaves at the end of next week." At Daisy's downcast look, he added, "And I made arrangements for all of us to spend the afternoon with their family tomorrow. I know it's our normal Bible study night, but Randall and I thought it would be a good way to part. We'll meet together for Bible study, and the kids can play for the evening."

"That's a good idea. Thank you for arranging all of that." Daisy appreciated Tucker's thoughtfulness.

"We get to ride our horses over there after supper and spend the night tonight," James spoke up. "This sure is good chili, Momma. Did you get the idea to cook it because I asked Mr. Paco if he knows how to cook chili? Because I really like chili."

"I'm glad you like it, son. Yes, the idea came from you. It was a good one." Daisy looked at Tucker. "What's this about spending the night?"

"The boys can ride over with Paco and Lawrence after we eat. They'll be safe with them. They can come back with us tomorrow night," Tucker explained. "There's little time left for visiting. For the time being, there won't be any kids at the ranch after the Thorntons leave."

* * *

The boys made bedrolls with clothes for the following day and rode over the fields with Paco and Lawrence to the Thornton ranch. The experience would make the twins feel like real ranch hands.

Daisy stood alone on the porch, watching them leave. She knew they were safe. They were all safe now.

She also knew the twins would appreciate the time with their friends. What she didn't know was how to straighten out her conflicts with her husband. Glad of the opportunity to talk with him alone, Daisy went in search of Tucker.

He wasn't in the front of the cabin. She went out the front door and crossed to the barn. He wasn't there, either. When she came out of the barn and looked toward the house, he came out of the front door.

"I want to show you something. Can you come in for a minute?" Tucker called to her.

"Where have you been? I've been looking everywhere for you."

"Are you answering my question with a question?" he teased her.

Daisy limped across the yard, her brows drawn together.

"We've got a lot to talk about. I'm hoping we can get some things figured out while we won't be interrupted." Daisy walked past him into the cabin. He followed her inside.

"Me, too. I want you to see something first." He crossed the room and opened the door to her bedroom. He gestured for her to come and look. When she stood in the doorway he asked, "Do you like it?"

Daisy was speechless. In front of the tub, he'd placed

a hand-carved, accordion-style wooden screen. Each panel was a series of intricately carved squares. Some were carved in the design of her father's seal of vines woven into a heart shape. Others were filled with daisies. Every imaginable configuration of a daisy was represented on the beautiful screen.

She frowned and said, "It's gorgeous, Tucker." She walked close and ran her fingers over the raised patterns. "Did you carve this yourself?"

"I worked on it at night. I got the idea when I decided to leave the corner in the front of the cabin set up for the boys and I to use. I thought you might enjoy some privacy when you change clothes or bathe." He touched the panel and smiled at her. "I'm glad you like it."

Daisy shook her head. "It's all too much, Tucker." She shook her head again, and her frown grew.

"What's too much?" He seemed confused by her response.

"It's all too much." Gesturing toward each item with her hands, Daisy continued, "The room, your mother's wedding ring, the furniture, the bathtub, the horses, the ranch next door, a ranch hand from Mexico, a young man who worked for my father, not to mention someone shooting at me today! And me shooting not one— but two—men!" She paused for a moment and fingered the carving again. "And now this beautiful carving…" Her voice became so quiet he could hardly hear her. She continued to shake her head. "It's just all too much."

Daisy turned to look at Tucker. "Where does it end? When will it stop? What's next?"

Tucker put his hands on her shoulders and looked into her sad brown eyes. "I did it all for you, Daisy. I want you to be happy."

"I don't need all this to be happy, Tucker." She kept shaking her head. "What I need to be happy is to know you value my opinions. To know we don't have secrets. I need to not be surprised by some grand gift that's so expensive I can't imagine where the money will come from to pay for it. I need to know you want me involved in your life. I want to know what's going on and not be overwhelmed by surprise when I'm blindsided by your next mystery project. That's what I need to be happy, Tucker. Not all this."

She gestured with her hands again and turned away from him, causing him to drop his hands from her shoulders. "I need a plan to follow. I need to know the plan is going to work. That's what I need Tucker."

With each sentence raw emotion ripped from her soul. Daisy felt as if she were literally unraveling before his eyes. She abruptly stopped and turned toward him, just inches from his face.

"I love you, Tucker." Daisy looked him straight in the eye. "Even when I'm so frustrated I don't know what to do, I love you. I don't need all this to be happy with you. I just need you to be happy with me." Daisy's lip trembled.

Tucker returned her stare. "You've wanted everything to go according to your plans and at your pace…" He paused and drew in a slow steady breath. "Well, Daisy, I have plans, too. I'm a man who's always followed his own pace. I've been patient with you because I loved you, but enough is enough."

"You said for me to set the pace. When we got married, you promised not to rush me." Daisy jumped on the first thing that came to mind. "What plans are you talking about?" She kept talking in a feverish rush to keep from thinking. "We never once talked about you buying the Thornton ranch. Unless you count that first week when you teased me about buying it without talking to me first."

Tucker put a finger across her lips to hush her. He looked deeply into her eyes.

She talked around his finger. "You're the one who came here when Papa asked you to."

"Daisy, I'm warning you." Tucker's voice was calm and steady. His eyes never left hers.

"What do you mean, enough is enough?"

Tucker wrapped his large hands around the tops of her arms and pulled her to him as she continued to rant. He silenced her with his lips. She sputtered and jerked her head back to look at him, her eyes wide with wonder.

"You loved me?" she said, her voice a hoarse whisper. "What do you mean 'loved'?"

"Years ago, I loved you." Tucker titled his head to one side and shrugged one shoulder.

She still couldn't grasp all he was saying. "But I was married to Murdock." The statement was a question. She frowned.

"Not then." He stroked her cheek with the back of one hand while wrapping his other arm around her waist. "Before."

"Before? Oh, Tucker, I'm so confused."

"I know," he said, "but I can explain." He kissed her again, taking his time about it.

"Stop doing that," she protested when he released her. "I don't know what to think!"

"You think too much." He kissed her again, and she melted against his chest without resistance.

"Really," she whispered, "you've got to stop doing that. I can't think straight."

Tucker set her back a step away from him and looked straight into her eyes. "Listen, Daisy."

She opened her mouth to speak, and he held up a hand to stop her. "I mean it, Daisy. I want you to listen, because I'm only going to say this one time." He waited for her to agree. She closed her lips, and at her nod he continued.

"I fell in love with you years ago. I can't even actually say when it happened." His eyes reflected the memories of all the years they'd known each other. "You were barely more than a child when we met, and then we became friends. You'd come to me for advice or comfort. I was good with that—in the beginning. Then I started liking that you needed me. You were so beautiful, and clever, and so much fun. Impetuous, but at the same time, delightful."

"Tucker..."

With a raised finger, he signaled for her to stay quiet. "And then Murdock came along." His brows drew together and downward. "At first I was jealous. Then I saw you together." His brow relaxed. "Any fool could see how in love you both were. I really believe God put the two of you together. I can't say I was happy about it, but I knew it was the right thing. So I locked my feelings for you deep in the recesses of my broken heart and resigned myself to working on your father's ranch and being alone. I actually got used to it and was content. When I thought of you it was a pleasant memory, without jealousy or envy."

Daisy tried again to speak, but he put his hand to her

lips. "Please let me finish. That's the only way you'll understand." She nodded again.

"I was happy for you when you got your farmland and had the boys. I wanted God to bless you and give you a happy life." She smiled slightly, and he continued. "And my heart ached for you when I found out Murdock had been killed." Tears slid from her eyes and spilled over her lashes at his words.

"I knew you'd be heartbroken, because I knew the depth of the love you had for him." He drew in a deep breath. "It was not unlike the depth of love I had for you all those years before." He smiled then. "That's why I came when your father asked me to help you."

Daisy saw a hint of sadness in him.

"And now I've grown to love you again. I thought that part of me was dead." Tucker continued, "I know you'll never be able to love me like you loved Murdock. But your friendship caused my heart to crack open so the sun could shine into my soul and that long-buried seed of love began to grow and flourish." He leaned in close to her face now and whispered, "I can be happy loving you to whatever degree or depth you'll let me."

"Oh, Tucker." Her voice was barely more than a whisper. "I had no idea." She stepped closer and snuggled into his embrace without looking away from his tender eyes.

"It wasn't our time then, Daisy. That was Murdock's time. I know he was your destiny." He nodded his head in the direction of James and John's bedroom. "Those fine young men wouldn't be here if it hadn't been for the love the two of you shared."

Daisy squeezed him with gratitude. "Thank you for saying that."

"I mean it."

"God has taught me so much in such a short time." Daisy's sober voice held his attention. "Murdock is gone. I can't go back to him."

"The twins are Murdock. You see him every day." Tucker's words were a clear attempt to comfort her.

"Do you think I love John more than James?"

"Of course not."

"I love them both." Her eyes never left his face. "But they are unique individuals. They each complete me as a mother in a different way." Her eyes softened, and she willed him to believe her.

"Like Murdock, you are my husband." A flash of pain crossed his gaze. "I loved Murdock. I will always treasure his memory and the sons he gave me." She lowered her voice. "I love you—in a completely different way. He was my first love. The love of my youth. He's gone." A smile pulled her lips upward. "Now you are the love of my life."

She tightened her hold around his waist, willing him to receive the truth of her words. "You fill a different part of my life. Murdock was my past. You are my future."

"Oh, Daisy, I love you now more than ever before." Tucker put a soft kiss on her temple. "Do you remember I told you God had taught me that when I couldn't fly, He wanted me to run, and He wanted me to walk when I couldn't run?"

"Yes," she said, nodding.

"For you that verse was about not having the energy to run or fly because of the suffering you were going through. For me, it was an instruction in patience to wait until it was the time for me to run or fly."

Understanding of his meaning dawned in her eyes,

and he continued. "I'd given up hope that I'd ever fly again." He paused. "Well, I'm ready to fly now. I've been walking in patience long enough. When our friendship began to grow, slowly at first, but deeper, I started to run. I'm letting you know now, my heart is about to burst with love for you, and I've got to soar like the eagle I am." He gave her a squeeze. "Do you think you can keep up with me?"

"Yes! Oh, yes!" Daisy stretched up to the tips of her toes to meet his kiss with her heart wide-open.

Daisy snatched her head back. "Wait!" She blurted out. "What about the money? Where did it come from?"

Tucker's eyes danced with mischief, and he started to laugh. "So you have to know now?"

"You've kept me in the dark long enough, Mr. Barlow. For this marriage to work, you're gonna have to fess up. No more secrets."

"I'll tell you. If you promise not to interrupt," he teased.

"But—"

"No *buts*. Promise?"

She exhaled. "I promise." Her smiled teased him back.

"It happened over a period of time. First, I learned that it pays to pay attention. All those years growing up in the hotel, listening to businessmen talk while I cleared away their dishes or carried their luggage, I heard a lot of good information. Especially about how important it is to save your money. And being a ranch hand, with no family or expenses for so long, gave me plenty of time to do that. Then your father gave me the opportunity to hone my business skills. He took me under his wing like the father I didn't have. I'll always be grateful to him."

"What kind of opportunity did Papa give you?" She grew more curious by the second.

"Everyone thought I was a simple ranch hand. No one knew that several years ago he partnered with me for an interest in his ranch. He taught me how to make business deals and land deals. Those lessons stood me in good stead. That's what took me so long to get here in the beginning. I was selling off some properties. Your father bought out my share in his ranch. I've actually built quite a nest egg."

"You're rich?" Daisy was befuddled.

"No. I'm not rich. *We,* however, are financially secure."

Tucker tilted his head to one side. "Are you satisfied? Is there anything else you want to ask me?"

"I think, dear Tucker, you have left me speechless."

"Finally." He smiled and claimed her lips. All other thoughts left her mind.

Epilogue

December 1880

"We better hurry, or we won't be there when the train comes." James jumped into the back of the wagon. "John, come on."

"There's plenty of time, son." Tucker set the empty Moses basket under the seat of the wagon. "Your momma is putting on her hat."

John climbed up beside his brother. "My stomach feels funny. I can't believe today is the day." His hat was freshly brushed, and he took extra care to keep his clothes neat.

"Are you ready, dear?" Tucker called to Daisy.

She came to the door of the cabin and answered. "Another question, Tucker? Really?" Her smile belied the tartness of her words. Daisy pulled the door of the cabin closed and descended the steps. She asked John to hop out of the wagon to help her.

"Here, John, hold your sister for me, please." Daisy carefully handed the small girl to her proud brother. Tucker offered his hand to Daisy, and she climbed into the wagon. Tucker took his new daughter from his son, kissed her soft cheek and handed her to her mother.

"Are you sure you want to make the trip to town, Daisy? We could just as easily meet the train and come back here. I'm sure you'll be able to hear the whistle from inside our cabin." Tucker waited for her answer while John climbed back into the wagon.

"I want to go. It's the first train to come to Pine Haven. I don't want to miss it."

Thirty minutes later, they were at the station. The new building had more windows than any other building in town. There was a giant clock on the platform. A huge water tank stood beyond the depot where the train would pull forward and take on water before leaving town. Everywhere they looked, they saw someone they knew. Many stopped to peek inside the blanket at the newest member of the Barlow family.

Daisy stood on the platform, her nerves in a tight bundle. Then they heard it. A distant whistle. It grew closer and louder. The earth began to vibrate with the power of the approaching train. Tucker put his arm around Daisy's shoulders.

"I'm glad we sold them the easement to the southern tip of our farm," he said.

"I am, too." She stole a glance at him. "I just wish I'd known then what a savvy businessman you were. I wouldn't have been worried about anything."

Tucker squeezed her shoulders. "I wanted you to love me for me, not for my money. I had to move carefully so you wouldn't find me out." He grinned and looked over her shoulder at the beautiful child she held.

"I still can't believe how quickly you got the Thornton place to the level it's at today, or how successful our cotton was this past season. You really do have the Midas touch." She looked around. "Speaking of the ranch, where are Paco and Lawrence?"

"They decided to skip the festivities. They're working on the new bunkhouse. It's got to be finished before the new ranch hands get here next week," he answered.

"How do you keep it all straight?" She smiled at him, expecting no answer.

James and John stood in front of her, watching as the train came into view. James hopped from one foot to the other, while John stood quietly and stepped closer to Tucker.

Tears formed in Daisy's eyes, and she blinked them away. She refused to cry on this happy day. She was even wearing her happy dress—the one she wore last year when she married Tucker.

The train roared into the station with great power.

"Papa Tucker?" John looked up expectantly.

"Yes, John?" Tucker was still moved by the name the twins had decided to bestow on him.

"Do I look okay?" John tugged on his hat and straightened his coat.

"You look fine, young sir," Tucker assured him.

The train stopped with a long blast of the whistle and a burst of steam as the brakes locked down. Almost before it stopped, people streamed from the line of cars. Daisy searched every face. And then she saw him. With a wave of her hand, she had his attention, and within seconds they were embracing.

"Papa!" she whispered against his wet cheek. "I've missed you so."

Daisy stepped back to look in his face and smiled at the man responsible for the happiness she enjoyed today.

If it hadn't been for Papa's letter, Daisy wouldn't have understood the wisdom of marrying Tucker that day.

Satisfied his health really had improved, she drew his attention to the bundle in her arms and pulled the blanket back. She placed the tiny babe in his arms and spoke to her daughter.

"Rose, meet your papa Warren."

James and John met Papa Warren for the first time, as he held his first granddaughter, named for his beloved wife, in his arms. True to their character, James had been excited, and John had been nervous about meeting their momma's papa. Both boys were soon reveling in the attention and joy of visiting with their grandfather. James led the way to the wagon, as the two generations shared excited stories and began to make new memories. This Christmas season would be a wondrous time for all of them.

Tucker pulled Daisy close to him and whispered against her ear, "Life really isn't fair."

"You're right." Daisy smiled her agreement. "Sometimes you get more than your share of good."

* * * * *

Dear Reader,

Thank you for joining me for *Conveniently Wed*. I hope you enjoyed Daisy and Tucker's story. Sometimes life's difficulties put us up against insurmountable challenges, even when the powers that be are on our side. Daisy's strength and Tucker's compassion and patience helped them renew their friendship from long ago.

Both characters reminded me of times when I wanted to run ahead of or lag behind where God wanted me to be. They needed God to help them as they journeyed into a new relationship toward their unexpected happy ever after.

I'd love to hear from you. You can reach me through my website at angelmoorebooks.com where you'll find the latest news and links to connect with me on social media.

My prayer is that God will bless you and guide you through life's situations with His wisdom and peace.

Angel Moore

Questions for Discussion

1. Marriage to Tucker came at the strong suggestion from Daisy's father. Has a parent or mentor every guided you in a direction you didn't understand? Did you heed the advice? Was it ultimately the right direction?

2. Because of his mother's lifelong loyalty to his father and his rejection from Alice, Tucker didn't think Daisy would ever love him like she had loved Murdock. Daisy didn't think she'd have another opportunity for the kind of marriage she'd shared with Murdock. Have you ever denied yourself a relationship because you didn't think you deserved a second chance at happiness? Have you ever resisted a new friendship or relationship because of the way someone treated you in the past?

3. Tucker married Daisy out of loneliness, with only the hope of friendship and companionship. Daisy agreed for the sake of her sons and to preserve the farm Murdock built for their future. Have you ever, due to circumstances, settled into a relationship that eventually grew to a treasured friendship or love?

4. The land agent was willing to use his power to manipulate Daisy's land away from her and the twins. Do you ever feel judged by your position or gender? How do you deal with those situations?

5. Tucker loved Daisy when she was a teenager but knew it wasn't his destiny to marry her then. He buried his feelings and moved on with his life. Daisy struggled with letting the love she'd shared with Murdock recede into her past. Have you ever gotten ahead of God's timing, due to desire or excitement? Have you ever wanted to lag behind due to weariness or pain?

6. Daisy loved her father and appreciated his efforts to raise her and her sisters after their mother died, but she'd secretly longed for feminine guidance and nurturing. As a boy, Tucker watched helplessly as his mother worked herself to death trying to provide for him. They didn't understand the value and price of their parents' sacrifices until they were adults. Have you learned to appreciate some aspect of your parents' methods or attitudes since becoming an adult? If you are not an adult, do you think you can look at your parents with a more open mind to see their motives?

7. James and John suffered the loss of their father, but within weeks had to adapt to a new father figure. As children, they had no say in the matter. How quickly do you adjust to new relationships? How do you feel when the circumstances are forced upon you?

8. Tucker and Daisy both trusted God for their lives in different ways. Daisy trusted God to help her regain her strength after the sorrow of Murdock's death. Tucker had contented himself to be alone, thinking

that true love had passed him by. Is it difficult for you to believe God is working for your good in the middle of terrible circumstances?

REQUEST YOUR FREE BOOKS!

2 FREE INSPIRATIONAL NOVELS
PLUS 2
FREE
MYSTERY GIFTS

Love Inspired

HISTORICAL
INSPIRATIONAL HISTORICAL ROMANCE

YES! Please send me 2 FREE Love Inspired® Historical novels and my 2 FREE mystery gifts (gifts are worth about $10). After receiving them, if I don't wish to receive any more books, I can return the shipping statement marked "cancel." If I don't cancel, I will receive 4 brand-new novels every month and be billed just $4.74 per book in the U.S. or $5.24 per book in Canada. That's a saving of at least 21% off the cover price. It's quite a bargain! Shipping and handling is just 50¢ per book in the U.S. and 75¢ per book in Canada.* I understand that accepting the 2 free books and gifts places me under no obligation to buy anything. I can always return a shipment and cancel at any time. Even if I never buy another book, the two free books and gifts are mine to keep forever.

102/302 IDN F5CN

Name	(PLEASE PRINT)	

Address		Apt. #

City	State/Prov.	Zip/Postal Code

Signature (if under 18, a parent or guardian must sign)

Mail to the **Harlequin® Reader Service:**
IN U.S.A.: P.O. Box 1867, Buffalo, NY 14240-1867
IN CANADA: P.O. Box 609, Fort Erie, Ontario L2A 5X3

Want to try two free books from another series?
Call 1-800-873-8635 or visit www.ReaderService.com.

* Terms and prices subject to change without notice. Prices do not include applicable taxes. Sales tax applicable in N.Y. Canadian residents will be charged applicable taxes. Offer not valid in Quebec. This offer is limited to one order per household. Not valid for current subscribers to Love Inspired Historical books. All orders subject to credit approval. Credit or debit balances in a customer's account(s) may be offset by any other outstanding balance owed by or to the customer. Please allow 4 to 6 weeks for delivery. Offer available while quantities last.

Your Privacy—The Harlequin® Reader Service is committed to protecting your privacy. Our Privacy Policy is available online at www.ReaderService.com or upon request from the Harlequin Reader Service.

We make a portion of our mailing list available to reputable third parties that offer products we believe may interest you. If you prefer that we not exchange your name with third parties, or if you wish to clarify or modify your communication preferences, please visit us at www.ReaderService.com/consumerschoice or write to us at Harlequin Reader Service Preference Service, P.O. Box 9062, Buffalo, NY 14269. Include your complete name and address.

"I think she likes you," Brady offered.

Really? Colt thought with a start. Brady thought Allie
liked him? "I like her, too." And he did, despite their on-
again, off-again sparring the past year.

"Are you taking her some ice for her ice cream?" Cilla
asked.

"I don't know. It depends." On the one hand, after not
seeing her all week, he was anxious to see her; on the other,
he wasn't certain what he would say or do when he did.

"On what?"

"A lot of things."

"But we will see her at the ice cream social, won't we?"

Fed up with the game of Twenty Questions, Colt, fork in
one hand, knife in the other, rested his forearms on the edge
of the table and looked from one of his children to the other.
The innocence on their faces didn't fool him for a minute.
What was this all about, anyway?

The answer came out of nowhere, slamming into him
with the force of Ed Rawlings's angry bull when he'd
pinned Colt against a fence. He knew exactly what was up.

"The two of you wouldn't be trying to push me and

Allison into spending more time together, would you?"

Brady looked at Cilla, the expression in his eyes begging her to spit it out. "Well, actually," she said, "Brady and I have talked about it, and we think it would be swell if you started courting her."

Glowering at his sister, and swinging that frowning gaze to Colt, Brady said, "What she really means is that since we have to have a stepmother, we'd like her."

"What did you say?" Colt asked, uncertain that he'd heard correctly.

"Cilla and I want Miss Grainger to be our ma."

Don't miss WOLF CREEK FATHER
by Penny Richards,
available January 2015 wherever
Love Inspired® Historical books and ebooks are sold.

SPECIAL EXCERPT FROM

*When a rodeo rider comes face-to-face with an old love,
can romance be far behind?*

*Read on for a preview of
HER COWBOY HERO by Carolyne Aarsen,
the first book in her brand-new
REFUGE RANCH series.*

Keira wished she could keep her hands from trembling as she handled Tanner's saddle. What was wrong with her?

Seeing him again, his brown eyes edged with sooty lashes and framed by the slash of dark brows, the hard planes of his face emphasized by the stubble shadowing his jaw and cheeks, brought back painful memories Keira thought she had put aside.

He looked the same and yet different. Harder. Leaner. He wore his sandy brown hair longer; it brushed the collar of his shirt, giving him reckless look at odds with the Tanner she had once known.

And loved.

She sucked in a rapid breath as she turned over the saddle on the table. Tanner seemed to fill the cramped shop.

Keep your focus on your work, she reminded herself.

"So? What's the verdict?" Tanner asked.

"I don't know if it's worth fixing this," she said, quietly. "It'll be a lot of work."

Tanner sighed. "But can you fix it?"

"I'd need to take it apart to see. If that's the case, two weeks?".

"That's cutting it close," Tanner said. "Is it possible to get

LIEXP1214

it done quicker?"

Keira would have preferred not to work on it at all. It would mean that Tanner would be around more often.

It had taken her years to relegate Tanner to the shadowy recesses of her mind. She didn't know if she could see him more often and maintain any semblance of the hard-won peace she now experienced. Tanner was too connected to memories she had spent hours in prayer trying to bury.

"I'm gonna need it for the National Finals in Vegas in a couple of weeks." Tanner continued.

"I heard you're still doing mechanic work, as well?" She was pleasantly surprised she could chitchat with Tanner, the man who had once held her heart.

"Yup, except last year I bought out the owner. Now I'm the boss, which means I can take off when I want. I took over the shop in Sheridan after a good rodeo run. The same one I started working on before—" He didn't need to finish. Keira knew exactly what "before" was.

Before that summer when she left Tanner and Saddlebank without allowing him the second chance he so desperately wanted. Before that summer when everything changed.

A heavy silence dropped between them as solid as a wall. Keira turned away, burying the memories deep, where they couldn't taunt her.

But Tanner's very presence teased them to the surface.

She looked up at him to tell him she couldn't work on the saddle, but as she did she felt a jolt of awareness as their eyes met. She tried to tear her gaze away, but it was as if the old bond that had once connected them still bound them to each other.

Will Keira agree to fix Tanner's saddle?
Pick up HER COWBOY HERO to find out.
Available January 2015, wherever
Love Inspired® books and ebooks are sold.